For more than forty years,
Yearling has been the leading name
in classic and award-winning literature
for young readers.

Yearling books feature children's
favorite authors and characters,
providing dynamic stories of adventure,
humor, history, mystery, and fantasy.

Trust Yearling paperbacks to entertain,
inspire, and promote the love of reading
in all children.

sammy KEYES

and the PSYCHO KITTY QUEEN

WENDELIN VAN DRAANEN

A YEARLING BOOK

Published by Yearling
an imprint of Random House Children's Books
a division of Random House, Inc.
New York

Visit us on the Web! www.randomhouse.com/kids

Educators and librarians, for a variety of teaching tools,
visit us at www.randomhouse.com/teachers

ISBN-13: 978-0-440-41910-5
ISBN-10: 0-440-41910-7

Reprinted by arrangement with Alfred A. Knopf Books for Young Readers

Printed in the United States of America

April 2006

10 9 8 7 6 5 4 3 2 1

OPM

For Tante Helen, who has lived amazing adventures of her own,
and has been a fan of Sammy's from the beginning

As always, special thanks to my lucky charms Nancy Siscoe and
Mark Parsons, who helped shape this book,
and to Michele Burke for her early comments and suggestions.

sammy
KEYES
and the PSYCHO KITTY QUEEN

PROLOGUE

There are things in life you can predict, and then there's my mother. And I swear it's on account of her that things happened the way they did. She just has that kind of cosmic power.

Grams says it's silly to blame her, but I know in her heart my grams has suspicions, too.

Strong suspicions.

I mean, the minute my mother hit town, one thing after another went wrong. I tell you, that woman's the Diva of Disasters.

And then all her little disasters sort of added up to a *big* disaster, which made me go and do something I *swore* I wouldn't do anymore.

Snoop around the seedy side of town.

ONE

I have to admit that it didn't *start* with my mother. It started on Hudson's porch. Hudson Graham is my favorite old guy in the whole wide world because he's got great stories, great advice, and he knows how to listen.

He's also got the coolest porch you'd ever want to hang out on, and when Hudson's home, it's usually equipped with iced tea and cake.

"Sammy!" he said when he saw me turn up his walkway on my skateboard. "How are you?"

"Starved!" I grabbed my board and trotted up the steps, eyeing the crumbs on his plate. In a flash I knew it had been a piece of his mega-maple upside-down cake.

He took one look at my face and laughed. "Your grandmother let you out of the house without breakfast?"

"She was preoccupied. And besides, I wasn't hungry then—now I am!"

"Why don't I fix you some eggs and toast. Then cake."

"Aw, come on, Hudson. It's Saturday." I plopped down in the chair beside him.

He looked doubtful. "Somehow I don't think your grandmother would approve. And you know I've been working hard to get out of her doghouse..."

3

"Forget the doghouse. If she asks, I'll just tell her it was an early piece of birthday cake."

"Birthday cake? When's your birthday?"

"Tomorrow."

"Tomorrow?" He jumped out of his chair. "Why didn't you mention it before?"

I shrugged. "I don't really like my birthday, that's why."

"You don't *like* it?" He was hovering over me. "Why not? Kids your age love their birthday!"

I kicked my feet up on his railing. "Well, let's see . . . When I turned twelve my mother celebrated by taking me to McDonald's, which is where she broke it to me that she'd be leaving me with Grams while she went off to Hollywood. Then, when I turned thirteen, she didn't even bother to call or send me a card or *any*thing. She finally called two days later gushing excuses, but it was pretty obvious she just forgot."

"Yes, but Sammy, I thought you had gotten past resenting your mother."

"I know, I know," I sighed. "I guess I just have negative associations when it comes to my birthday." I swung my feet down and laughed. "So could you help me get over it? I want some cake!"

He laughed. "Coming right up."

I followed him inside, saying, "Actually, Grams always tries to surprise me with a really nice cake on my birthday. She goes all out and is totally secretive about what she's concocting. I'll bet that's what she's doing right now."

Hudson handed over a giant piece of mega-maple cake. "So you're double dipping, huh?"

I laughed. "I'm entitled, don't you think? I mean, given the circumstances and all."

He chuckled and opened the fridge. "Can I at least insist on milk?"

"Perfect!"

When we were seated back outside, he said, "So catch me up. What's going on at school? And with Heather! You haven't said anything about her in a while."

"That's because there's absolutely nothing going on with Heather." I laughed and took a bite of cake. "Can you believe it?"

Actually, I was finding it hard to believe myself. Ever since my first day of junior high, Heather Acosta has worked hard to make my life miserable. That rabid redhead has done everything from jab me in the butt with a sewing pin to frame me for vandalism. But for the last couple of weeks, there's been nothing.

Well, nothing serious, anyway. I don't count glaring and sneering and catcalls. That's just junior high stuff that everyone goes through. I'm talking diabolical, evil, twisted plots to take over the world. Or at least the school. Elections aren't for another month, but she's already angling to be elected William Rose Junior High's "Most Popular Seventh Grader," or "Class Cutie," or whatever other stupid category she can con the rest of the seventh graders into believing she should win.

Too bad they don't have a "Most Likely to Psycho." I'd vote for her in a hot second.

Hudson shook me from my thoughts, saying, "Two

5

months until summer vacation. Is that what you're thinking about?"

I laughed. "Actually, I wasn't."

"Aren't all kids in countdown mode by now?"

"It's only the first week of April!"

He gave a knowing nod. "Ah. Maybe I'm confusing the kids with the teachers."

I said, "Huh?" but then he said, "So what else have you been up to?" and I remembered what I had come to tell him about. "Oh!" I said, swigging down some milk. "Holly and I have been checking out Slammin' Dave's. Hudson, I've got a whole new perspective on pro wrestling."

He raised a bushy white eyebrow. "You do, do you?" Then he grumbled, "I still can't believe that Bargain Books is now a pro wrestling shop—"

"Slammin' Dave's is not a *shop*, Hudson, it's a *school*." I almost added that having wrestling dudes across the street from where I lived was a whole lot safer than having a bookstore, seeing how the guy who used to own Bargain Books got hauled off to jail for theft, attempted murder, and arson, but I didn't. I just said, "And Slammin' Dave takes his *school* very seriously."

Hudson grinned. "Can I deduce from your apparent knowledge base that you've been spying on him?"

"I wouldn't call it *spying*," I said through a mouthful of cake. "Just, you know, watching."

"Through binoculars?"

"No! You can't see anything from the apartment. I just go down to the school and look."

"Doesn't that place have heavy black curtains covering the windows?"

"Well . . . yeah."

He grinned at me. "So they let you just stand in the doorway and watch?"

"Hudson, quit it!"

He laughed. "I just want you to be able to admit it, that's all."

"All right, all right," I grumbled, scraping up cake crumbs with the back of my fork. "I've been snooping, okay? You happy?"

"Through cracks in the curtains?"

"Yeah," I muttered. "Or the back door. They prop it open for ventilation."

"Mm-hmm," he said.

"There's nothing illegal about it, it's just interesting."

"Interesting? How so?"

"Well, you've got all these beefy guys in these totally cheesy wrestling suits doing flips and body slams and rope dives. It's like they're catapulting cattle in there."

"And you find catapulting cattle interesting?"

I laughed. "Well, yeah." I leaned toward him and said, "There's this one guy who started showing up last week. He wears an orange-and-black-striped caveman suit and a hooded *cat* mask. It covers his whole face. His whole *head*. I mean, once in a while some of the guys will wrestle in full-on costumes, but this guy wears his mask all the time. He shows up in it, he wrestles in it . . . he never takes it off."

"So?"

"So does he sleep with it on? Does he eat with it on? Does he take a shower in the thing?" I leaned back. "What *doesn't* he do in his mask, that's what I want to know."

Hudson laughed, then said, "Sammy, it's just part of his character."

"His character?"

"You know, pro wrestlers create personas—the character they play in the ring. Like Mark Calloway was The Undertaker, Robert Remus was Sergeant Slaughter, Terry Bollea was Hulk Hogan—"

"Wait a minute! How do you know these guys' real names?"

He shrugged. "I've been around for seventy-two years. I'm bound to have picked up a thing or two."

Now, when he said that, it hit me that Hudson had been seventy-two for a really long time. So I was about to ask him, "When's *your* birthday?" only just then something catches my eye. Something *pink* off to my left. Behind some bushes. Along the far side of Hudson's porch. So instead I whisper, "What was that?"

"What was what?" Hudson whispers back.

I stand up and tiptoe the length of Hudson's porch. And when I sneak a step down the side stairs and peek around the bushes, I choke out, "Aaarrh!" and jump back. Right on the other side of Hudson's bushes is one of the scariest sights I've ever seen.

A super-sized, batty-eyed Barbie.

She isn't exactly a *doll*, though. She's more like a Barbie gone to seed. She's middle-aged, with super-bleached hair and a mountain of makeup—thick black eyeliner that curves way up at the corners, three-inch fake eyelashes, sparkly gold eye shadow, and pink lipstick. She's wearing a halter top that matches her lips, high heels, and jeans that are so tight they look shrink-wrapped on. And as if that's not enough of a fashion statement right there, on the top of her head is a tiara.

A *tiara*.

"Who are *you*?" she snaps, and her voice sounds really...snotty.

"Who am *I*?" I ask. "Who arc *you*?"

Hudson steps around me, saying, "Katherine Brown? Why, to what do we owe this pleasure?"

"Don't play nicey-nice with me, Hudson Graham. And it's no longer Brown. Or Truesdale or Stewart. It's just Kitty. *Miss* Kitty."

Hudson is such a gentleman. In a heartbeat he says, "Well then, Miss Kitty...to what do we owe this pleasure?"

"I *said* don't play nicey-nice. You know exactly why I'm here!" Her gaze shifts from Hudson to me, and back again. "You're harboring a criminal, and I intend to do something about it!"

My life flashed before my eyes: My suspensions. My detentions. My breaking-and-enterings. My run-ins with Officer Borsch. My illegal living situation at the seniors-only apartment complex.

I'd never seen this woman before in my life.

How did she know?

But Hudson says, "A criminal? What on earth are you talking about?" He motions over the back gate to his rental unit. "There's not even anyone living back there at the moment."

"I'm not talking about your renter," she says, all huffy-like. "I'm talking about that vicious *beast* of yours!"

Hudson's eyebrows reach for the sky. "Rommel?"

"I hear him howling at night! Do you think I don't know he's roaming the streets, thirsting for blood? This is the third of my kitties that's disappeared in two weeks, and I intend to get to the bottom of it!"

"But—"

"If your beast got ahold of Snowball, I'll sue you, you hear me, Mr. Graham? I'll have your heinie in court so fast you won't know what bit you!"

Hudson and I look at each other, and although Hudson manages to keep things under control, I can't help it—the thought of Rommel taking on a cat just busts me up.

"You think this is funny?" she says, stepping toward me. "All you dog people are alike. You look down your noses at cats, but you think it's A-okay to let your monsters jump up on people and sniff in their privates and do their business in their yards —"

"Hey!" I said. "I've *got* a cat. I just happen to know that there's no way Hudson's dog attacked *yours*."

"Oh, is that so?" she says, locking eyes with me. "Well, excuse me if I don't believe you."

Hudson says, "Miss Kitty...," but I'm not about to let her get away with how she's acting. "Watch who you call a liar, lady."

She didn't reply, and she didn't respond to Hudson,

either. She just kept staring me down through those ridiculous eyelashes.

"Miss Kitty?" Hudson tried again.

"Is this sassy brat a relative of yours?" she asks without taking her eyes off me.

"I am *not* a brat," I tell her, still staring her down.

Hudson says, "Kitty—"

"*Miss* Kitty!"

"Miss Kitty, please listen to me. Rommel couldn't possibly have attacked your cat. He's old and arthritic."

"He's a *canine*," she says. Like she's hacking up a fur ball. "It doesn't matter how old they get, a dog's got it in for a cat."

Wow. This woman could stare. My eyes were watering, but no way was I going to blink.

"Miss Kitty!" Hudson says. "If you would please just follow me, I have something to show you." He backhands me softly and says, "Quit it, will you?" under his breath.

So, okay. For Hudson I let her win the stare-down. Then I turn away and blink a gazillion times to clear my eyes before following along into the house.

Hudson leads Miss Kitty over to a corner of the kitchen, where Rommel's sleeping in a little wicker bed on the floor. "There he is," he says, "my bloodthirsty beast."

A wiener dog is not real ferocious-looking to begin with, but at this stage in his life, Rommel's got more sausage than spice, if you know what I mean. It's a wonder he can walk anywhere at all. Especially without scraping bottom.

She frowns. "That can't be him."

"It's the only dog I've got," Hudson says, putting a piece of mega-maple cake onto a plate. "How long has your cat—you said her name was Snowball, right?"

"*His* name," she snaps, sort of circling Rommel's bed. She was dying to poke him to see if he'd spring into action, you could just tell.

"Ah. Well, how long has Snowball been missing?"

"Since yesterday." She nudges the wicker bed with her shoe. Rommel doesn't budge, so she mutters, "He's playing possum."

"No, he's just old," Hudson says, laying a fork on the plate alongside the cake. "He's thirteen."

"Thirteen? Really?" I ask.

"That's not so old for a dog," ol' Bleachy Brain says. "Especially not a beagle."

"You mean dachshund," Hudson says.

"Same difference," she mutters, frowning at Rommel.

Hudson hands her the slice of cake. "So if a cat happens by, how will we know it's Snowball?"

Her face pinches at the sight of the cake. Like she thinks Hudson's trying to poison her. She waves off the offer and says, "He's black."

"*Black?*" I choke out. "Why'd you name him Snowball if he's black?"

"Because he's mine and I could." She turns to Hudson. "Snowball's fluffy, with green eyes and a long, bushy tail."

"Does he have a collar? Tags?" Hudson asks.

"Just a Zodiac."

"Pardon?"

"A flea collar," I whisper.

"Oh," Hudson says.

"Not that he *has* any of those nasty beasts," she says. "But since there are flea-ridden *dogs* in this neighborhood, you can't be too careful." She scribbles her phone number on a napkin and says, "Call me if you see him." And just like that she clomps out of the house. No, Sorry I accused your dog of mauling my cat. No, Thank you for listening. No nothing.

"Wow," I whispered when she was gone. "She's something." Then I asked, "And what's with the tiara?"

Hudson shrugged. "She was once rodeo queen."

"Her? When? A hundred years ago?"

He pinned her phone number to a small bulletin board by the table. "Don't be cruel, Sammy."

"Cruel? I'm not trying to be cruel. But she must be, like, *fifty*. Are you saying she's still wearing the crown she won when she was a teenager?"

Hudson nodded. "That's what I've heard."

"Hudson, that's crazy. Why would anybody want to go around wearing—"

"Because she's trying to hold on to the past, Sammy." He sighed and shook his head. "I can only feel sorry for her."

"Feel *sorry* for her? Why?"

"Because it's pretty obvious that the high point of her life was that crowning moment at seventeen or eighteen. You can't relive your glory days—and there's no living new ones if you're a prisoner of the past."

I thought about that a minute, then said, "So why haven't I ever seen her before?" I laughed and added, "Believe me, I'd have noticed!"

"It's been a good five years since *I've* seen her. She lives in that orange adobe place down the street."

My eyes bugged out. "*That* place? Every time I go by, there are cats everywhere. On the fences, on the porch, in the yard . . . that place is just creepin' with cats!"

"Very well put," he laughed.

"And she wants to be called *Kitty*?" I shook my head. "I think she's more like *crazy*."

Hudson gave a little nod. "She's definitely someone who could use a little help."

I snorted.

And that, I thought, was the end of that.

TWO

After the Kitty Queen left, Hudson invited me to watch him develop some pictures in his darkroom. Now, if it had been a school day, I might have gone. But it was Saturday, and it was beautiful outside. Flowers were blooming, birds were chirping, there were little puffer-belly clouds all across the sky. And the air smelled sweet—like pine resin and honeysuckle and . . . sawdust. I love the smell of sawdust. Don't ask me why, I just do.

Anyway, the point is, I didn't feel like being cooped up in a dark little room with stinky developer and a bare red safety bulb. I wanted to go *do* something. And normally I would have ridden over to Marissa's house, only Marissa had been kidnapped by her parents for a weekend of "family love and reacquaintance" in Las Vegas, of all places.

So instead I headed over to the Pup Parlor to see if I could get my friend Holly to break away from her chores. But as I was cruising up Broadway, clicking along the sidewalk past the Heavenly Hotel, this lady I know named Gina—or Madame Nashira, as she's called by her clients—steps out of the lobby.

"Sammy," she sings. "How *are* you, girl?"

"Great," I tell her. "How about you?" I size up all her scarves and bracelets and her mountain of shellacked hair. "You going to work?"

"Yup," she says. "The House of Astrology awaits." She grins and adds, "Got a birth chart to finish — some classy lady's paying me double to do a rush job."

"Cool," I tell her, 'cause even though I don't believe in all that stuff, Gina makes it seem interesting. I mean, listening to her talk about the twelve houses of the zodiac, and conversions into sidereal time, and all the other stuff she jabbers on about when she's telling you what she does as a fortune-teller, well, it almost makes you believe that she really is a star scientist.

Anyway, she says, "Don't be a stranger, girlfriend. Stop by and see me sometime." And she's hurrying off, tippy-tap-tapping her way down to Main Street in her spiky high heels, when all of a sudden she turns and says, "You're an Aries, aren't you?"

For a second I just stare, but finally I nod and shrug like, Yeah, so what?

She tippy-tap-taps back to me, then tilts my chin up and looks deep into my eyes. "And you have a birthday coming up real soon, don't you?"

I break free of her and shrug again, saying, "Yeah. Tomorrow," as I toe at microscopic rocks with my high-top.

"Tomorrow! Well, hey. I know you think it's bogus, but you ought to let me do your birth chart. I promised it to you way back in what? September? Let me give it to you for your birthday. All I need is a birth certificate."

She laughs. "You got one of those, right? Everybody's got one of those."

I shake my head. "Well, actually, no."

"Well, your *mom* does, right? She's got to. So get it from her. Then come in and see me." She starts walking down the street, calling, "It'll be fun!"

So I head up to the Pup Parlor, trying to shake off the thought of my birthday. And when I jingle through the door, I call out "Hi, Vera. Hi, Meg!" to Holly's guardians. "Is Holly around?"

Meg was combing out a cairn terrier, and Vera was busy soaping down a golden retriever. Both of them said, "Sammy!" and then Vera added, "Holly's out back, dumping the trash."

"Probably peeking in on that carnival next door," Meg said.

Vera blasted on the water sprayer, calling, "Go on back and see!"

"Thanks!"

I went through the grooming room, turned left at the register, and made my way past pet carriers and stacks of towels to the back door. And sure enough, there was Holly, crouched behind the bumper of a long white van, peeking in Slammin' Dave's back door, a big plastic garbage bag at her side.

"Hey!" I whispered when I got up close.

She jumped a little, then laughed. "You should never have gotten me started on this."

I laughed, too. "I know. But how can you *not* watch?"

There were guys pumping iron over to one side and bodies smacking onto mats on another. The guy with the cat hood was there, talking to a man wearing a white T-shirt and jeans. Slammin' Dave was coaching two wrestlers in the ring. One had a good-sized gut hanging over tight black wrestling shorts. The other guy was in skimpy red shorts and had the biggest outie I'd ever seen. I swear, it looked like a little fleshy toilet plunger, without the stick. Both of them were wearing tall black wrestling shoes, knee pads, and elbow pads.

"That's Ronnie Reaper in black and The Blitz in red," Holly whispered.

Ronnie Reaper dragged The Blitz along, spun him around, then lifted him up and dropped him so The Blitz's stomach squashed across his knee.

Holly cringed, "Oowww," as The Blitz collapsed onto the mat.

Slammin' Dave pulled Ronnie Reaper back, and when The Blitz straightened up, I was sure his outie would have been plunged to an innie, but there it was, poking way out.

I whispered, "I always thought pro wrestling was so bogus, but man, they are really hurting each other."

Holly nodded. "Meg and Vera call it a carnival—which it kind of is—but they won't even give it a chance."

Just then Slammin' Dave comes charging toward us, saying, "How many times do I have to tell you? This is not a peep show!"

"Hey!" I call as he's shutting the door in our faces. "I'm thinking about signing up!"

He hesitates, and looks me over. "You?"

"Yeah!" I flex a biceps at him. "I've got potential, don't you think?"

He snickers.

"C'mon!" I flex a little harder and turn from side to side like a body builder. "I may be scrawny, but I'm tough. And Holly here's a real gymnast. She does flips and stuff like you wouldn't believe."

Holly looks at me like, I do? but Dave doesn't seem to notice. Instead, he stops scowling and actually opens the door a little wider.

"Besides," I tell him, "everyone's always saying how bogus pro wrestling is, but I tell them you're for real."

Now he's grinning. "You do, huh?"

"Yeah! So come on. Don't close the door."

All of a sudden the guy in the cat mask is standing behind him. "We're ready," he says to Slammin' Dave. His voice is low and raspy, which is kind of creepy right there. But then he looks at me, and I about freak. He's got *cat* eyes—yellowish gold with long black pupils. And I know he's just wearing a pair of those wacky contact lenses you can buy for parties and stuff, but the whole package of him in his cat hood and those eyes is giving me chills.

"Well," Slammin' Dave says to us. "We do need the ventilation, so as long as you're interested in the sport, and not just gawking..."

"We'll be cool," I tell him. "And don't worry, we won't put up bleachers or anything."

19

He laughs and wags a finger at me. "Start pumping some iron—someday we'll put that spunk of yours to good use." Then he props the door all the way open and heads back inside.

The cat guy, though, doesn't follow him right away. He waits until Dave's out of earshot, then steps toward me and whispers, "Go away!"

"Dave said we could stay."

He glances over his shoulder, then says between his teeth, "Curiosity kills the cat, so scat!"

Now, I'm not big on being bossed around. Especially not by potbellied cat dudes. So I lean forward a little and—just because it seems like a good way to get my point across to this guy—I bare my teeth and let out a low, doggy growl.

He doesn't say a word. He just squints his cat eyes at me, then follows Slammin' Dave back to the ring.

"Wow," Holly whispers. "That guy's got issues."

"No kidding."

Anyway, we keep watching for a little while, and we get totally into the way The Blitz and Ronnie Reaper are going at it in the ring. Holly and I even try a couple of moves that they're practicing on each other. One's a block, and the other's this slick twisteroo–hammer-hold–make-'em-bite-the-mat move. It takes us a couple of tries to get that one, but when we do, Holly and I both go, "Oh, that's cool! Let me try it again."

So we're in the middle of twisting each other around when the guy in the white T-shirt and jeans comes out with some trash.

He sees Holly and says, "Hey, chiquita. What's shakin'?"

"Hey, Tony," she says back. "We're just watching."

"Looks like you girls are preppin' for the big leagues."

Holly and I both kind of blush, but he doesn't make a big deal out of it. He throws the trash bags into Slammin' Dave's bin and says, "So when you gonna get your old ladies to hire me? I'm quick. I'm cheap. Lots of people around here use me." He takes her trash sack and flings it on top of his heap. "Let Tornado Tony do your work— you girls should be at the mall."

Holly laughs. "Thanks, but we do fine on our own."

"Don't you even want to know my rates?"

Holly shakes her head. "It's never gonna happen, Tony."

"Hey, I don't believe in never, so expect me to keep trying." Then he nods and says, "Cha-cha, girls," and goes back inside.

Holly eyes Slammin' Dave's trash bin, which is now overflowing. "I'd better not leave that there," she says, more to herself than to me. "Vera'd have a fit."

I follow her over to the Pup Parlor trash bin, asking, "So, do you think you'll have any time to cruise around today?"

"Maybe." Her trash-bin lid won't stay propped open, so I hold it up while she hefts the sack. And she's in the middle of swinging it into the bin when all of a sudden she stops and moves some papers aside. Then she gasps. It's a weird gasp, too. With a little squeak to it.

So I look inside the trash bin to see what she's so wide-eyed and gaspy about, and in a heartbeat *my* eyes are popping and *I* let out a little squeak, too.

And in my gut I just know.

We've found Snowball.

THREE

It was the ugliest dead thing I'd ever seen. The top lip was curled back in a sneer. The eyes were glazed open, and the fur was matted and gooey-looking. This cat looked like it had been slimed by a giant snail, then tossed off the Empire State Building.

"Ohhhh," Holly says. "Poor *thing*."

"Tell me that's not a Zodiac collar on him," I whisper.

Holly looks at me with disgust. "The poor thing's dead and you're worried about fleas?"

"No! It's just that..." I reach in and check the collar. "Rats!"

"Sammy, what's with you?"

So I give her a quick rundown of my morning with Hudson and the Kitty Queen, and when I'm all done, she looks back at the cat and says, "And you think *that's* Snowball?"

"Green eyes, fluffy black fur—well, before it got wet anyway—and a Zodiac collar."

"But...what happened to him? And how'd he get in *our* trash bin?"

We look around. With a big vacant lot straight ahead and Wesler Street to the right, the back side of the Pup Parlor was wide open.

"Anyone could've dumped him here," Holly whispers.

"Yeah," I said. And for some reason it seemed kind of spooky. Like if someone could dump a cat, they could also dump, you know, a body.

"So what do you want to do?" Holly asks.

I thought about it a minute. "I guess I should find out if it really is Snowball."

"You want to go get that cat lady?"

I shook my head. "Believe me, you don't want her coming here. She *hates* dogs."

Holly hesitates, then asks, "So you're thinking about taking it *to* her?"

"It's probably the easiest thing to do." I shrug. "Wanna come?"

She shrugs back. "Sure. You want me to get a Hefty bag or something?"

"Yeah. And some rubber gloves."

Of course, the minute Meg and Vera find out what's going on, they've got to check out the cat and talk about everything *we've* just talked about. But we finally get the cat in a Hefty sack and head out.

The cool thing about Holly is, she's tough. Well, except when it comes to animals, then she's like butter. But stuff like being too cold, or bugs, or scrapes and bruises, she doesn't let faze her. She also has her own skateboard, so we made good time carrying the Ugliest Dead Thing Ever across town.

When I turned onto Cypress Street, Holly asked, "Are you stopping in at Hudson's?"

"Good idea!" I called back. "We could use rein-forcements!"

"You're not really afraid of her, are you?"

"Afraid? No. But she's strange, Holly. You'll see what I mean."

Hudson didn't answer his door, though. Then I remembered he was going to develop pictures, so I went around back and knocked on his darkroom door.

No answer.

So I pulled up the garage door and peeked inside.

His car was gone.

"You want to wait for him?" Holly asked.

"Nah." I shifted the Ugliest Dead Thing Ever under my other arm. "Let's go."

So we took off again, and when we got to the orange adobe house, I said, "This is it."

The grass was dry and patchy, and the shrubs had long branches shooting out everywhere. Like Pippi Long-stocking hair, only green.

And of course, there were cats. I noticed three right away, but as we made our way up the walkway, more cats appeared. From under bushes, from around the house, from under the porch, they were all coming toward us, *staring* at us.

"Wow," Holly said, picking up her board. "This *is* creepy."

Then I heard the Kitty Queen's voice calling, "What do *you* want?" from behind the screen door.

"Uh . . . I think we found Snowball," I called back.

The screen door whipped open and Kitty pounced onto the porch. "What? Where?" she demanded. A sleek white cat and a calico followed her out of the house, and behind them came a string of kittens.

"Um . . ." Two *more* cats came down a walkway on the left side of the house. I held the Hefty sack out. "I . . . I'm not positive, but . . . but it fits the description." I put down the bag and started backing up.

The Kitty Queen came down the porch steps, squinting at us. "Are you telling me Snowball's in that *bag*?"

"Well, I . . . I really hope it's *not* Snowball, but . . ."

She snatched the sack and opened it, glaring at me the whole time. Then she turned the dead cat out onto the ground and wailed, "Noooo!"

All of a sudden I felt terrible. "Are you sure it's him? Maybe it's just a cat that—"

"Of course I'm sure!" she wailed. The cats surrounding us had quit staring at me and were now twitching their noses around Snowball. Miss Kitty said, "Ebony, Biscuit, get inside! Shoo, kitties, shoo! You, too, Moonie, Jeepers . . . inside!"

Now, the amazing thing is, one by one, every single cat turned and padded away. They didn't streak off or even hurry along, either. They walked. And as they walked, they kept turning their heads to look over their shoulders. Not at Snowball or the Kitty Queen.

No, at *me*.

It was creepy, let me tell you. It was like they were thinking that *I* had killed their friend, and they were going to figure out a way to get me back.

The Kitty Queen had been inspecting Snowball, and now she snapped, "Where'd you find him?"

"In a . . . in a trash can," I said.

"In a *trash* can?"

"Uh-huh." The cats were all gone, but I was still feeling a little freaked out.

"Where?" She was checking out his neck. His back. His flank.

"Um . . ." I looked at Holly, trying to figure out exactly how much I *didn't* want to say. "In an alley by Broadway. Off Wesler."

She was prying open his mouth now. "By that hideous hotel?"

She was calling the Heavenly hideous? Had she looked in a mirror lately? But I just bit my tongue and said, "Yeah. Right around there."

She pulled something out of Snowball's mouth, then turned to squint at us. "And why were you looking in trash cans back there?"

She was really unnerving Holly, so I said, "Holly works over there. She was just taking out the trash and happened to notice him."

The Kitty Queen looked at Holly with a sneer. "I doubt you work at the Heavenly. Or that wrestling place. And you're too young to work at the bank." Her eyes flashed. "Unless . . ." She stood up and crept in on Holly. "Unless you work at that nasty Pup Parlor!"

"It's not nasty!" Holly said. "It's—"

"Evil!" she shouted, pouncing forward. Then she

wagged something in Holly's face and screeched, "Do you know what this is?"

We both jumped back, but she pounced again. "DO YOU KNOW WHAT THIS IS?"

"No!" Holly cried.

"It's the ear of a dog!" She wagged it again. "You see it? Huh? This is what killed my kitty!"

I said, "But—" but she turned and pounced *my* way, screeching, "But nothing!"

"Hey!" I shouted, trying to stand my ground. "It's not *our* fault!"

"If it weren't for *you,* my cat would probably still be alive!"

She was staring me down again, but boy, I wasn't going to let her win this time. I stared right back, saying, "How can you say that? We didn't have anything to do with this!"

"You expect me to believe that?" She pointed at Holly but still locked eyes with me. "*She* pampers killers! She washes them, she dries them, she puts little bows on them. She fools the general public into believing that they're cuddly, friendly companions when what they are is kitty killers!"

"You're crazy, you know that?" Her eyes flared when I said that, and it flashed through my brain that maybe she was actually possessed. She sure looked like it! But I tried not to act scared as I said, "You don't even know that's part of a dog's ear. You can't tell anything from that! It's way too small. Maybe it was another cat! Ever think of that? Maybe some tomcat killed him!"

"Maybe some *dog* killed him," she said, keeping her

eyes locked on mine as she lifted the piece of ear between our faces.

Now, even with my eyes on hers, I could see the tattered tan hide, crusted in blood. That was plenty gross to begin with, but then she started rubbing it between her fingers, saying, "This feels like dog..." She brought it closer to her face and her nose twitched. "It smells like dog..." Then very slowly, she brought it to her lips and *licked* it. "And girl, it *tastes* like dog."

"Eeeew," I said, and turned away. How could anyone win a stare-down against that?

Before she can gloat, though, a voice behind me says, "Sammy?"

I spin around. "Officer Borsch!"

"Took you long enough," the Kitty Queen snaps.

"I just got on shift, ma'am." He sizes up the situation. Me. Holly. Kitty-the-Dog-Licker. The dead cat. Then he lets out a deep sigh and says, "Why do I get the feeling that this is going to be more complicated than a simple missing cat?"

"There's no such thing as a simple missing cat!" the Dog Licker says down her nose at him. "And because of all your attention to my last two reports"—she points to Snowball—"*this* is what I have to face today!"

"I'm sorry for your loss, ma'am, but—"

"Oh, you don't give a hoot! There's a dog out there, and he's mauling my kitties! I expect you to find him, catch him, and destroy him!"

Officer Borsch hikes up his gun belt and nods. "We are doing the best we—"

29

"Oh, let me guess," she says. "You've got your *canine* patrol on the case, right?"

Officer Borsch takes a deep breath, then goes over and stands by Snowball, looking down at him. "Who found him?"

So I tell him the story about Holly taking out the trash, and when I'm done he *hmm*s and makes little sucking noises through his teeth. Then finally he lets out a weary sigh and says, "None of that gives me much to work with."

The Dog Licker wags the piece of ear in his face. "Well, this should!"

"What's that?"

"A *dog* ear! I pried it out of my poor kitty's mouth."

Officer Borsch squints at the fragment of fur. "A dog ear? Ma'am, how can you be so sure..."

"Don't ask," I whisper to him. "You don't want to know."

He eyes me, then takes another deep breath and goes back to his squad car for a Ziploc. And when he's got the piece of fur bagged, he takes off, saying, "We'll be sure to contact you if we discover anything."

"You can't just leave!" the Kitty Queen screeches after him. "You have to write a report! You have to—" but Officer Borsch just keeps on trucking. So she takes it out on us. "Well?" she says. "What are you brats hanging around for?"

I snort and grumble, "You're welcome," and head for the sidewalk. But before we can reach it, that crazy cat woman cranks up a hose and shouts, "Here's the thanks you deserve!" and soaks us with a power nozzle.

"What did you do *that* for?" I scream, charging back at her.

But she just blasts me until Holly drags me away, saying, "Sammy, come on!"

I was soaked from my head clear down to my butt. Water was actually running down my legs, inside my jeans. "Hold up a minute," I said when we were on the sidewalk and out of reach. I wrung out my hair. I wrung out my shirt.

"Wow. She nailed you!"

"She's psycho!"

"You can say that again."

So I'd wrung out all the water I could, and we were about to head up Cypress when I spotted a police car cruising toward us. "Don't forget," I whispered when I saw that it was Officer Borsch, "he can *not* know where I live."

Officer Borsch powered down the window, then leaned across the seat and called, "Wow. What happened to you?"

"That psycho hosed me down!"

He shook his head and chuckled, then nodded over to Holly. "I remember you now. New Year's. Sisquane. That whole business with the pig."

Holly nodded and tried to keep a straight face. Not an easy thing, thinking back to how a two-hundred-pound pig had followed the Borschman all over Sisquane.

We'd called it Oinkers in Love.

"Hey," I said. "Do you really think that piece of fuzz was the tip of a dog's ear? Since when do cats chomp down on dogs? Don't they just hiss and claw and run up trees when dogs chase them? I mean, it looked more like a mouse ear to me."

He nodded. "It could be anything."

"And why'd she call you about her cat, anyway? Why didn't she call the pound, or the Humane Society, or put up lost-and-found posters? This is the third one she's missing? How many does she *have*? They're all over the place!"

He nodded and moved his tongue along the inside of his bottom lip. Like he was shifting around a wad of chew, deciding which, if any, of my questions he was going to answer. Finally he said, "I don't know, I don't know, I don't know, and enough for the neighbors to complain regularly. So you see, I get the joy of dealing with this from both sides of the fence. And why me?" He frowned. "I ask myself that every day."

Just then a staticky voice came from inside the squad car. Officer Borsch sat up, said, "Ten-four, copy that," into his radio, then called, "Stay out of trouble!" and zoomed off.

My clothes and hair were still wet when we reached the intersection of Broadway and Main. And since it was about time for me to be getting home anyway, I said bye to Holly and snuck around the Senior Highrise to the fire escape.

Now, if I hadn't been soaked to the spine, I might've gone in the front door. But I didn't want the manager, Mr. Garnucci, to ask me a bunch of questions later. Like why I was so wet coming in and dry going out. Or how my grandmother happened to have an extra shirt and jeans in my size just lying around the apartment. So up the fire escape I went, to the fifth-floor door, which I've jammed with bubble gum so it doesn't latch.

And as I hurried down the hall to the apartment, I started wondering what kind of cake Grams had baked me. Maybe I'd be able to tell by smell! Yum!

But as I eased open the apartment door and said, "Can I come in?" I discovered that Grams had been up to a whole lot more than baking a cake.

FOUR

"Mom!" I cried when I saw my mother in the kitchen.

"Surprise!" she said, coming over to give me a hug.

"Wow!" I pulled back and looked at her. "You're really here!"

She laughed. A tinkly, sparkly laugh. Like it had been tapped with fairy dust.

"And oh!" I called to Grams in the kitchen. "That smells wonderful!" I inched a little closer. "I smell chocolate! And candied oranges! And toasted walnuts. And . . ."

"Stop!" Grams said. She was scrambling around like crazy. "It's supposed to be a surprise."

"It is!" I laughed, and hugged my mother again.

But after a second she backed away and said, "Samantha, you're soaked! What happened?"

"Oh," I said. "It's kind of a long story."

Grams laughed and called from the kitchen, "Prepare yourself, Lana."

My mom smiled at me like, well? So I shrugged and said, "I was hosed down by a crazy cat lady."

"For?"

"For returning her dead cat."

Mom's smile started to fade. "For returning her dead cat?"

But just then, out of nowhere, *my* cat jumps right over my feet, dives under the kitchen table, and pounces on something in the corner.

My mother puts one hand to her heart and catches her breath. "What on earth...?"

"Hey, Dorito," I say, moving toward my cat. "What'cha got there?"

Now, I can tell he's not just playing with a kitty toy— he's being way too intense. So I crouch beside him, and when he turns to face me, there's something long and skinny sticking out of his mouth. And it's *twitching*. Like some sort of freaky alien tongue.

"That's a *tail*," Mom squeaks.

I clamp onto Dorito's muzzle and try to pry his teeth apart, but Grams kneels beside me and says, "It's a mouse, Samantha—just let him have it!"

"But Grams...!" I felt so sorry for the mouse, trapped inside jaws of death, twitching like crazy to get free.

"Oh! Eeeew!" my mom squeals, and believe me, she's looking around for a chair to jump on.

"Samantha," Grams says gently, "this is what cats do. This is what they're for."

I frown at her. "This is what they're *for*? You mean you got me Dorito so he could catch mice?"

She sighs. "Look. If there are mice in the building, they're going to have to exterminate them anyway."

"Oh! Eeeew!" Mom says again with her hands to her cheeks.

35

I've got Dorito's lips peeled back, but he's not giving up the mouse. His big yellow eyes are actually glaring at me. And Grams is still coaching me, saying, "Samantha, mice can carry salmonella or hantavirus or Lyme disease, not to mention fleas. They're not animals you want in your house!"

By now the tail has stopped twitching, but I pry Dorito's mouth open anyway. "Let go, Dorito!"

Grams grumbles, "You are so stubborn...," and Dorito gives me a disgusted look, but finally he opens up and lets me have the mouse.

I hold it out, letting it dangle by its tail. It's so little. So cute.

So dead.

"Oh eeeew!" my mom says again. "You have *mice*."

"It's just a baby, Lana," Grams says to her. "And it's the first one I've ever seen."

"But...," my mom says, giving her a panicked look, "a baby means there's an entire *litter* somewhere. It means—"

"Oh, Lana. Don't get yourself all worked up. It's just a mouse."

"But you yourself said they can carry salmonella or hantavirus or Lyme disease. Not to mention"—she shudders, nose to toes—"fleas."

So I'm dangling a tiny dead mouse by the tail, with a disgusted cat on one side and a flea-phobic mother on the other, when Grams says, "Just take it downstairs, would you?"

"Take it downstairs?" I ask. "And do what with it?"

"Throw it out!"

"But—"

"And don't use the trash chute. Millie in five-oh-two says it's plugged up again."

"But—"

"Just go!" Grams whispers, eyeing my mother, who's looking like she's about to faint.

So okay. I sneak down the fire escape and over to the Dumpster. And maybe I should have just tossed the little flea-infested, hantavirus-carrying rodent in and forgotten about him, but he was so cute. And it just felt so . . . wrong.

So I wound up saying, "Sorry, little guy. I hope mousy heaven's a really nice place. With lots of crackers and cheese and . . . and whatever else you like." And since one side of the Dumpster was open like it always is to catch trash from the chute, I was just reaching in to lay the mouse on something, you know, soft and not too smelly—like that made any sense, I know, but that's what I was doing—when I noticed the tip of something sticking out from underneath a grocery sack of trash.

It was orange. And furry.

I just stood there holding the mouse by its tail, thinking, It *can't* be. But when I pushed aside the grocery sack, there it was.

A big dead cat.

Not only was it a big dead cat, it was a big dead cat that looked like it had been hurled off the Empire State Building. Its eyes were glazed open, and its fur looked gelled out in spots. Like it had been electrocuted.

I thought about tracking down Officer Borsch but nipped that idea right in the bud. I sure didn't want to have to deal with nosy questions about why I was digging through the Highrise Dumpster.

But I didn't want to just leave the cat. For one thing, I could see a collar and a tag—this was somebody's pet. But I didn't really want to touch it, either. Something about it was really...creepy.

Finally I decided to zip over to the Pup Parlor and get Holly. So I lay the mouse in the Dumpster, ran across the Highrise lawn, jaywalked Broadway, and jingled through the Pup Parlor door. "Hey, Vera. Hi, Meg. Can I borrow Holly?"

"Again?" Meg asked.

Holly appeared from the back of the shop. "Hey, I thought you went home to change."

"Yeah, but, well..." I decided to cut to the chase. "I found another dead cat."

"You're kidding, right?"

"No. And it looks a lot like Snowball did." I spazzed up my arms, stuck out my tongue, and cranked open my eyes.

"Where is it?"

"In the Highrise Dumpster."

"Are you going to tell Officer Borsch?"

"I...don't know."

Meg nodded. "That would open up a can of worms, wouldn't it?"

"Exactly. But the cat's got tags, so I want to at least check it out."

"Okay," Holly said. "Let me get some gloves and a plastic liner."

So Holly and I dashed back to the Senior Highrise, and when she saw the cat, she said, "Wow. It looks like the same thing killed both cats."

I snapped the gloves on. "I know. But why would someone put one here, and one over there?"

"So maybe they're not connected."

"But what are the odds that there's a dead cat in *my* trash can and another in *yours*?"

"So what are you saying?"

I hopped up and leaned into the Dumpster. "I don't know. I'm just thinking out loud."

I had a little trouble reaching the cat, and since I didn't want to actually climb into the Dumpster, I wound up pulling the cat toward me by its tail. I felt a little bad about doing it, which was stupid—it was way beyond feeling a thing.

But then all of a sudden Holly cried, "Look! There's a dead *mouse,* too!"

I pushed off of the rim, saying, "I put him there. Dorito caught it—which is how I found the cat."

"Oh! For a second there I thought . . . well, I don't know what I thought!"

I read the cat's tags. "His name's Mr. T."

"Phone number?"

"Yup." I scooped him into the bag and tied it closed. "Something about this is just too weird." My spine was tingling, which, believe me, is never a good sign. It means I'm either in serious trouble, or about to put myself there. But I couldn't ignore what I was thinking, so finally I just said it: "Holly, what if these aren't the only cats?"

"Huh?"

"What if there are *more* of them? What if there are cats in trash cans all up and down the block?"

"But . . . why?"

"What if the Psycho Kitty Queen's right? What if there's someone in town who *hates* cats? What if they're going around killing them?"

"Sammy! Who in their right mind would do that?"

I pulled a face at her. "We live in Santa Martina, remember? This town is full of wackos."

"Good point."

"So what if someone's killing cats and putting them around town in different people's trash cans?"

She shrugged. "Well, why not just put them all in one Dumpster?"

"Because if someone happens to notice one cat in a trash can, that's one thing. It's no reason to call the police, right? But if there are two, or three, or *four,* you're going to think, Whoa now! Something weird is going on."

"But—"

"Is your trash pickup on Mondays?"

"Yeah."

"Ours, too. Which means we've got today and tomorrow to check around. And tomorrow . . . well, tomorrow's out for me."

"So you're saying you want to go snooping through trash cans?"

I nodded. "That's what I'm saying."

She laughed and shook her head. "Isn't that ironic."

I grinned at her and said, "Yeah, it's ironic," because back before Meg and her mother, Vera, took her in, Holly was a foster-home runaway. She lived her life digging through trash, and even after she wasn't homeless any more, she *still* did it. I finally had to yell at her to stop, because it was so embarrassing walking around with someone who snooped through everyone's garbage.

She laughed. "So when do you want to start?"

"Well, my mom's here—"

"Your *mom's* here?"

"Yeah. And I should get back up there, but I already need a shower so . . ."

"So you want to go now?"

"Just for a little while. Why don't we start behind your building and take a quick check around the block?"

"Sounds good to me." She nodded at the plastic sack. "What about Mr. T?"

"Can we leave him behind the Pup Parlor for now?"

She shrugged. "Don't see why not."

So we raced back across the lawn, jaywalked Broadway *again,* and after we'd shown Meg and Vera the Unfortunate Mr. T, we grabbed a couple of plastic liners and some clean gloves and got to work.

There was nothing in Slammin' Dave's trash. Nothing in any of the trash cans on Wesler. Nothing down the next street or in the alley or the Heavenly Hotel's Dumpster. We ran from can to can, got barked at by a lot

41

of dogs, and got some pretty strange looks from people, but we didn't find any cats.

Well, not dead ones anyway.

When we got to Main Street, I sighed and said, "It sure *felt* like we were on to something."

"We've still got the whole Maynard's area and down that way," Holly said.

"Yeah, but I've got to get back home." I handed her my gloves and sacks. "Thanks for doing this with me."

"Sure," she said as I took off running. "I'll call you later!"

"Bye!"

When I got home, my mom said, "There you are!"

"Sorry!" I said. "I found another dead cat down in the Dumpster—"

"Another dead cat?" My mother's face crinkled up. "What on earth . . .?"

"I know. So I went over to Holly's 'cause—"

"Enough talk of dead things," Grams said. "Why don't you take a quick shower and I'll make us some lunch. We've got lots we need to talk about." Then she looked over at my mother and said, "Right?"

My mom smiled politely, then looked away.

Lots to talk about? As I went to Grams' dresser and got a change of clothes, my whole body started feeling disconnected. Like my ligaments weren't holding my bones together right. Had the day finally come that my mom was going to tell me who my father was? Did she finally think I was old enough?

I was going to be fourteen! Of course I was old

enough—I'd been old enough for years! I just hadn't had any luck convincing *her* of that. And Grams had always insisted on staying out of it. "It's not my place to tell you, Samantha." How many times had I heard *that*?

But now...well, there was obviously *something*, and what else could it be? So as I took my shower, I started getting nervous. Almost panicky. Why had my father been such a secret all these years? Was he a criminal? A jerk? Slimy? *Dead*? I mean, what was taking so long for her to tell me if there *wasn't* something weird about him? She wouldn't be keeping it from me if he was just some normal guy, right?

But then maybe that wasn't it at all. Maybe she was just going to share how...oh no! What if she wanted me to come live with her! No! It had to be my dad. It just had to be.

I got out of the shower and got dressed quick. And I'd worked myself into such a state that I just barged into the kitchen, where Grams and Mom were putting together sandwiches, and said, "Are you here to tell me who my father is?"

"Your"—Mom's face turned white as she looked at Grams—"father?"

"Mom! I'm going to be fourteen—I can handle it!"

My mom gave me a quivery smile. "Well...no. That's not why I'm here."

"It's not?"

"No! I'm here because it's your birthday, sweetheart."

All of a sudden my mind flashed with an idea. "Okay, then, for my birthday I want my birth certificate."

"Your what?"

"My birth certificate."

"But...it doesn't say who your father is."

"You wrote Unknown?" I blinked at her like mad, then said, "*Is* he unknown?"

Grams had been trying to stay out of it, but when she heard that, she scolded, "Samantha!"

"Well?" I asked. "What else am I supposed to think?"

"You're supposed to think...you're supposed to think...." Grams looked to my mom for help.

I shook my head. "Mom, in a few hours I'll be fourteen. *Fourteen.* Why is this such a big secret? Do you have any idea what kids my age talk about? Believe me, talking about who my dad is, is not going to shock me." Then, since she was just standing there like a fish out of water, I said, "And even if it doesn't tell me anything, I still want my birth certificate."

"But...but why?" she stammered.

"Because I have a friend who's an astrologer and she needs it to do my birth chart."

"Your birth chart? What's that?"

"It's a way astrologers map out...you know, things about you. She usually gets a lot of money to do them because they're really complicated, but she's going to do mine for free."

"Why?"

"Because I helped her get her watch back."

"Her watch?"

"Never mind, Mom. The point is, I want my birth certificate."

"But I thought you didn't believe in the zodiac."

I studied her a minute. "That's not the point."

"Then what *is* the point?"

"For my birthday, I want my birth certificate."

Finally Grams steps forward and says, "I think we can work that out, Samantha, but first, there's something else your mother wants to talk to you about." She picks up a tray of sandwiches and heads into the living room, whispering to my mother, "It's time, Lana."

My mom fidgets. She flutters. She blinks and she sputters. Then she sits in the armchair, picks up a sandwich, looks at me, and says, "Funny you should ask about your birth certificate."

"Why's it funny?"

"Because I have a little confession to make."

My head starts racing with the craziest ideas. If it wasn't about my father, then what could it possibly be? Wait! Maybe I wasn't really hers. Hey, why hadn't I thought of that before? It made perfect sense to me! It explained everything. But why would she adopt me when, let's face it, she didn't really *want* me. So maybe I was stolen? Maybe...but why would she steal something she didn't want? Or maybe they found me in a Dumpster. Yeah! Maybe they found me in a Dumpster and couldn't figure out what to do with me so they kept me. Or...

Grams eyes my mother and prompts, "Lana..."

"Don't push me, Mother," my mom says back. Then she turns and gives me a quivery smile and I can tell—this is it.

FIVE

So there I am, holding my breath, waiting for my mom to drop her bombshell, and you know what she says? She says, "Do you remember what a rough time you had in kindergarten?"

"Kindergarten?" I squint at her. Leave it to my mom to bring up a completely unrelated, very sore subject. "What's kindergarten got to do with anything?"

"Well, I made a mistake."

"About *kindergarten*? You mean you shouldn't have let them hold me back?"

"No, no. It was true—you weren't ready."

"Kindergarten was stupid," I grumbled. "The first time and *especially* the second time. Like I didn't know my ABCs? Like I couldn't count to twenty?"

"I know, Samantha. You *were* smart. Which is why I did what I did."

"Did what you . . . what did you do?"

Her eyes were fluttering like crazy. Her mouth was in hypertwitch. But she didn't answer my question. Instead she said, "To this day I don't understand why you couldn't have just sat still. Squirm, squirm, squirm. And you'd talk out of turn and tackle other kids. There was this one boy, Tyrone, do you remember him? Big kid, and nice as can be. You'd tackle him and steal his scooter. One time you even gave him a black eye!"

"Mom! WHAT DID YOU DO?"

"Well, I...I..." She gave me a cross look. "And there's no need to shout." Then she composed herself and said, "You have to understand, I thought you were ready! You were so precocious. Your vocabulary was astonishing! And even though you were a little small, I thought you could handle it. I thought waiting another year would make you so *bored*. Besides, I was having trouble making ends meet and...and...it seemed like the perfect solution!"

It felt like a cold drop of water was trickling down my spine. "Are you saying...do you mean that..." I knew she was trying to tell me something big, only I wasn't quite getting it.

Then Grams rolls her eyes and says, "Just tell her, Lana."

"All right, all right," Mom snaps. Then she does a total diva pose, with her hand to her forehead as she sighs and looks down. "Samantha, it was the wrong thing to do and I'm sorry. But I did it, and it's time you knew."

"Knew *what*?"

She drops her hand and sighs again. "The reason you weren't ready for kindergarten was because you actually weren't ready for kindergarten."

"*What*?"

"You were only four years old."

Like two ice drifts heading for each other, my life and my mother's lie crashed together. I felt cold. Helpless. Destroyed. It was worse than being adopted.

Or stolen.

Or found in a Dumpster.

Finally I choked out, "That means I'm only *twelve*?"

She gave me a helpless little look and tried to smile. "But tomorrow you'll be thirteen ... "

"So you what? Doctored my birth certificate? I mean, the school makes you give them a birth certificate, right?"

She nodded. "And then when they had you repeat kindergarten, I just ... well, I couldn't bring myself to tell them the truth."

"But what about *me*? Why didn't you tell *me*?"

"I was afraid you would spill the beans. And because you were always so proud of turning another year older. I didn't have the heart to—"

I sprang to my feet. "I can't *believe* this! I can't believe that you would *do* that! All these years I thought I'd failed kindergarten! Do you know how *embarrassing* that is? But no, I didn't really fail—you just put me in too early! It was easier for you to stick me in school than it was for you to take care of me!"

"Samantha!" Grams said. "Samantha, that's just not true. Try to understand that your mother—"

"No!" I shouted. "And why didn't *you* tell me, Grams? I can't believe you've gone along with this all these years!"

"Please try to understand. Your mother wanted to—"

"I don't care what *she* wanted! This is *my* life! You should've told me!"

And before either one of them could stop me, I bolted out the door.

Nobody should have to be thirteen twice. It's not like I really believe in bad luck, but for me thirteen had not been a very good year.

Scratch that—it'd been downright rotten.

Plus, in the back of my mind, turning fourteen was like quietly turning the corner on bad things. Like escaping bad luck. Being fourteen was a lot more "almost sixteen" than being thirteen. It was a lot closer to driving and earning my own money and just being, you know, independent.

But now all of a sudden I was twelve. Twelve! How could I be twelve? I felt like such a little kid! Twelve-year-olds don't do the things I'd been doing for the past year. They're too...young. This meant I'd been sneaking up the fire escape since I was *eleven*? What kind of insane mother did I have?

I stumbled across the Highrise lawn, jaywalked Broadway, and burst through the Pup Parlor door.

"What's wrong?" Vera asked when she saw my face. She put down a dog brush and hurried over. "What happened? Are you all right?"

"No!" I said, shaking all over. "I'm...I'm..."

She put her arm around me. "You're what, dear?"

"I'm...I'm..." I felt like I was choking.

Meg was there now, too. So was Holly.

I looked from one to the other to the other. "I'm . . . I'm . . ."

"Sammy, it's okay," Holly whispered. "Just say it."

"I'm . . ." They all hung on the word until I burst into tears, crying, *"twelve!"*

"You're . . . twelve?" Vera asked, and her arm loosened around my shoulders.

I nodded.

"What?" Meg said.

Tears were springing out everywhere.

"I don't understand," Vera said. "Aren't you *supposed* to be twelve?"

"No!" I cried, and I actually stamped my foot. "I'm supposed to be thirteen! I'm supposed to be turning fourteen tomorrow!"

"But . . ." they all said, then asked, "Tomorrow?"

"Yes! They held me back in kindergarten! Why? Because my mom told everyone I was five when I was only four! Only she never told *me* that! Not until today! Happy birthday, Samantha! And oh, by the way, I've been lying to you for eight years." I flung back tears. "Why am I surprised? Why am I even surprised? I hate her I hate her I hate her!"

Vera wrapped me in her arms and said, "There, there," as I bawled into her shoulder.

"Oh man," Holly said. "Your mom sure knows how to mess with your head."

"But you don't hate her," Vera said gently. "You're just hurt."

I pulled away and said, "And Grams! She's known all along."

Vera sighed. "I'm so sorry."

I needed air. Lots of air. I dried my face and said, "I'm going for a walk. I've got to get out of here."

"I'm going with you," Holly said. And Meg and Vera nodded like, Absolutely! Go!

So I tore out of there, going who-knows-where, with Holly trailing along trying to make me feel better, saying stuff like, "So look at the bright side—you *didn't* flunk kindergarten," and "You're the same person you always were—it doesn't really matter," and "Hey! Get your grandmother to make it up to you by telling your mother that she's a couple of years *older* than she really is. That'll freak her out good!"

I almost smiled at that last one. My mom's such an age-aphobic that it would be a great thing to pull. But I was too mad to actually smile. I wanted to hit something. Kick something. Smash something to bits.

Instead, I started looking in trash cans.

"Are we looking for cats?" Holly asked.

"Yeah, I guess. I just want to stop thinking about my stupid mom and her stupid stunts."

Holly shrugged. "Well, if dead cats will help you do that, I hope we find some."

I laughed. Then I laughed again. Then I looked at her and said, "Am I being that pathetic?"

"No!" she said. "I don't blame you a bit."

"But for you to be hoping we find dead cats . . ."

"Well, you know what I mean. And I have been think-ing about it all day."

"Yeah?"

"The look on Mr. T's and Snowball's faces... I don't know... it's just been haunting me."

So we stopped talking about my stupid mother, cut down a service alley, and started looking in trash cans for real. And before too long we found ourselves coming up to the propped-open back door of Maynard's Market.

There was a faded yellow El Camino parked out back, so we knew that Maynard's loser son, T.J., was working the counter. And just our luck, T.J. spotted us. "Hey!" he yelled as I pushed open his trash lid. "What do you *garbage* girls think you're doing?"

"Lookin' for dead bodies," I threw back with a glare.

"Well, that'll be *yours* if you don't scram!"

Now, for T.J. that was a really good comeback, so I actually appreciated the humor in it. "Hey," I said with a grin, "good one, Teej."

He pushed between me and his trash and slammed the lid down. "Get lost, ya hear me? I'm sicka youse."

"Of youse, T.J.? *Youse?*"

"Shaddup! I said scram!"

"We're scrammin', we're scrammin'." Then I Terminatored him with, "But we'll be back."

When we got to the sidewalk, Holly said, "Man, he's even uptight about his garbage."

"So where do you want to go now?"

Holly shrugged. "Maybe Mr. T and Snowball were the only two cats."

I shook my head. "If you had two dead cats, would you go through all that trouble?"

"But you said—"

"Well, I'm revising my theory. I mean two cats, okay, dump them in the same bin. Cover them up, no one'll know. But more than two cats, you'd want to spread them around. Reduce the risk of someone getting suspicious."

Holly sighed. "You're not ready to call it quits yet, are you?"

"I'm not ready to go home," I grumbled.

"All right," she said. "One more block."

So we dug through the trash of a travel agency.

Nothing.

We dug through the trash of a bank.

Nothing.

We tried a bridal shop and a jewelry store and a Mexican restaurant.

Nothing.

Everywhere we went, we were striking out. And by the time we were down to a carpet store, a restaurant, and a tattoo parlor, believe me, I was totally sick of digging through garbage.

"Want to just skip it?" I asked, but Holly said, "Might as well finish the block."

So we checked out the Kojo Buffet Dumpster, and the minute Holly opened the lid, we both jumped back. "Oh gross!" Holly cried. "It sure *smells* like something's dead in there!"

I held my breath as I poked through rotten vegetables

and fish heads, and brought the verdict in early. "Nothing!"

"Pee-yew!" Holly said, lowering the lid.

"Okay, how about I do Tiny's and you do the carpet place? I've had about enough of this."

"Fine by me," Holly said.

Tiny's Tattoo Parlor had the opposite sort of trash as the Kojo Buffet. It was tidy trash. All in white bags with knotted red drawstrings. It was a cinch to go through, too. I pulled out one sack, then the next, then the next. They were all light and just . . . tidy.

And I was about to say, Nothing here, only when I pulled up the fourth sack, well, I did sort of a mental double take. There wasn't a cat under it or anything, but all the other sacks in Tiny's trash had been light.

This one was heavy.

And okay, I didn't think it was a cat, because I'd already carried around a cat in a sack twice and pretty much knew what that felt like.

But still, I was curious. So I worked open the knot and spread apart the sides. And in a flash I knew—there was a sicko on the loose in Santa Martina.

"Hey, Holly!" I called, but then *she* called, "Bingo!"
"What?"

"I found one!" She waved me over to the carpet-store trash bin. "Come here!"

I closed the sack and hauled it over to where Holly was proudly pointing out a dead cat. "We weren't crazy after all!"

Hers was a big cat. Dark gray. Smooth coat. White

paws. Well fed. And even though there was dried blood on it and chunks of fur were missing, you could tell it had once been a real handsome cat.

"What's the tag say?"

Holly turned it and read, "Prince." Then she noticed my trash sack. "What's that?"

"Two cats."

"*Two?*"

"Yup. And it's not a pretty sight."

She checked them out and said, "They look heavy. We'd better get a different trash bag for Prince."

So we emptied one of the tidy sacks from the tattoo parlor, and we'd just worked it around Prince when a guy in a blood-stained apron came out of the Kojo Buffet.

Now, this guy's apron was bad enough, but when he started coming at us, shouting, "Hey, you girls there! What you doing?" and waving a *cleaver* in the air, well, Holly and I shot a look at each other, grabbed our sacks, and *ran*.

SIX

Holly and I ducked down the first driveway we came to and charged toward Main Street as fast as we could. I figured that once we got out in the open we'd be safe, but when I looked over my shoulder the guy with the cleaver was still chasing us, and gaining.

"Aaarrh!" came out of my throat, because with his bloody apron and his gleaming knife, the guy looked demented.

So there I am, running for my life with two dead cats swung over my shoulder, when all of a sudden I realize that there's a car pacing alongside me. It's not right next to me or anything, but I can tell it's there, kind of hovering behind me. And when I glance over my shoulder, who do I see?

Officer Borsch.

He's grinning through the windshield at me. And since he's looking like such a, you know, *smarty*-pants, I almost stop and hurl my dead-cat anvil right through his windshield.

But in a flash I realize that, smarty-pants or not, Officer Borsch tailing me means that Butcher Boy won't dare carve me into buffet bits right there in the street. But then when I glance behind me, Butcher Boy's gone. No bloody apron, no gleaming knife, no nothing. Just Officer Borsch grinning at me like a doggone smarty-pants.

So I drop the sack off my shoulder and sort of crumble to a halt while Officer Borsch lowers the passenger window and calls, "You know how ridiculous you look? All you need's a striped shirt and a mask to make the whole burglar-look complete."

Before I can tell him that he's being about as helpful as a ball and chain, Holly's beside me, saying to him, "Did you see that guy with the butcher knife?"

Officer Borsch's eyes open a little wider. His lips push forward a tad. Finally he says, "A guy with a knife?"

"He was chasing us!"

"Ah," he says. "And why would a man feel compelled to chase the two of you with a butcher knife? Did you, perhaps, *take* something of his?"

That did it. I picked up my sack, walked over to his car, and shoved it through his open window. "Yeah. We stole his *cats*. But not until after we *killed* them."

Holly followed up with her sack, shoving it in right after mine. Then we both stepped away and I called, "And since he's so hot to get them back, why don't you go be a hero. He works at the Kojo Buffet."

"Yeah!" Holly calls. "And while you're there, ask him why his Dumpster smells like dead bodies!"

"Wait a minute, wait a minute!" Officer Borsch says, struggling to lean past the sacks on his passenger seat. But I was too ticked off to wait a minute. I just dusted my hands off and headed up the sidewalk.

Holly was right beside me, laughing under her breath. "Man, you've got a lot of nerve."

"Me? Like you didn't just shove a dead cat in a policeman's car?" Officer Borsch had thrown his squad car in gear and was following us, so I picked up the pace, grumbling, "After all the times I've helped him, he *still* thinks I'm a criminal."

"Ladies!" Officer Borsch was calling out the window.

I spun around and snapped, "Oh, now we're ladies? A minute ago you accused us of *stealing* stuff." And before he could say anything back, I started running. Not running-like-I'm-guilty kind of running. Just an easy jog away from him.

But ol' Borschhead floors it to catch up, and get this— he puts on his revolving lights. Like he's pulling us over for jogging on the sidewalk.

I just roll my eyes at him and keep on running. But then I about jump out of my pants, because he chirps his siren at me. "Sammy!" he yells out the window. "Stop right now!"

I spin on him and punch my arms down at my sides. "You stop! Stop accusing me of stuff I didn't do! Stop implying that I'm guilty of something when I'm only trying to help! Holly and I have spent hours digging through trash cans for evidence and all I get from you is attitude."

"Attitude? *Me?*" Then he says, "And what evidence are you talking about?"

"What do *you* care? You probably never even owned a cat in your life. You probably—"

"Hey. Hey, I don't know what this is all about. Why don't I meet you at the Pup Parlor, okay? We'll straighten everything out."

I just stood there, sputtering and spattering like an egg in hot oil, until finally I said, "Fine!" and stormed off.

Now, when you're a cop, you don't have to worry about red lights or double yellow lines or illegal U-turns. You just put on your siren and boogie. Which is why Officer Borsch was already waiting in front of the Pup Parlor with the sacks unloaded when we arrived. "You weren't kidding about what's in here," he said.

I felt like saying Duh! but rolled my eyes instead.

"Look, Sammy, I thought we were past all this hostility. What's going on? Is puberty kicking in?"

"Puberty?" I flew at him. Just launched myself at him and started pounding on him with both fists. "What kind of *stupid*—"

Holly grabbed me. "Sammy!"

"pea-brained—"

All of a sudden Meg and Vera were there, too, scrambling to help pull me off him.

"ignorant—"

"Sammy!" Vera shouted.

"chowder-headed—"

"Sammy!"

"thing is that to say?"

Officer Borsch held my wrists and kept me at arm's length while I struggled and flailed and turned red in the face.

"Take a deep breath, Sammy," Officer Borsch said, his voice calm and low. "Take a *deep* breath."

I wasn't used to him being calm. I was used to *him* being the one to get red in the face and lose it. So I just stood there a minute, looking at him, then Holly, then Meg, then Vera. Then I noticed that cars were slowing *way* down on Broadway, checking out the action in front of the Pup Parlor.

So I did take a deep breath. And another. And another. But they were choppy, and hurt going in. And pretty soon my chin was quivering and my throat was pinching off and my eyes were stinging.

"Come on," Vera said, taking me by the shoulders. "Come on inside with me."

She took me through the Pup Parlor and upstairs to their apartment, where she parked me at their kitchen table. And I tried so hard not to cry, but it was hopeless. I just sat there and sobbed.

"Oh, sweetie," Vera said with her arm around me. "This has been one rough day, hasn't it?"

I nodded.

"Is ol' Borschhead causing you grief?"

I grinned through my tears. How sweet was that? Trying to get me to smile by calling him ol' Borschhead.

"Is he?"

I shrugged and nodded. But she knew it wasn't really him.

"It'll all work itself out," she said gently. "Give it time. You'll see." She walked me over to the couch and said, "You rest here a minute. I'll bring you some juice."

The juice did help. A lot. Vera just sitting beside me helped, too. But even when I was calm on the outside, inside I felt all . . . sputtery. Like some wild-haired chemistry professor was playing with steaming test tubes inside me, going, Hmm, I wonder what'll happen when I mix *these* together. . . .

But I tried to lock the chemistry guy up because I did want to feel better. I mean, Officer Borsch can get to me sometimes, but it was no reason to *pound* on him.

So I nodded and I got up and I smiled, and when we joined the others outside and Officer Borsch asked me if I was feeling okay, I nodded and muttered, "I'm sorry about before."

"No problem," he said.

"Where'd the cats go?" I asked, looking around.

"I had Animal Control take them away," Officer Borsch said.

"But . . . I want to find out what killed them! Did you see them? They look like they've been electrocuted!"

"Sammy, Sammy," Officer Borsch said, trying to calm me down. "We'll investigate. I just thought we should get them out of here, because they've obviously upset you."

"But—"

"And I promise you I'll let you know what we find out, okay?"

"But—"

He turned to Meg. "Watch after her, okay? And keep her out of the trash!"

"Will do," Meg said.

And with that, Officer Borsch went back to his car and zoomed out of sight.

"Did you guys see the cats?" I asked Meg and Vera.

They nodded.

"What do you think happened to them? Who do you think's doing this?"

"Not some ordinary predator, that's for sure," Meg said.

"Is that what Officer Borsch said?"

"He doesn't know what to think."

"They weren't drowned, either," Vera said. "Drowned cats are much more matted than that."

Meg turned to Vera. "When have you seen drowned cats, Mom?"

"Oh," Vera said all matter-of-factly, "when I was growing up our neighbors used to drown whole litters."

Meg eyed me, then said through her teeth to Vera, "Watch what you say!"

"Well, you asked!" Vera said back. "It used to be a very common practice."

"Well," I said, "I'd better get going."

They all fluttered around a little, saying stuff like, "Are you sure you're all right?" and "Are you going home to straighten things out with your mother?" and "Promise us you won't go looking for more cats?"

I told them, "Yeah, yeah, yeah," like everything was cool and I was fine, but the truth is, I just wanted to get out of there.

And no, I didn't go back to the apartment. I walked past Slammin' Dave's and the Heavenly Hotel, crossed the street, and headed for the one place I always go when I feel like I'm caught in a twister—Hudson Graham's.

But as I was trucking along Main Street, a bright red convertible tore by, zigzagging through traffic like it was part of a video game instead of real live downtown traffic. And it wasn't just the car that distracted me. It was the car along with the bright red hairdo behind the wheel. See, there's only one person in Santa Martina who looks and drives like that—Candi Acosta, Heather's mom.

Let's just say the lemon didn't fall far from the tree.

Anyway, half a block ahead of me, Mrs. Acosta flipped a U-ie across Main Street and started coming back my direction.

My instinct was to dive in some bushes, but before I could, Mrs. Acosta parked along the curb right out in front of the Red Coach.

The Red Coach?

Whoa, now! I moved a little closer. And let me tell you, my mood was doing a U-turn about as quick as Mrs. Acosta had. I mean, the Red Coach is the seediest bar in town, and believe me, that's saying something. Men hang out there from the time it opens 'til closing—I'm talking one or two in the morning. The kids at school call it Wino World, and Grams doesn't even like me walking on that side of the street.

And Candi Acosta was going in *there*?

Boy! Was I going to have some great ammo against Heather!

Now, the minute she hits the sidewalk, Mrs. Acosta

gets a whole chorus of catcalls from the slobs hanging out front. And she sticks her nose in the air and pretends to ignore them, but boy, she's shaking her back end from side to side like she's on a fashion show runway instead of a puked-on sidewalk.

Only she doesn't go to the Red Coach. She struts right past it and goes into the place next door—Madame Nashira's House of Astrology.

Rats! But, I tell myself, that *does* make sense. People like Mrs. Acosta *believe* in fortune-tellers. Shoot, she probably decides what to do each and every day based on the astrology column in the paper. But still, something about her going in there made me feel uneasy. Like she was trespassing into *my* territory.

Which I know is stupid, okay? It's not like Gina's really a friend or anything. And just because I've been inside her House of Astrology a few times doesn't mean I own the place.

But still. It bugged me. And I actually considered sneaking down to the House of Astrology and taking a peek inside, but there were all those guys hanging out in front of the Red Coach, and what did I care? I had bigger problems than Heather.

Which, believe me, is saying something.

So I got back on track and headed over to Hudson's. Trouble is, when I got there, who was sitting on his porch?

The Psycho Kitty Queen.

I turned right around. I was not in the mood for another run-in with her! But Hudson chased after me, calling, "Sammy, don't rush off. Wait!"

"Forget it, Hudson."

"Sammy, please come back! Your grandmother called and told me what's happened."

I pointed back at the porch. "That maniac blasted me with a hose! I tried to help her, and that's how she thanked me! If she's here, I'm gone."

He waved his hands back and forth a little, telling me to calm down. "I'll tell her to go."

I looked at him, then the porch. She was sitting in *my* chair. Man! I wanted to hose *her* down! "What's she doing back here, anyway?"

"She claims to have seen a man snatch her cat."

I hesitated. "Another cat? Really?" But then I scowled and said, "Like I should even care."

He put his arm around my shoulders and started leading me back to the house. "That's one of the many reasons I like you, Sammy. You *do* care."

"You're going to make her leave, right?"

"Absolutely."

"So what did the guy look like?"

"According to her? A bulldog."

I let Hudson lead me up to his porch. And I don't know if she was daydreaming or what, but the Psycho didn't seem to recognize me until I was coming up the steps. And then, boy! She jumped up and said, "You? *Again?*"

I rolled my eyes at Hudson, who cleared his throat and said, "I was just telling Sammy about the fella you saw snatch your cat—how he looked like a bulldog."

"That's right!" the Psycho said. "He snatched Ebony right off my back fence. He was gone before I could stop him."

She was staring at me, but I wasn't about to lock eyes with her again. I looked away, saying, "Ebony's the white one, right?"

Her eyes narrowed. "How'd you know that?"

"You called him that when I delivered Snowball."

"Snowball?" Hudson asked. "You found Snowball?"

"She delivered him *dead*," the Kitty Queen said.

"I shouldn't have delivered him at all," I shot back. "Not for the thanks I got."

Somehow we had locked eyes again. So rather than break down and look away, I started talking really fast. "And I don't know why I'm going to *tell* you this, 'cause you've been nothing but *mean* to me, but yours aren't the only cats being killed. My friend and I found four others in trash cans around town this afternoon!"

"See?" she said. "There's a cat killer in town! Why don't they *do* something about it?"

"Why don't you go home and call the police and *ask* them!"

Our eyes stayed locked until finally Hudson tugged on my arm and whispered, "Sammy, that's not polite!"

"Tell *her* that! She's the one who starts it!" But him tugging on me distracted me, and I blinked.

She stood. "I'll be going now," she said. "I've got a phone call to make."

When she was gone, Hudson let out a sigh of relief. "Well, now. You've had quite a day, haven't you?"

"Yeah." I flopped down in *my* chair. "How can so much go wrong in one day?"

"All I know from your grandmother is that your mother's in town and you're upset."

"Do you know why, Hudson? Do you know what that selfish airhead did this time?"

He cringed but didn't reprimand me. He just shook his head and said, "I have no idea."

So I told him about my mom changing my birth certificate and how I'd been held back and all of that, and when I was done, I said, "So I had to do stupid ol' kindergarten twice, and now I've got to do lucky thirteen twice."

"Oh, Sammy," he sighed. "I can certainly see why you're upset." He smoothed back his left eyebrow. Then his right. Finally he said, "Your mother's mistakes aside, your age is relevant only in how it affects your state of mind."

"That's just theory, Hudson. I'm living the reality!"

"Well, okay," he admitted. "It does matter more before you're independent, I'll grant you that. But really, Sammy, the best thing you can do for your happiness is to live in the here and now. If you dwell on the past, or long too much for the future, you can't enjoy the present. A lot of happiness comes from your outlook—if you change the way you *think* about being thirteen, thirteen might not turn out to be so bad." He shrugged and said, "Look at this as getting another shot at it for free."

"That's like saying I get another headache for free!"

He shook his head. "Oh, it's not so bad, is it?"

I sighed. I mean, I understood what he was saying. But

I couldn't seem to shake the feeling that my life was some crummy board game where I kept having to go back to the beginning and spin again.

Then Hudson said, "I'd really like to meet that mother of yours."

I snorted. *"Why?"*

He shrugged. "I just would." He eyed me and said, "I watch her from time to time on *The Lords of Willow Heights*."

"You've got to be kidding!" I could not imagine someone as smart as Hudson wasting time watching a soap opera as dumb as *Lords*.

He grinned. "Your grandmother got me started." Then he shrugged again and said, "Your mother's really quite good in the role of Jewel."

"I know," I muttered, because it's true—my mother plays an amnesiac aristocrat to the hilt.

"So you do watch it, then?"

"No. Grams tapes it. And sometimes she makes me, but no." I sat up a little. "It's a *soap*, Hudson."

"A little overly dramatic for you?"

"It's just stupid. No one's ever happy. Everyone's always sabotaging their relationships. People leave and then come back with really lame excuses about why they were gone."

"Not nearly as credible as say...*your* life?"

I blinked at him a minute, then backhanded him. "Hey!"

He laughed. "So what are you going to do about your birthday?"

"Avoid my mother," I grumbled.

"Come on, Sammy. You can't and shouldn't do that."

"Why not?"

"She knows she was wrong, and she apologized. Now it's up to you to show her how mature you really are. Can you do that?"

I let out a grumbly laugh. "No."

He laughed, too, then said, "Say, why don't I take all three of you out to the Santa Martina Inn for brunch tomorrow."

I scowled at him. "Because I don't want to worry about which fork I'm supposed to be using."

He leaned forward like he was sharing a secret. "I'll help you." Then he added, "Besides, that way I'll be with you. I'll act as a buffer. Otherwise, I have a hunch it'll be just you and the ladies all day."

Talk about a persuasive perspective! "Okay," I said, then pulled a face. "But does it have to be the Santa Martina Inn?"

"Special occasions require special ambiance."

I knew he was just trying to make my stupid birthday special. So I sighed and said, "Thanks, Hudson."

"Okay! So how about I pick the three of you up at nine-fifteen?"

"Sounds good to me."

"Great! Now go home and impress your mother with how mature you are. Believe me, she won't know what hit her."

"You're not even gonna offer me a piece of cake?" I cringed. "I really don't feel like going home."

"You've got to, Sammy. You're just delaying the inevitable. Go home and resolve things with your mother. Focus on the fact that she did come home to see you. And that at least she told you now instead of later." He shook his head a little. "Imagine how bad it would have been if she'd waited until you were ready for your driver's license."

My eyes totally bugged out at the thought of how mad I would have been.

He laughed. "See? You've got to look at the positive. And really, Sammy, it's just a number. It doesn't change who you are."

So off I went, dragging myself back to the Highrise. And the whole way I was sort of refereeing a battle in my head—one side of me was totally mad at my mom and Grams and didn't want to see them for, oh, maybe a year or two. But the other side was thinking about what Hudson had said about getting an extra year for free and shocking my mom by being, you know, *mature*.

And I was clear up at the intersection of Broadway and Main, still duking it out with myself, when I noticed a kind of strange-looking guy walking along Broadway. He was big—thick, with a heavy jaw. His shoulders were kind of hunched, and his arms swung a little ahead of him, his body sort of careening from left to right as he moved down the sidewalk.

At first he reminded me of a little albino gorilla. But when he reached Slammin' Dave's and opened the door, I thought, No, he looks more like an albino caveman.

The light changed, so I crossed over Main Street thinking that maybe that was even his wrestling name—The Albino Caveman. Or maybe just The Caveman. Or wait—The *Arctic* Caveman. Yeah! That'd be a cool name—The Arctic Caveman.

It wasn't until I was clear across Main Street that it hit me—he didn't look like a caveman.

No, he looked like . . .

A bulldog.

SEVEN

Holy smokes. A bulldog! Just like the Psycho Kitty had said! And there had been a dead cat in the Pup Parlor trash. Right next door to Slammin' Dave's!

But...why would the Bulldog be killing cats at Slammin' Dave's?

It didn't matter how much sense it *didn't* make, in a flash I was crossing Broadway, heading straight for Slammin' Dave's.

Now, instead of sneaking peeks through the curtains, I decide to get gutsy and go inside. The place is pumping with music and steaming with big men wearing small amounts of spandex and lots of sweat. And you'd think they'd notice a scrawny thirteen—scratch that—*twelve*-year-old girl, but no one seems to.

I scan the place looking for the Bulldog but don't see him anywhere. There's a class of guys doing hill climbers on the floor mats, and Slammin' Dave's got his back to me as he's pacing in front of them, yelling, "Get your knees up. Get your knees *up*. Benny! I'm talkin' to you! No slackin'! You can be a wrestling-school dropout, or you can sweat some bullets and get to the big ring. It's all on you, man, all on you!"

72

Benny kicks into gear a little bit, but it only lasts a few steps. No doubt about it, the guy's ready to drop.

"Where are we?" Slammin' Dave shouts over the music. "I can't hear you!"

"Seventy-eight, seventy-nine, eighty, eighty-one . . . ," the guys on the mats bark as they move, but their voices fade fast.

Now, I know that any second, someone's going to spot me and throw me out. Trouble is, there's nothing to use for cover. No trash can, no plant, no wall—nothing. And I'm thinking I *could* hide behind the curtains, but not only would people outside be able to see me, something about it seems really, you know, *stupid*. Like it's what a *six*-year-old would do.

Being twelve was bad enough.

Then I notice something: The wrestling ring isn't solid to the ground—it has a red vinyl skirt around it. And the mat's off the ground, way higher than a bed.

A door to my right starts to open, so I don't waste another second thinking about it—I scurry under the ring. And after waiting a minute for my eyes to adjust, I start crawling through the jungle of junk that's stored there. I maneuver around two-by-fours, and pieces of drywall, and plywood, and spools of wire, and buckets, and paint, and extra mats, and just . . . garbage. And I start asking myself, Why? Why are you here? And now what? How are you planning to get *out* of here?

Then I hear the music cut off, and all of a sudden there are heavy footsteps above me and Slammin' Dave's voice is calling, "All right. Today I'm gonna teach you how to take a back bump."

I crawl forward until I get to a split in the skirting, and when I peek through it, I can see a bunch of students standing on the floor mats. Their bodies are shiny with sweat, and some of them have rivers of it running down their temples. Their eyes are all totally fixed on Dave, who's giving them instructions from inside the ring. "What's *key* is, don't hit the back of your head. If you do that, you'll see colors. Or stars. Or, if you do it hard enough, the night sky."

So while Dave's talking, I'm checking out all the students.

No Bulldog.

I check to the left. And to the right.

No Bulldog.

"First thing you do," I can hear Dave saying, "is squat like this."

All the wrestlers squat, still looking at Dave.

"Then cross your arms like this."

They all cross their arms.

"Bring in your chin and rock your hips." All the wrestlers try it, and then Slammin' Dave calls out to one of them, "What'cha got down in your shorts, Benny, cement? You gotta *move*. Roll *up* on the balls of your feet."

Benny rocks up on the balls of his feet, but he still looks really stiff.

"All right!" Dave says. "Now don't try this down there, just watch. What you do next is imagine someone's pulling a rug from under you. Then throw your shoulders back and—" BAM! The mat slams above me.

A second later Dave's voice is back. "And when you get up, remember, no open hands! You want to get your fingers pulverized, do like this. You want to keep 'em intact, make a fist, lean on your forearm, and spin up like we drilled on last time." After a few seconds of silence Dave says, "All right. One more time. Squat down, cross your arms, tuck your chin, rock your hips, and—" BAM! The mat slams again. Then Dave calls, "Rick, get in here!"

A guy with frizzy blond hair steps forward and climbs into the ring. Ten seconds later the mat goes BAM!

"Again!" Dave shouts. "Keep your head tucked!"

BAM!

"Again!"

BAM!

"All right, Hector! Your turn!"

So a guy who looks like a marine climbs into the ring as the other guy comes out. And I *was* trying to keep an eye out for the Bulldog, but it was hard to concentrate because every time the mat slammed, I jumped. It was *loud,* and the mat wasn't like a mat on the ground. Whenever I watched through the window or back door, it always looked like the wrestlers were hitting hard, but now I could see that the floor of the ring was springy. Not like a trampoline or anything, but springy enough to absorb a lot of the impact.

Anyway, I didn't see the Bulldog anywhere. Maybe he'd gone out the front door again. Maybe he was in the locker room changing. Maybe he was in the office making phone calls. Who knew? All I knew is I was stuck and feeling very stupid. What was I *doing* there? What did I think? That the Bulldog had a stash of cats at Slammin' Dave's? That he was going to *wrestle* them to death?

Please.

And why did I even care? The Psycho Kitty Queen was mean. Why should I be trying to help her?

But it wasn't for *her*, exactly. It was the cats that bothered me. And besides, it wasn't just her cats. Mr. T and Prince were somebody else's cats. They could even have belonged to some kid.

Like Dorito belonged to me.

So there I am, trapped under the ring with the floor going BAM...BAM...BAM every few seconds, and wacky thoughts about cats and kitty killers running through my head, when all of a sudden I hear a deep, loud, rumbly *growl* in my ear.

Before I can think, my body shoots out from under the ring. And as I'm scrambling to my feet, the place goes quiet. Big sweaty bodies everywhere are staring at me. And I start backpedaling for the door, but two of the wrestlers grab me by the arms and yank me back.

Then the flaps of the ring's skirt push apart, and out comes the guy with the crazy cat mask. His creepy yellow cat eyes are fixed on me as he rasps, "I saw her dive under. She wasn't doin' nothin'. Just watchin'."

Now Dave's looking down at me from the ring like, Well, well, well, while the rest of the wrestlers are checking me over, not really knowing what to think. "Good work, El Gato," Dave says to the cat dude.

"Thanks," he says, then jerks his head toward me.

Well, I jump, 'cause the guy's a freak, you know? Stupid cat mask, yellow eyes, striped potbelly...

He laughs and rasps, "Skittery ain't'cha?" then whispers, "I told you to stay away!"

Slammin' Dave laughs and says to me, "I've heard about wantin' a ringside seat before, but *underneath* it?"

"You want I should throw her out?" El Gato asks him.

Dave shakes his beefy tan neck. "Uh-uh. Throw her up here."

"Up there?"

"Uh-huh."

And with that, El Gato lifts me by the back of my jeans and my shirt and passes me through the ropes.

"You must want to wrestle bad, huh?" Slammin' Dave says with a grin.

I look from side to side. "Uh—"

"Well, come on. Let's see you take a bump."

"But—"

"What do you say, guys?" he calls to the class. "Think this girl can be the next Chyna?"

All of them snort and snicker, and one of the plumper guys even laughs and says, "Not in this lifetime!"

"Shut up, Tubby," I grumble at him.

"Oh," Dave says. "She's got attitude!" I start to say something back, but he cuts me off with, "That's a *good* thing." He puts an anvil arm around me. "You learn anything, being under there?"

Now what my brain wants my mouth to say is, No sir. I'm sorry, sir. And I promise I won't do it again, sir. But instead I pop off with, "Yeah. That you need a new janitor. It's a dump under there."

He laughs, then calls, "Hey, Tony! Yo! Tony, you still back there?"

The guy who'd tossed Holly's trash when we'd been spying through the back door appears from around some lockers. "Yeah?" he says, and when he recognizes me, he says, "Hey, chiquita." Then he turns to Dave. "What's up?"

"Tony," Dave says, "this young lady's calling your professional services into question."

"That so?" Tony asks, raising an eyebrow at me.

Now, this is all making me pretty nervous. So I say, "Look, I'm sorry, okay? I didn't mean anything. And I'm sorry I snuck in. I just wanted to, you know, *experience* it."

"You want to experience it?" Dave says, spreading his arms. "Go ahead—take a bump."

Me and my big mouth. And from the grin on his face I can tell—the idea is definitely growing on him. He says, "You saw what I was teaching, right? Let's see what you learned."

Well, the whole thing seemed pretty stupid to me, but I just wanted *out* of there. So I said, "Fine."

"Uh . . . ," El Gato says, stepping forward. "You think that's such a hot idea?"

Well, forget him! Stupid creepy cat. I toss him a look, then squat, cross my arms, and tuck my chin. And before I can even think about what I'm doing, I rock on my toes, imagine someone's yanking a rug from underneath me, throw back my shoulders, and BAM! I hit the mat.

I just lay there for a second. It hadn't hurt at all. Well, not like you'd expect, anyway. Then I rolled up and bounced on my toes. "Wow. That really works!"

Dave's eyes were wide. His jaw was dangling. And after all of two seconds of gaping at me, he turns and says, "See that, Benny? *That's* how it's done."

"Beginner's luck!" Benny calls back.

Slammin' Dave snickers. "You could use some of that, my man." Then he turns to me and says, "Again."

Again? Uh-oh. It probably *had* just been beginner's luck. But I wanted to try it again—something about doing it right felt really good. So I squat, cross my arms, tuck my chin, rock up, and . . . BAM! I hit the mat again. And man, I gotta tell you, it felt great. I felt, I don't know, tough.

I rolled up, and before Dave could stop me, I tried it again.

BAM!

I rolled up again and said, "That is so cool!"

"Bet she can't take a front bump," Benny yelled.

"Oh yeah?" I called back. Then I turned to Dave. "What's a front bump?"

Dave shakes his head and says, "We don't have time for that," but Benny calls out, "Sure we do! Huh, guys?"

Now you can tell that the other guys aren't big on the idea, but Benny says, "Twenty-five bucks says she can't do it."

"On what?" the guy who looks like a marine asks. "Her first try?"

"*Fifty* bucks says she can't do it on her first try."

There's a minute of silence where everyone seems to be staring at me. But then Tony says, "Fifty says she can."

The Marine calls, "I'm in!" and before you know it, lockers are slamming and Tony's collecting money, jotting down notes on a scrap of paper.

"They're *betting* on me?" I whisper to Dave.

He grins. "The pressure's on, kid."

"Why? Someone's gonna lose either way. And it's not like *I* get anything out of it."

"Hmm," he says, then calls down to Tony, "Hold back ten percent."

"You takin' a cut?" Tony asks.

Dave shakes his head. "She is."

Everyone seems to freeze for a split second, and then Tony says, "She can't do that."

"Hey, who's runnin' the show here, huh?" Dave asks, like there's no way he's going to let his *janitor* call the shots. "Front bump or fail, she gets ten percent for trying."

Tony shrugs and says, "Whatever you say," and gets back to collecting bets.

Now in my head I'm thinking, Wow! If all these guys bet fifty bucks each and I get ten percent...that'll be a *boat*load of money for me.

So when they've got the money all squared away and Slammin' Dave says to me, "Ready?" I say, "You bet!"

It was too late to back out when he showed me what I had to do.

EIGHT

A front bump is nothing like a back bump. Well, except that you land flat on your back on the mat. A front bump is basically an airborne somersault. No hands, no shoulders, you just launch yourself forward through the air, tuck your head in, and land BAM! on your back.

The whole ring shook when Slammin' Dave demonstrated. Then he broke it down for me and demonstrated again. And my face must've been looking pretty chalky, because he took me aside and said, "Don't freak. There's really nothing to it."

"Oh right," I choked out.

"Listen. As far as I can tell, you've got no fear of the mat."

"Well . . . no. It's not *soft*, but it's got springs—"

"Shhh," he said, grinning. "So it's not cement, right?"

"Right."

"So in your mind, make it a trampoline. See yourself flippin' over—" He noticed me eyeing the guys lined up ringside and El Gato, pacing around behind them. "Hey," he said, blocking my view, "concentrate." He moved me so my back was to the wrestlers and said, "Close your eyes."

I closed them.

"Think of the mat as a trampoline. You ever been on a trampoline?"

I nodded.

"You ever been *hurt* by a trampoline?"

I shook my head.

"Good. Now picture yourself...you're taking a step, your arms are swinging back as you tuck your chin and flip over. And then, *slam*, you land loud, but not hard. Your arms are out, your head is up."

I stood there with my eyes closed, going through the steps, seeing him do it, seeing me do it. Visualizing just like Coach Rothhammer taught us to do about hitting home runs in softball.

He talked me through the steps about five times. Finally he said, "You got it?"

I nodded.

"Good," he said. "If I were a betting man, I'd put my money on you." Then under his breath he added, "Just don't land on your head."

Tony got a nod from Slammin' Dave and called, "Time to rock 'n' roll!"

"Don't I get even one practice try?" I asked.

"No!" Benny said. "The bet is first try."

Slammin' Dave nodded. "Give it your best shot, kid."

It always irritates me when someone calls me kid like that. It's like they don't give me credit for knowing anything, or how to *do* anything. And maybe Slammin' Dave didn't mean it that way, and maybe I did look totally scrawny standing next to him. But him calling me kid reminded me how I was back to being twelve again, and I don't know—it made me more than irritated. It made me *mad*.

But instead of snapping, I am *not* a kid! like I normally would've, I just glared at him. And before I had time to doubt myself or get scared, I took a step, hurled my body forward, and BAM! I hit the mat on my back.

At first I was stunned. The backside of my arms had hit hard, and even though I wasn't seeing stars, there was a little, you know, visual static.

I also thought I'd gone deaf. But then it hit me that it was just dead quiet from everyone else being stunned, too.

I rolled onto my forearm and stood up.

I'd done it!

The first thing I saw was El Gato. Even with his hood I could tell that his scary cat eyes were bugged way out. Then the Marine punched a fist into the air and whooped, "Yes!" But Benny shouted, "Hey! Is this some kind of a con? There's no way that girl's never taken a bump before!"

"No one's conning you," Tony said as he began passing out money to the winners. "You called the bet, remember?"

Slammin' Dave was grinning at me but good. He shook my hand and said, "What's your name, kid?"

"I'm *not* a kid!"

He gave a soft snort. "Sure you are. And take my advice—enjoy it while you can." Then he says, "So? You gonna tell me your name or am I gonna have to make one up?" And before I can even say, It's Sammy, *he* says, "I got it! You're The Tiny Tiger."

"The Tiny Tiger? I'm not a—"

He laughs, "Oh yes you are!" Then he calls over to Tony, "Hey, give The Tiny Tiger her cut!"

Now, I'm expecting all these musclemen to laugh and roll their eyes at my new, stupid name, but they don't. They all just sort of nod like, Yeah. Fits.

Tony smiles as he peels off two twenties. "Nice going, chiquita."

"Thanks," I tell him, taking the money.

Slammin' Dave calls, "Intermission's over, boys! Time for some pain!" He spreads the ropes for me to climb through and says, "You're welcome back anytime, Triple-T."

"Triple-T?"

He's grinning, boy. Grinning big. "The . . . Tiny . . . Tiger."

"I am *not* a tiny tiger!" I tell him as I climb out of the ring, but really, how mad can I be? I've got forty bucks in my hand, and I took a front bump on my first try.

Now the truth is, with everything that had happened, I'd completely forgotten why I was at Slammin' Dave's to begin with. But as I was heading for the front door, it all came flooding back. The Psycho Kitty Queen's cat. The Bulldog cat snatcher . . .

I looked over my shoulder. El Gato was busy talking to Dave on the far side of the mats, so I decided to take a quick peek into the room that's to the right of the front door. Maybe that's where the Bulldog had gone.

It turned out to be an office. I went inside and whispered, "Here, kitty-kitty-kitty" under the desks, but I didn't find any cats. Just roll-around chairs, a computer, wrestling posters, and papers. Papers *everywhere*—newspapers, printer paper, legal pads, maps, receipts—I'd never seen such a messy office. And boy, did it smell!

"Take a wrong turn?" a voice behind me rasped.

I jumped and turned. El Gato was standing there, staring at me with his creepy cat eyes. I kind of smiled at him and said, "Uh . . . I was just going to use the phone real quick. My mom's probably, you know, worried."

He took me by the collar. "Quit prowling around and get out."

"But—"

"You heard me," he said, then dragged me along and tossed me outside.

Oh well. It's not like I'd found any evidence of kitty-napping. But what had happened to the Bulldog? I stood on the sidewalk thinking for a minute, then decided to go next door to the Pup Parlor.

When Vera saw me, she said, "You're back! Are you doing better than you were before?"

I laughed. "A lot better." I showed her the forty bucks. "And richer!"

Meg and Holly were paying attention now, too. "Where'd you get that?" Holly asked.

"At Slammin' Dave's," I said with a grin.

"Slammin' Dave's?" Meg asked. "How on earth . . . ?"

So I started running off at the mouth about going to Hudson's and having another encounter with the Psycho

Kitty Queen and what she had said about some bulldog-looking guy stealing her cat, and how that got me sucked into *following* some bulldog-looking guy into Slammin' Dave's, and how I hid under the wrestling ring and got flushed out by El-Gato-the-Freaky-Cat-Dude and wound up winning forty dollars by doing a front bump on my first try.

Holly's jaw was dangling, but Vera frowned and said, "They sound like a bunch of basement bookies."

"Basement bookies?"

"You know, gamblers."

I thought about it a minute, then said, "Was that illegal?"

Meg snorted. "I'm sure it was. You were like a horse at the races..."

Vera nodded. "Or a bird at a cockfight."

"Or a bull at the rodeo."

"Wait a minute," I said. "A bull at the rodeo? People bet on *bulls*?"

Meg shrugged. "People bet on just about anything."

Vera was still nodding. "And if they know lucky, they'll bet on girls who *are* lucky."

"Lucky? *Me?*" I couldn't believe my ears. "I'm not lucky, I'm *cursed*."

Meg and Vera both rolled their eyes. Then Meg said, "I've never actually known anyone who's managed to go *down* in age."

"That's right," Vera added. "I'd give what's left of my teeth to go down a year."

"But not to be thirteen!"

"Honey," Vera said, "if I could do thirteen again, believe me, I would. And this time I'd do it right."

"Right? You can't do anything right when you're thirteen. Seems like everything you do is *wrong*."

Meg laughed. "I might do the same things, I'd just go about them different."

Vera said, "Well, I wouldn't be in such a dad-gum hurry to grow up. Why, I remember when I was thirteen, the one thing in the world I wanted was this ruby red lipstick at the five-and-dime. I was mad for that lipstick. But Mother wouldn't even let me try it on! For three years I heard, 'When you're sixteen. Not until you're sixteen!' When I finally did turn sixteen, she bought it for me, and do you know what? It looked god-awful on me. I waited three years for a tube of lipstick that I wore but once."

Then Meg said, "You never told me that story before, Mom. It reminds me of those boots I wanted. Remember those?"

"Those white go-go boots?"

"Yes! And you would absolutely not get them for me?"

"Oh, Meg, honestly. You cannot compare go-go boots to a lipstick—"

Now, while the two of them are going on about go-go boots and lipstick, Holly pulls me aside and whispers, "Personally, I'm with you."

I chuckle and say, "Thanks." Then I ask, "Can I use your phone?"

She nods and takes me into the kitchen, whispering,

"There are worse things than being thirteen, but still, I cannot believe your mother."

"Tell me about it."

She hands me the phone and says, "Is that who you're calling?"

"No way." I punch buttons on the dial pad and say, "I'm calling someone much more reliable."

When Hudson answers the phone, I say, "Hey, Hudson. I need your psycho neighbor's phone number."

There's a moment of silence, then he says, "You mean Miss Kitty's?"

"You got more than one psycho neighbor?"

He laughs. "Actually, yes. But here, let me get you her number." A few seconds later he's back. And after I jot down the number, he says, "Now, Sammy—"

"Don't worry, Hudson. I'll be polite."

"Good girl. I take it you have some information for her?"

"Maybe. I spotted a guy who looks just like a bulldog."

"Oh," he says, and believe me, it's a real skeptical oh.

"Well, he went into Slammin' Dave's, but I lost him after that. I'm just going to tell her about him—she can check it out herself if she wants to."

So we say bye, and while I'm punching in the Psycho's number, Holly says, "I don't get why you want to help someone who's so mean."

"I don't know. I guess if it was Dorito that had been snatched, I'd want help tracking him down." Then all of a sudden, "Hello, Miss Kitty speaking" comes purring in my ear.

"Uh, hi. This is Sammy. Hudson's friend?"

Her tone turns sour. "*You* again? Ebony better not be dead!"

"Well, I haven't exactly *found* him. I—"

"Then why are you calling? I didn't give *you* my phone number. You have no right to bother me this way. I have—"

"Will you please just listen?" She was suddenly quiet, so I said, "You know how you said you saw a guy who looked like a— "

"Pit bull," she spits out. "A vicious, good-for-nothing pit bull!"

"Wait—a *pit* bull? Before you said he looked like a *bull*dog!"

"Pit bull, bulldog—same difference."

"No, it's not! A pit bull doesn't look anything like a bulldog."

"Oh, come on. They're dogs!"

"So's a Chihuahua and a Saint Bernard!"

"Quit harassing me! Don't you ever dare call this number again!" *Click.*

After I put the phone down, Holly said, "She thinks a pit bull looks like a bulldog?"

"She probably doesn't have a clue what either of them looks like." I stood up and shook my head. "I can't believe I went through all that because she said 'bulldog.'"

Holly smiled. "Look at the bright side—you won forty bucks."

I grinned. "True."

Then the phone rang, which made us both jump. But right away we laughed, and Holly answered it, saying, "Pup Parlor." My heart sank, though, when she pulled a face at me and said, "Uh, yes, she is," and handed the phone over, mouthing, "It's your grandmother!"

I hesitated, then took the phone. Dead cats and back bumps couldn't delay me forever. It was time to go home and try some of Hudson's advice.

NINE

Grams was calm enough on the phone, but when I snuck through the apartment door, my mother attacked me with, "Where have you *been*?"

I gave her a surprised look. "Why, visiting with Vera and Meg and Holly and let's see...spending time at Slammin' Dave's...discussing things with Hudson..." I nodded and headed for the fridge. "Yeah. That pretty much covers it."

She followed me. "You mean to tell me you've been running around all over town discussing our business with other people?"

I shrugged and hung inside the refrigerator. "Just seeking an objective perspective."

"Sa*man*tha!"

I took out a leftover sandwich and cocked my head at her. "Yes?"

My mother rolled her eyes and threw her hands in the air, which was actually very interesting to observe—it was the exact same move Grams makes when *she's* fed up with me.

"So," I asked, taking a bite of sandwich, "did you two have a nice afternoon?"

"A nice . . . ?" Grams was looking at me like I'd lost my very last marble.

I walked into the living room, saying, "Well, I'm sure you had lots to discuss."

Mom crossed her arms. "All right. What's the game?"

"Game?" I shrugged. "Just making polite conversation."

Grams stepped forward and said, "Samantha, you may not believe this, but your mother is pretty torn up about what she's done."

"Oh, by the way," I said, ignoring her comment, "Hudson has invited us all out for brunch at the Santa Martina Inn tomorrow." I took a giant bite of sandwich. "To celebrate my birthday."

Grams' brow furrowed into unhappy rows. "But . . . your mother and I wanted to take you out to brunch ourselves."

"Oh," I said, then chewed for the longest time. Finally I swallowed and said, "Well, I'm sure you want to make *me* happy on *my* birthday, right? And what would make me happy is to accept Hudson's generous invitation to take us all to brunch." I gave my mom a forced smile. "He's really looking forward to meeting you."

Mom looked uncertain. "Because of all the terrible things you've said about me?"

"No, because he's a fan of yours. He says you're really good in *Lords*."

Grams was blinking like crazy. So was Mom. And inside I felt great. Almost calm. Maybe there really was something to this acting mature stuff.

If only I could keep it up.

I made it through the whole evening without complaining, criticizing, or making one sarcastic remark. And my reward for this nearly impossible feat?

My mother accused me of being "aloof."

Whatever.

My big decision that night was whether to sleep on the floor in the living room with my mother, or on the floor in Grams' room. I was madder at my mom than I was at Grams, but Grams can be a pretty fierce snorer. I considered crashing on the bath mat, but Dorito didn't seem to like it in there, so I wound up on the floor of Grams' room. Way off in a corner.

Grams and Mom stayed up talking, which I eavesdropped on for a while, but they were being very careful about what they said, and then they started talking about *Lords*. And believe me, once my mother starts up about her soap, that's it. You can kiss talking about anything else goodbye. Besides, it had been some day, and I was exhausted. So I just curled up with Dorito and thought about everything that had happened. About the cats in the trash and the Psycho Kitty and the whole adventure at Slammin' Dave's. I still couldn't quite believe I'd won forty bucks. Forty bucks! I could actually buy myself a birthday present.

But what?

Everything I own fits in Grams' bottom drawer—you name it, and I probably don't have it. So what did I want? What did I really want?

Besides a normal mother.

Or being fourteen instead of thirteen.

That was stuff forty bucks couldn't come close to buying.

So I made myself think about *things*. You know, *tangible* items. And after a while I decided that I'd really like to have my own portable CD player. Marissa had a jack splitter and two sets of headphones for hers—which was fun, but I never really got to listen to music when I was alone. And believe me, Grams is not into the kind of music I like, and vice versa.

But after I figured out what I wanted, my brain went back to being mad about having to be thirteen twice. Maybe it would be all right to be *Vera's* age and *then* go back to being thirteen. But being thirteen twice back-to-back? That was teenage torture!

I also thought about Vera's first lipstick and Meg wanting go-go boots. You have to understand—Meg is not the go-go boots type. She's about five-eight and stocky. Not fat, just big boned and, you know, strong. So the thought of her in white go-go boots and a miniskirt or hot pants or whatever you wear with go-go boots was a little, uh, scary?

Eventually I drifted off to sleep, because the next thing I knew it was morning and Grams was standing in front of her open closet, trying to decide what to wear.

So I stumbled into the bathroom, but my mom was already in there, messing with makeup.

"Good morning," she sings out.

I just grunt and act like I'm still asleep as I tinkle in the toilet.

"I'm looking forward to meeting Hudson."

"Grmmm."

She drops her voice. "Your grandmother became...flustered when she talked about him. Is there something going on between the two of them?"

"Grmmm-ummm."

She pulls a face. "What does that mean?"

"Grmmm-ummm."

She screws her mascara tube closed and snaps, "Why can't we ever have a normal conversation?"

I just flushed the toilet and mumbled, "Happy birthday to you, too," and went back to bed. And as I curled up with Dorito, I knew I hadn't been very mature in the bathroom, but I told myself that my mom deserved every bit of sarcasm I dished her way. It was her own fault for having a thirteen-year-old twice.

But I couldn't go back to sleep, and the truth is I felt kinda guilty. Hudson's voice kept murmuring through my brain... *She knows she was wrong, and she apologized. Show her how mature you really are....*

So I got up, got dressed, and joined Grams and Mom in the living room, where they were having tea.

"Happy birthday, darling," my mother says, and Grams smiles and nods. "Happy birthday, Samantha."

"Thanks," I tell them, sitting down cross-legged by the coffee table. "Can we have cake for breakfast?"

Grams laughs, "Cake?"

"You don't want to spoil your appetite for brunch," my mom says. "If it's anything like it used to be, their brunch will fill you up for the entire day."

I look at her and ask, "When have you been there?"

"Oh...it was years ago."

"Years ago?" I wait for a second, then ask, "Is that all I'm gonna get?"

My mom shrugs, and I can tell she's about to give me some lame story instead of the truth, so I just shake my head and mutter, "Why can't we ever have a normal conversation?"

"Samantha!" my grams snaps.

"Sorry. Sor-ry! But she asked me the same thing when I wouldn't answer about you and Hudson."

"About me and...," Grams says, her cheeks turning all red.

I face my mother and say, "I think you can look to each other for the answer to your question."

"My question?" my mother asks, looking all confused.

"About why we can never have a normal conversation! You guys have way too many secrets. Why can't you just tell me who you went to the Santa Martina Inn with?"

"Because it's really irrelevant," my mother says.

"Well, was it my father?"

My mother's lips pinch together for a second, then she says, "Stop with the third degree, would you?" and all of a sudden she spills some tea and has to run to the kitchen for a rag.

Now, there are all of four drops spilled, but of course Grams gets up to help her. And then they notice how late it's getting, so my mom disappears into the bathroom to fix her hair and makeup while Grams goes back into her bedroom.

So I curl up with Dorito on the couch. And after flipping through a dozen magazines, I finally call out, "We're gonna be late!"

Like magic they both appear, but they must've drunk the same evil potion, because they take one look at me and at the same time they say, "You can't go to the Inn like that!"

I look at my sweatshirt and jeans and high-tops, then brush off some cat hair. "There. That's better."

"No!" Grams says. "That is not better!"

I shrug. "It's *my* birthday, right?"

"But . . . I think the Inn has a dress code!"

I roll my eyes. "Oh, it does not."

Grams sputters a bit, then finally says, "Why don't you wear that sweater your mother gave you for Christmas?"

"Oh, she doesn't have to wear that," my mother says, then smiles at me like she completely understands why I don't want to be caught dead wearing pink angora.

But what flashes through my mind is that if I wore the stupid sweater, I would totally blow them away. I mean, how mature would that be of me? So I said, "You know what? I'll wear the sweater. And I'll put on better jeans."

Grams blinked.

Mom blinked.

I smiled and went into the bedroom to change.

But as I snuck down the fire escape to meet Grams and Mom out front, I couldn't help grumbling to myself that so far the second thirteen was just like the first thirteen, only pinker and itchier.

Little did I know that it was about to get a whole lot more uncomfortable.

TEN

The Santa Martina Inn has a large circular drive that lets limousines drop prom and wedding people off at the front doors so they don't get their hairdos blown apart by the wonderful Santa Martina winds. My mother, of course, was all for Hudson dropping us off. So we females got out and stood around the lobby checking out the scrolled wood and chandeliers and stained-glass partitions until the male showed up.

How nineteenth century can you get?

The hostess led us into the dining room and seated us at a square table with thick white linens, an arsenal of utensils, and enough drinking glasses to drown yourself. And then a waiter in a white coat and black bow tie came over and said, "Four buffets?" through his nose. I felt like saying, "Dude, get a grip—this is Santa Martina," but Hudson just smiled and said, "Yes," then added, "it's my young friend's birthday."

"Happy birthday," the waiter said to me, like he had thorns on his tongue. Then in a flash he started picking up side plates, glasses, and utensils, until all we had left was your basic plate, glass, fork, knife, and spoon. "Enjoy," he said, and hurried off.

"Enjoy?" Grams asked, looking around.

Hudson laughed and pointed to a side room. "The buffet's right back there." He smiled around the table. "Shall we?"

Now, as I'm getting up to follow Hudson over to the buffet, I notice who's sitting two tables away from us. And let me tell you, I about fall over.

Grams grabs me by the fuzzy pink arm. "Are you all right?"

I look again, and it's no hallucination. It's them, all right. All four of them.

Together.

"The *Acostas* are here," I whisper through my teeth.

Casey's straight ahead, with his dad to his right and his mom right across from him, with her back to us. And seated between Casey and his mom is his sinister sister.

Heather.

Casey spots me and grins, sending me a "hey" with the twitch of his fork. I turn my back, and believe me, my instinct is to bolt from the building.

Now, Grams has seen Candi Acosta and her daughter in action before and knows exactly why I'm petrified. But she says through *her* teeth, "They're in public. They'll be civilized. Just ignore them." Then, as she works me toward the buffet, she asks, "Is that Casey?"

"Stop looking over there!"

"Who's Casey?" my mom asks. "Who are the Acostas?"

Grams shakes her off and asks me, "Is that the father?"

"Yes! Now stop staring!"

"But I thought they were divorced!"

"They *are*."

"So why are they all having a fancy brunch together?"

"How should I know?"

"There are presents on the table!"

"Grams!"

"Would somebody please explain to me who these people are?" my mother demands.

I duck inside the buffet room saying, "My archenemy, her wicked mother, her brother, and her dad."

"So what's the big deal?" my mom asks. "What are they going to do to you here?"

"Nothing," Grams says firmly. "They're going to do nothing at all."

Hudson was already halfway down the buffet table, his plate heaped high. So I walked along the chafing dishes and tried to calm down. I told myself that it didn't matter. That it was a free country and people I hated could eat here if they wanted to. But something about seeing all four Acostas together had totally shot my appetite. I mean, when I first found out Casey was Heather's brother, that was it—I never wanted to talk to him again. I figured if he was an Acosta, he was sure to have venom in his veins.

But then he'd sort of worked his way back into my life—mostly by sticking up for me around his sister. And it was kinda fun having him as a . . . well, friend, I guess. I mean, it's not like I have a *crush* on him or anything, and even though friend is really too strong of a word, I don't know what other word to use.

But seeing all four of them together at a fancy restaurant as a *family,* well, it brought back into focus what I'd thought in the first place—he was, and always would be, Heather's brother.

"Sammy?" Hudson was standing beside me, looking at my plate. "You've barely taken a thing!"

"I'm sorry. I'm . . . I'm . . ."

Grams whispered, "Heather's here."

"Where?" Hudson asked, and it made me laugh. I mean, even though he was carrying a plate of food, he was willing to do battle right then and there.

All of a sudden I felt better. Hudson Graham was a real friend. Not some part-timer. Not some pretender. He was *always* there when I needed him. So I said, "Thanks, Hudson," and decided that there was no way I should let the Acostas ruin my birthday brunch.

I got busy putting food on my plate. Lots of it. And I was in the middle of dishing up some home-style potatoes when a voice over my shoulder said, "Try that with verde sauce and sour cream—it's god-like."

It was Casey's voice, and it tickled my ear. Tingled down my spine. And before I could say, "Go away," he said, "I never thought I'd see *you* in pink."

"Blame her," I said, and scowled in my mother's direction.

"Your mom?" he asked.

I shrugged and nodded.

"So where's your dad?"

I shook my head. "Let's not go there. . . ."

He was following me along the table, filling up a plate of

his own. "Divorce City, huh? Fun place to live, I know."

I faced him. "So why are the four of you having a chummy Sunday brunch? Doesn't look like Divorce City to me."

He made a friendly smirk and shrugged. "They try to be civilized on our birthdays."

"On your...birthdays?"

"Uh-huh." He put two pieces of bacon on his plate and two on mine. I just stood there staring. Finally I choked out, "Are you saying it's your birthday?" My heart was pounding, because somehow I knew what he was going to say next.

And he did.

"Nah—it's Heather's. Her thirteenth." He laughed. "Now she's *officially* bad luck."

Normally I would have laughed, but nothing about this was funny. "But...but it's not *today*, is it? I mean, you're just celebrating today, right?"

"No, it's today." He cocked his head and asked, "Why? What's the big deal?"

I just stared at him like a zombie.

"Sammy?"

I sort of shook my head, and it barely came out a whisper when I said, "Never mind."

"Hey, you okay?"

"Yeah. I just...I need to go sit down...."

My mother was waiting in the wings and was all aglow as she walked with me back to our table. "He is *very* cute, Samantha! And the way he put food on your plate and was attending to you...my!"

I sat down and pretended to eat, but my stomach was all in knots.

Heather Acosta and I had the same birthday.

How could this *be*?

"Mom?" I whispered. "You know how you keep secrets from me?"

"Well, I wouldn't exactly say—"

"Mom!" I snapped, looking at her all intense-like. "If today isn't really my birthday, you have to tell me right now."

"Isn't your birthday? Why wouldn't it be your birthday?"

"Well, it isn't my *fourteenth* birthday! Maybe you changed the whole thing—you know how you changed your birthday so people in Hollywood would think—"

"That was a completely different situation!"

I leaned in and said through my teeth, "But you've been known to change entire birthdays! Not just the year! I need to know! Was I born today or not!"

My mother looked from side to side, assessing the amount of social damage I'd caused. "It *is* your birthday, Samantha. You are now thirteen years old."

My face crinkled up. "Please tell me that's a lie!"

"Why?"

I looked from her to Grams, then Hudson, and finally I choked out, "Because today is *Heather's* birthday."

There was a moment of silence, and then Grams whispered, "You must be joking," as she turned to look at the Acosta table.

Mom looked, too, whispering, "She doesn't look like a very pleasant person. . . ."

"No duh! Which is why I do not want to have the same birthday as her!"

Mom shrugged. "Well, there's nothing I can do about *that*." Then she added, "But the boy is cute, and the father is certainly handsome."

"Like that has anything to do with anything?"

By now Hudson was turned around in his chair, studying the Acosta table, too. And I told them to quit staring, but they all kept looking back, making comments about the Acostas.

That is, until the Acostas started looking at us.

It started with Casey's dad catching Casey flash me a peace sign. Pretty soon *he's* looking over, and then Heather gets in on the action, flashing angry eyes our way. Then Mrs. Acosta turns around in her seat and gets all spun up.

"Great," I said. "Just great."

I tried to eat, but I just couldn't. And Hudson kept giving me reassuring smiles and winks, but it was hopeless—my stomach was knotted like a hangman's noose, slipping tighter and tighter, until it felt like it was going to kill me.

Everyone else did okay, and Hudson was great at keeping a conversation going with Grams and Mom. He complimented Mom on her portrayal of Jewel on *Lords,* and my mom was super sweet to Hudson, saying things like, "This is such a treat!" and "You're delightful!" and "No wonder my mother likes your company!"

Grams kicked her under the table good for that one.

And then my mom saw somebody walk by with a

strawberry cream-cheese tart and said, "Oh! I haven't had one of those in ages!" She turned to me. "Why don't you come with me?"

I almost said, Nah, but Hudson caught my eye and gave me a wise nod. So I got up and followed my mom back to the buffet room. And silly me, I thought my mom wanted to be with *me,* but no—she wanted to gossip about Hudson. "Don't you think he's perfect for her? Don't you think—"

"God, Mom, where have you been?"

"What do you mean?"

But all of a sudden Casey's *dad* is standing there. He smiles at my mom and says, "Excuse me—I don't mean to intrude..." He looks my way and says, "How are you, Sammy?" But before I can tell him, Totally freaked out, thank you very much, he puts out his hand and says to my mother, "I'm Warren Acosta and I was wondering, well, the resemblance is uncanny and I just have to know...do you play the part of Jewel on *The Lords of Willow Heights?*"

My mom shakes his hand, and I can tell she is totally flattered that he's recognized her and is about to say, Why yeeeeees, only what kind of mess would *that* be? Pretty soon Heather would figure out...everything!

So real quick I laugh and say, "Why does everybody think that? She doesn't look anything like that airhead." And before either of them can say a word, I add, "And I can't believe you watch that show, Mr. Acosta. I mean, you're a man...what are you doing watching garbage like that?"

"Samantha . . . ," my mother says, and believe me, she is not looking too happy.

In a flash I turn my back on Mr. Acosta and give Mom a look like, Don't be an idiot—he can't know you're Jewel!

Mr. Acosta laughs and says, "Actually, I got hooked when I was preparing for an audition for a part on *Lords*. I didn't make it, but at least I got a callback."

"You're an actor?" my mom asks, and that's when I notice it—she can't take her eyes off him any more than he can take his off her.

His shoulder makes an aw-shucks move, and he says, "Mostly just community theater . . ."

"Shakespeare?"

"Aye, m'lady," he says, and makes a grand bow.

Now believe me, I'm thinking, Oh, *brother*, but my mom's positively blushing. Then, like an allergic rash, Mrs. Acosta appears and says through a phony smile, "Warren, our daughter would like to open her presents." She grabs him by the crook of his arm and says to Mom, "If you'll *excuse* us?"

Mom says, "Of course," but she's still smiling at Mr. Acosta, and believe me, he's still smiling at her.

"Mom!" I say through my teeth as I yank her over to the strawberry tart zone. "What do you think you're *doing*?"

"What am I doing?" she asks all innocently. "Why I . . . I'm not doing anything."

"Get him out of your mind! You cannot even be thinking what you're thinking!"

She laughs, then she smiles at me real sweetly. "And what do you think I'm thinking?"

I throw my hands around like mad, saying, "That he's dashing and charming and..."

"Cute?"

"Yeah, cute! And you cannot be thinking those things!"

She laughs again. "They're harmless things to think, Samantha."

"But they can lead to dangerous consequences!"

In a flash I knew what she had to do—she had to go back to using the fake name she'd used when she'd landed the part of Jewel. So I step between her and the tarts and say, "Change your name back to Dominique Windsor."

"What?"

"You've got to! He recognized you, Mom! How many other people here might recognize you? And what if they start asking questions? What if he watches *Lords* and sees your name in the credits?"

She wasn't hearing me, I could tell. She reached around me for a tart and said, "That was the first time that's happened."

Now the way she said it was like she was *pleased* that it had happened. And all of a sudden it hit me—this was her first celebrity moment.

I shook my head and said, "Do you have any idea what a mess you've made of my life? First you dump me at Grams', then you pretend to be someone named Dominique Windsor and won't even admit you're my mother just so you can get a part on a smarmy *soap*. Then you waltz back into town to tell me I'm twelve when I thought I was thirteen, and now you fall in love with my archenemy's father!"

She laughs again and says, "You do love to exaggerate, don't you?"

"No!"

"Oh?" She turns to face me. "Well, I didn't *dump* you at your grandmother's. And if you recall, I dropped the Dominique Windsor persona to make *you* happy. The soap is far from *smarmy*. And I'm certainly not in *love* with Warren."

"With *Warren*? You remember his name?"

"Oh please, Samantha. Can you stop with the melo-dramatics?"

I grab her by the arm. "Mom, listen to me—you have got to go back to using Dominique Windsor for *Lords*."

"Why? I already went through all the trouble of revert-ing to Lana Keyes. I can't keep bouncing around! Besides, I rarely come to Santa Martina, and nobody reads the credits anyway. They just fly by!"

"Haven't you ever heard of videotape?" I say through my teeth. "Or freeze-frame?"

She laughs. "Who's going to do that?"

"Heather!"

"Heather? And so what if she does?"

"Don't you get it? I'll be busted! Grams'll be busted! How can I be living with you when you're on a soap that's taped a million miles away?"

All of a sudden she starts taking this a lot more seriously.

109

She leans in a little and whispers, "I can't believe anyone would be that...meddlesome. What's it matter to them? It's the people at the Highrise who would care, not anyone else."

I snort. "You have no idea what we're dealing with here."

"Well, fine. If changing my name in the credits will fix all of this, that's what I'll do."

So we're heading back to our table, and I'm trying my best not to look over at the Acostas, but I slip up, okay? I look, just for a second, and there's Casey, grinning at me, while Heather's unrolling a large scroll.

Now believe me, she's not unrolling a copy of the Declaration of Independence—Heather could give a rip about life, liberty, and the pursuit of happiness.

She's more into inflicting pain.

But aside from that, I know it's not the Declaration of Independence because the scroll is black. With tattered edges. And even without moving in any closer, I know exactly what's inside it. Silver writing. Silver moons. Stars. Suns. Astroglyphics.

Heather's got one of Madame Nashira's birth charts.

ELEVEN

All of a sudden things clicked together. Mrs. Acosta going into the House of Astrology... Gina telling me she was doing a rush job for a "classy lady."

Candi Acosta *classy?*

That's like saying Hannibal Lecter's a gentleman.

But still. It made me sick to my stomach all over again. *I* was the one who should have a birth chart, not her.

Which was stupid, I know. I was always saying I *didn't* want one, so why did I care that Heather had one?

Now, thinking all that as I walked back toward our table took no more than three steps. Which is about as long as it took for Heather to put the birth chart aside and start opening the next present. And before I could even figure out why *that* was bugging me, my mother grabbed my arm and whispered, "They are so cute together!"

"Who?" I asked, all in a panic.

She nodded at our table. "Your grandmother and Hudson!"

Their heads were sort of close together, and they were laughing. And it *was* really nice to see them like that. I mean, the two of them have had their ups and downs, and it's a lot more fun to be around either of them when they're getting along.

Mom whispered, "So *is* there something going on with them?"

"Nothing official, okay, so don't say anything stupid." Then I added, "And you know, you'd know a whole lot more about what's going on with her—and me—if you'd *ask* once in a while." She looked sort of shocked, so I said, "No offense, Mom, but you're sort of self-absorbed."

"I am not!"

I laughed. "You don't know about Hudson, and you don't know about Heather. I think that says it all."

When I sat down, Grams said, "There you are!" Then she reached into her purse and pulled out a small rectangular box. It was white with a gold ribbon, and she slid it across the table to me, saying, "This is from your mother and me. We really hope you like it . . . and will *wear* it."

I looked from Grams to my mother and back again. Then I checked across the dining room to the Acosta table. Heather was up to her ears in tissue paper, but I didn't care. I liked my little box with the gold ribbon. And I liked that Heather wouldn't know I was opening a gift—there was no way I wanted her to know we shared a birthday.

I rattled the box a little, trying to figure out what it was. If my mom was involved, it was probably some sort of dainty jewelry. But if Grams was behind it, it was probably something more practical.

"Just open it!" my mom said with a laugh.

So I did. And what was inside was the most amazing thing—a softball watch. The minute hand was a bat, the hour hand was a ball, and a baseball diamond connected the 12, 3, 6, and 9.

"This is so cool!" I said, strapping it on. "I love this!"

Grams clapped her hands and said, "I knew you would!" and since I could tell it was her idea, I gave her the biggest smooch ever on her cheek. She kissed me back and said, "I'm hoping it'll help get you home on time."

I laughed. "It's gotta help."

I showed it off to Hudson, who said, "A home-run watch—very nice!"

Then I noticed that my mother was looking kind of hurt. And since the watch was supposedly from her, too, I said, "Thank you, too, Mom." I held my wrist out to her. "Isn't it cool?"

She smiled and sort of shook her head. "I don't know how you can tell time with that, but I'm glad you like it."

So for a moment there, I was just actually *liking* my birthday. But then a bunch of waiters and waitresses marched through the tables singing, "Happy birthday to you, happy birthday to you . . . ," and I froze. Could they know it was my birthday? Yes! Hudson had mentioned it when we were seated. But . . . maybe not. The waiter had barely paid attention.

I let out a huge sigh of relief when I saw that they weren't headed for our table—they were going to Heather's. And when they put the piece of cake in front of her, she looked my way to make sure I'd noticed that she was queen for the day. And—this is how relieved I was—I actually acknowledged by giving her a little smile and a wave.

But all of a sudden the waiters start singing again, and that's when I see that they've got *another* piece of cake.

Everything warps into slow motion. Their bodies moving toward me, their voices distorted and stretched out as they sing, "Happy birthday to you, happy birthday to you . . ."

My heart starts racing, and I want to charge out of there, but it's too late—the waiters are already at our table.

I check the Acostas, and sure enough, they're looking at us. And although Casey seems puzzled in an amused sort of way, Heather's chin has dropped to her chest and her eyes are as big as baseballs. And then, when the waiters put the cake down in front of me, she actually shoots out of her seat and screams, "No!"

Her mother yanks her down and has some frantic conversation with her that spreads to Mr. Acosta and then to Casey. And even though Mr. Acosta's shrugging like, What's the big deal? and Casey's grinning like the pages of *Mad* magazine are coming to life in front of him, Heather and her mother are looking downright savage.

I wanted to shout at Heather, Hey! I don't like this any better than you! But inside I knew—no matter what I said, no matter what I did—in the end, there'd be no escaping her.

Heather didn't come after me right then. But I knew

114

there'd be fallout, probably at school. Not that it was *my* fault that we had the same birthday. Actually, I was having trouble believing we were born on the same day, too, but when I said so in the car, Hudson told me, "It's not as strange a coincidence as you might think. It takes only twenty-three people in a room to create a fifty-fifty chance of two sharing the same birthday."

"No way!" I said.

"But it's true," he said. "And considering the number of people having brunch there today, plus the fact that a lot of people go to the Santa Martina Inn to celebrate special occasions, I'm surprised there weren't more."

"I wouldn't care about sharing my birthday with anyone else . . . but Heather?"

He shook his head. "I'll admit, that's one unlucky coincidence."

When we got to the Highrise we all thanked him high and low for taking us out, and he was real polite to everyone, but as my mom and Grams went up the walkway to the front door, he pulled me aside and said, "I am sorry, Sammy. I thought the Santa Martina Inn would be a special treat. But I'm afraid it—"

"Hudson, no! It was great. And I'm sorry I got so spastic about Heather." I toed the ground. "And so riled about my mother . . ."

"Your mother is trying to be nice, Sammy."

"I know. I know." I looked up at him. "And you should have seen me last night. I was so mature you'd have been puffing with pride."

"It felt good, didn't it?"

115

"Yeah," I said, "but it's hard work."

He laughed and said, "So true," then told me to come visit him sometime soon.

"Will do!" I said, and headed around the building to the fire escape.

Now, by the time I got to the fifth-floor landing, I'd actually convinced myself that even though she's lied to me and deceived me and hidden things from me, I *could* be nice to my mother. For my own sake, if not for hers. Only then, just as I'm opening the fire-escape door, I hear her *scream,* and Grams shout, "Lana, close the door!" And suddenly Dorito is streaking my way.

At first I thought he was racing toward me because he was happy to see me. But then I see that he's got another mouse in his mouth. And before I can stop him, he shoots between my legs and ditches it out the door.

"Dorito!" I shout, but he doesn't stop. He charges down the fire escape like he's done it all his life. And I'm racing after him shouting, "Dorito, no! Dorito!" but he ignores me. And then I hear Grams above me crying, "Oh no! There he goes!"

I look out across the lawn and there's Dorito, streaking toward Broadway. "No...no...no...," I whimper. "Dorito, please...not the street!"

But he goes straight for the street. Right into the street. And even though I don't want to watch, I do. Tires squeal, horns honk, Dorito zigzags, and I can almost not believe it—he makes it to the other side. Then, cool as can be, he starts strutting up the sidewalk toward Wesler Street.

I fly down the rest of the stairs and charge after him. And by the time I get across the street, Holly's in front of the Pup Parlor, asking, "What's going on?"

"Dorito! He got away!"

She runs with me up to Wesler, saying, "I knew it had to be something big—you making a scene like that on the fire escape." She eyes me. "In a pink sweater."

"You could hear me? Up in your apartment?"

"Oh yeah," she says, then adds, "Well, the window was open."

"*Maaaan.*"

"Forget it. No one around here's going to think about it. Or care." Then she says, "I take it wishing you a happy birthday would be sorta stupid?"

"Don't remind me!" I almost told her about Heather, but I decided to save it. I had to concentrate on finding Dorito.

When we got to the corner of Broadway and Wesler, we looked around, then hung a left, even though Dorito was nowhere in sight.

"How'd he get out?" Holly asked.

"We were coming home from brunch, and I think my mother freaked out when she saw he had a mouse." I checked down an alley. "And then he charged past me as I was coming in the fire escape!"

We ran up the block, then agreed to split up, Holly going north, me going south around the neighboring blocks. When we met up again, we were both totally out of breath. "Maaaan!" I wailed. "Where'd he *go*?"

We headed back toward Broadway, and inside I was

totally panicked. What if I couldn't find him? What if he got hit by a car?

What if he wound up in a trash can, slimed and shocked out of his mind?

"Holly, we've got to find him!"

"I know," Holly said, and I could tell she knew exactly what I was thinking. "Does he have tags?"

"No! He never leaves the apartment!"

"Uh-oh." We were on a corner, looking up and down both streets. "He could be in a tree, he could be down an alley, he could be in someone's backyard. He could be anywhere!"

"I know," I said, and it felt like someone had put a tourniquet around my heart.

We searched the neighborhoods again. We *kitty-kitty-kittyed* down alleys, around porches, up trees. We asked people on the street if they'd seen a big orange cat. No one had.

And after we'd been looking for hours, I spotted someone down the block *kitty-kitty-kittying* her way toward us. She was wearing a ball cap. Blue jeans. Red high-tops.

I stopped in my tracks and stared.

Holly stopped, too. "Who's that?"

It came out sort of a gasp when I said, "Grams."

"Your *grand*mother? Are you sure? It doesn't look anything like her."

For a second the tourniquet loosened and a bubble of happiness floated through my heart. I'd surprised Grams with the high-tops and jeans, but I'd kind of given up hope that she'd ever wear them. I guess to some people jeans and high-tops are like pink angora sweaters are to me. But there she was, looking high and low for my cat, ready to put those high-tops into action if she spotted Dorito.

"Grams!" I called, and waved as we ran her way.

"Any sign of him?" she asked, and I could tell she was really worried.

Holly and I shook our heads. "We've looked everywhere."

"We'll find him," Grams said, but she looked like she was about to cry. "Your mother feels just awful about this."

"Is she out looking, too?"

Grams shook her head. "Her bus left about an hour ago."

"Wait a minute—she's gone? She lets my cat out and *leaves?*"

"You knew she had to leave, Samantha."

I squinted a little and shook my head. "Why do you always stick up for her?"

"I don't always stick up for her. . . ."

"Yes, you do!"

She frowned a minute, then looked me square in the eye. "Well, when you're not around, I always stick up for you."

"Why don't you ever do that when I *am* around?"

She sort of shrugged. "You seem to do a pretty good job of it yourself."

"No, I don't!"

"Hey," Holly said, getting us back on track. "Do you think we should start putting up some posters?"

I hesitated. Putting up posters seemed so . . . desperate. "You think so? Already?"

"I can't think of what else to do," Holly said. "The Humane Society's not open, and neither is the pound. Would he be able to find his way home?"

"I have no idea." I turned to Grams. "What do you think?"

Grams shook her head. "I wouldn't count on it. Posters would probably be a good idea, but I don't think we have a picture."

Holly said, "Well, how about if I make it just MISSING: SPECKLED ORANGE CAT and your phone number. It's better than nothing."

"And Dorito's front right paw is white," I said. "Put that in."

Holly nodded. "Okay. I'll go home and print up some flyers, you two keep looking. Meet me back at the Pup Parlor in about half an hour. If you haven't found him, we'll put up the posters." She started to take off but stopped. "You want to offer a reward?"

I looked at Grams, wondering if she'd want to ante up, but then I remembered. "Forty bucks!" I dug the twenties out of my pocket. "It's not a lot, but at least it's something."

"I'm on it," Holly said, and took off running.

"So," Grams said as we started walking. "Where'd you get the forty dollars?"

Uh-oh.

"Samantha?"

"Uh...can I tell you about that later? It's kind of a long story and I'd really like to concentrate on finding Dorito."

She didn't look real pleased with that, but she finally nodded and said, "Okay."

We didn't move as fast as Holly and I had, but Grams was a more careful looker. She stopped and talked to people. She checked between houses. Under parked cars. Behind hedges. We *kitty-kitty-kittyed* until our tongues couldn't *kitty* anymore.

But by the time we were due back at the Pup Parlor, we'd seen no sign of Dorito, and I was getting the sinking feeling that I would never see my cat again.

TWELVE

Meg and Vera needed Holly's help, so Grams and I went around with the flyers on our own. And you'd think that putting up flyers would go quick—a little tape, a quick staple—you'd have the town plastered in no time. Trouble is, people *complained*.

Grams was around the corner taping a flyer to a newspaper stand when T.J. came out of Maynard's and ripped down the flyer I'd just stapled to a phone pole. "Put another one up and I'll call the cops," he snarled.

"The cops? Teej—I'm missing my cat!"

"Cat-schmat," he said.

Now, if it had just been T.J., I'd have said, Stupid, heartless jerk. But other people told us, "Hey, that's illegal."

I asked, *"Why?"* and was told, "It just is."

Well. Since I don't consider that to be a very good answer, we put them up anyway. And believe me, Grams fretted plenty. At one point she said, "I don't know about this, Samantha. I don't want to wind up in jail."

"Jail? Come on, Grams. They're not gonna lock you up for posting flyers about a *cat*."

"But what if they fine me? I can't afford a fine!"

"Grams, they're not gonna fine you."

"But I'm asking for it, aren't I? My phone number's right on the poster!"

"Proof that you didn't know any better."

So Grams was pretty nervous about it, but we went ahead anyway.

Now, the West Side is a weird combination of residential and industrial. So in one block you've got houses, and the next you've got businesses that make ice. Or that rebuild engines. Or box broccoli. And who knows what came first, the houses or the jobs? All I know is that it's always weird walking through the West Side. You never know what you're going to come up against. And since the streets are laid out funny—some are diagonal, some wind around and then just dead-end, some take you right into gang territory—well, it's easy to get lost. And scared.

And it's one thing being in the heart of the West Side by yourself or with your friends—when you're thirteen, you can *run*. But now I was there with my grandmother, and high-tops or not, running was not an option.

Grams must've been a little nervous about it, too, because as I was taping a flyer to the wall of a brickyard, she looked around and said, "I think we should make our way home after this one, Samantha."

But when I finished anchoring the paper to the wall, a man came out of the building next door. He didn't startle me or anything, but I did do a double take, and *he* did a double take, because we knew each other.

Kind of.

I gave a little nod, and he called, "Hey, chiquita" as he locked the door.

I read the sign above the door—Kustom Heat and Air. "You work here, too?" I asked.

He nodded. "I work everywhere and at all times. How else you supposed to get ahead?" He stuck his hand out to Grams. "Tornado Tony, at your service, ma'am. No job's too big, no job's too small. I'm quick, I'm fast, I'm cheap. If you got a mess, I'm your man!"

Grams laughed and said, "Pleased to meet you. But I'm afraid I don't have any work for you, if that's what you're after." She handed him a flyer and said, "But here's a way to earn some easy cash."

"What's this?" He read the flyer and said, "No picture?"

I shook my head. "I don't have one."

"This your cat?"

I nodded. "His name's Dorito. And I'm really worried about him because he's never been out in the wild before."

"Oh, he'll be all right," he said. "Cats've got nine lives and all that."

"You don't understand! There's a cat killer on the loose! He's—"

"Wait a minute—a cat killer?"

"Well, that's what this cat lady over on Cypress says. And at first I thought she was nuts, because she's got like a gazillion cats, but then Holly—you know the girl at the Pup Parlor?"

"Sure."

"She and I found a bunch of dead cats yesterday."

He was sort of squinting at me. "You found a bunch of dead cats? Where?"

"In trash cans! All over town. And since tomorrow's trash day—at least for around here, right?"

"Yeah . . ."

"Well, if some crazy cat killer gets ahold of Dorito and trashes him, how will I ever know? He'll get hauled off to the landfill and bulldozed with Pampers and cardboard boxes and half-eaten Twinkies! He'll be—-"

"Shhh-shhh-shhh!" Grams says, putting her arm around me. "We'll find him—we will!"

Tony looks at the flyer again. "Well, seeing how I work twenty-four–seven, and seeing how I know this neighborhood and everybody in it like the back of my hand, I'll ask around and keep my eyes open."

Grams tells him, "That's very nice of you," and as Tony heads up the street toward his van, he says, "You'll find him, chiquita!" Then he laughs and calls, "Or should I say Triple-T?" and gets in his van.

"Triple-T?" Grams asks. "What's that about?"

I shrug. "You know that forty bucks?"

"Yes . . ."

"Well, I won it."

So I tell her about my adventure in the ring. And it's a good thing I didn't add details—like about following the Bulldog or getting flushed out by El Gato—because I'd barely made it through telling her about taking the *back* bump when she said, "Wait—did you *bet* with those men?"

"Well, I didn't bet *with* them. They bet on *me*."

"And they gave you a cut?"

"Right."

"Samantha! That's against the law!"

"Really?"

"It must be!"

I shrugged. "Well, so is putting up flyers about your lost cat."

"That's completely different! That's—"

"Grams, I'm fine, okay?"

"But oversized men were betting on you! Don't you understand that that's just *wrong*?"

I laughed and shook my head. "I've got forty bucks in my pocket, Grams. And if it weren't for that worthless *mother* of mine, I'd be able to buy myself a birthday present instead of post it as reward money."

"But don't you see? That's how it starts! Win a little, bet a little more. Lose a little, bet a little more! Pretty soon you're in so deep you can't stop!"

"Grams! Get a grip! *I* wasn't betting. I took a bump, earned some cash, that's it! No big deal. And it's a handy thing to know how to do, all right?"

"Why? For the next time you're in a wrestling ring with he-men?"

"Grams, stop it!"

"But you like the way that easy money feels, don't you? I can see it! You would do it again, wouldn't you?"

"For forty bucks? You bet I would!"

"Samantha!"

Now, the whole time we're talking, I'm putting up flyers. And by the time I'm down to my last one, we're outside Tiny's Tattoo Parlor, and Grams is still badgering me about losing my soul to the evils of gambling. And I'm about to tell her, Stop already! when some guy comes out of Tiny's, saying, "Hey—none of that here."

I spin on him and snap, *"Why?"*

"City ordinance."

"So how am I supposed to find my cat, huh?"

"Your cat?" He takes the flyer and looks it over. Then he looks *me* over. And yeah, I'm checking him out, too. He's only about five foot two, but from his knuckles to his nose he's got everything from Jesus on the cross to *Eat at Pappy's* etched on him.

"Are you Tiny?"

"Uh-huh," he says. "And you are ...?"

"Sammy. This is my grams."

He nods and checks out my high-tops, then says, "You don't seem like the fuzzy pink sweater type. Ever think about ditching that look and getting a tattoo?"

Before I have the chance to say it myself, Grams spits out, "No!"

He raises an eyebrow my way like he wants to hear it directly from me, so I tell him, "Nah." Then I ask, "Why are you open so late on a Sunday, anyway? You giving half off on religious tattoos, or what?"

He laughs. "I'm not officially open, but if you're wanting a pretty cross or something, I'd give you a deal, yeah."

Grams says, "She is not in the market for a tattoo! She just wants to find her cat!" She calms herself with a deep breath. "Would you consider posting the flyer *inside* the window? There's no ordinance against that, right?"

He nods and says, "I'll do that," but there's something else on his mind, you can just tell.

"What?" I ask him.

He cocks his head to the right. "You might want to check next door."

I follow his gaze. "At the Kojo Buffet?"

He nods slowly and says, "I've heard that the health department has closed them down for that before."

"For what?" I ask him, but Grams' eyes get wide and she seems to know *exactly* what he means. "Are you saying...?" she starts, then shakes her head. "They don't really do that. That's just an urban legend...isn't it?"

I look at Grams, then Tiny. "Do what? What are you talking about?"

Tiny takes the flyer and backs into his shop, saying to Grams, "I'll let you explain it to her. And I will post this, but please let me know if you find him so I can take it down."

Now, I'm glad he's willing to put my flyer in his window, and I don't want to make him mad or anything, but I can't help asking, "Uh, Tiny?"

"Yeah?" He grins at me. "Change your mind? I could do a real pretty one on your ankle, or your shoulder... wherever you want."

"Uh, no. What I'm wondering is, why were there dead cats in your trash bin?"

I watch his face real carefully, but it barely even twitches. "In *my* trash can?"

"Uh-huh."

But then he squints at me. "Hey, why were you going through my trash?"

"I was looking for dead cats."

"But...you just told me you were looking for *your* cat."

"I am, but the reason I'm so worried about him is because there's been a slew of dead cats around here."

He shakes his head and says, "Look. I don't know anything about any dead cats, and I don't really want to." He wags the flyer as he heads for the door. "I'm willing to post this, but other than that, leave me out of it. And stay out of my trash!" He hesitates, then adds, "There's needles in there—I wouldn't want you to get stuck."

When he's gone, I turn to Grams and say, "So, explain."

"Explain what?"

"What he thinks, that you understand and I don't."

"Oh." She looks left. She looks right. Then she looks down and says, "Well, not all cultures view cats—or dogs—the same way we do."

"Meaning?"

"Meaning some places don't see them as pets."

"So...? What do they see them as? Work animals?"

"Well, that..."

"And?"

The corner of her mouth twitches down. "Some cultures also see them as...food."

"*Food?* You mean they *eat* cats?"

"And dogs."

"But Dorito's my pet!"

She was looking at the Kojo Buffet. "I know. And I always thought that sort of talk was just nasty rumors, but maybe we should call the police and see if this place *has* been in trouble for that in the past."

There was no way I was going to wait for the police while someone turned Dorito into Kung Pao Kitty! I wasn't waiting around for a search warrant, either. Or for the food inspector! And I sure wasn't going to go through the front door and *ask*.

No, this situation called for alley walking.

Evil stalking.

This was a back-door mission.

"Come on!" I said to Grams, then charged down the same driveway I'd charged *up* when ol' Butcher Boy had chased me earlier.

Grams followed, and she did it a lot faster than I would have guessed she could. "What's the plan?" she asked when she was beside me, peeking in the open back door of the Kojo Buffet.

"I want to check the Dumpster first," I whispered. "Can you signal me if someone comes toward the back door?"

"I'll do this," she said, and her mouth made an airy noise that sounded like a metal blade whipping through the air.

I looked at her. "That was cool! How'd you do that?"

She made the sound again, then crouched beside the door and nodded for me to get to work.

My grams, the closet ninja—who knew?

Anyway, I opened the Dumpster, and man, was it putrid! I didn't have gloves and sure didn't want to dig around, but I figured if they'd gotten ahold of Đorito, they couldn't have had him for very long. If they'd skinned him, his fur would be near the top.

The thought was plenty gross, but the smell was even grosser, if you can imagine that. I looked around quick as I could, then put the lid down and joined Grams.

"Nothing," I whispered.

"The more I think about it," Grams said, "the more I think we're overreacting. The cats you found were intact, weren't they?"

"Yeah, but—"

"So this is just a wild-goose chase."

"But Grams, what if?"

"What if what?"

"What if they've got him and they're *gonna* skin him?"

"Oh stop. Don't even think that. What are the chances that they saw Dorito, *caught* Dorito, and plan to serve Dorito? It sounds like something from a war movie."

We'd been watching the action in the kitchen area. There were two men working the griddles, going in and out of a big walk-in refrigerator. One of them was Butcher Boy.

"Far-fetched or not," I whispered to Grams, "by tomorrow it'll be too late."

Crouched like she was, she reminded me of Dorito ready to pounce a mouse. "So what are you thinking?" I asked her.

She took a deep breath. "I'm thinking that if it makes

you feel better, I'll go around front and create a diversion so you can take a look inside." She stood up, took off her ball cap, and placed it right outside the back door. "The signal is, you're inside if the hat's here—once you come out, pick up the hat and I'll know to meet you at Maynard's."

"But . . . what are you going to do?"

"Have a heart attack? Faint? Break a hip?" She laughed softly. "I'm old—the options for credible medical failure are wide open."

She meant it to be funny, but I didn't laugh. "Grams," I whispered, "be careful."

She kissed my forehead. "I love Dorito, too, you know."

I nodded, then watched as she disappeared around the corner.

THIRTEEN

I waited by the back door for what seemed like forever. I couldn't see into the dining area, just the kitchen and the beginning of a hallway. The one guy looked like he was having a head sauna, flipping piles of steaming food over and over with a long spatula, and Butcher Boy was going crazy with a cleaver, cutting up meat on a long wooden counter. I'd never seen a knife move so fast in my life, and I couldn't help wondering what he was slicing and dicing. It was red meat—not chicken or fish. But it didn't look like beef, either.

What *did* cat meat look like?

Just as I was grossing out about that, I heard a *crash,* a *scream,* and after a second Butcher Boy and the other guy dropped what they were doing and funneled down the hallway.

I zipped inside and took a quick look around, then went into the walk-in refrigerator. All it seemed to have in it were vegetables—onions, peppers, heads of cabbage, that sort of thing. But straight ahead were thick plastic strips that ran floor to ceiling. So I pushed through those, and all of a sudden the temperature dropped way down and I found myself surrounded by

133

sides of meat. I'm talking hanging hunks of butchered animals. Some were big, some were kinda small, and I sure couldn't tell what they were. They could have been cows or pigs or lambs.

Or dogs or cats or *monkeys*.

There wasn't any blood dripping, or whole carcasses with eyeballs bulging out or anything like that. But being surrounded by big sides of what used to be living animals was gross.

Creepy.

I made myself check around for a secret compartment where they might be storing to-be-butchered pets, but didn't see a thing. So I pushed back through the plastic strips, hurried past the vegetables, and opened up the walk-in door.

And lucky-thirteen me, I bumped right into Butcher Boy.

"Hey!" he croaked. I tried to bolt for the back door, but he grabbed me by the hair. "You!" he shouted, yanking me back. "You the one who messed in my garbage!"

"Ow!" I cried.

"What you doing here! What you want!"

I tried to pry his hand off my hair, but he clamped on harder.

"You thief?"

"No!"

"Then what you want?"

"My *cat*!" I cried.

"Cat?" he asked, then shook my hair. "You put cat in cooler? Who pay you?"

"Nobody!"

"Who pay you?" He shook my hair so hard it felt like he was pulling off my scalp. "Guy next door?"

So I kicked him in the shin with all my might.

"Waaaowww!" he wailed, and let go of my hair.

I took off running, but he chased after me, shouting. "I find cat again, I kill you!"

I snagged the ball cap and tore down the alley. But when I looked over my shoulder, Butcher Boy wasn't chasing me, he was just watching from the back door, shaking his fist in the air.

When I got to the street, I looked for Grams but didn't see her. And I didn't really know what to do. I didn't want her going back down the alley to see if the ball cap was gone. And I didn't think she'd go straight to Maynard's without knowing I'd gotten out okay. So I walked up the street back toward the restaurant, keeping in the shadows and hiding behind trees.

And I was just thinking that maybe I should go up and peek in the window when the Kojo door opened and Grams hobbled out. "I'll be fine, sir," she said, "but you should be glad I'm not the suing kind. Honestly, you should get that carpeting fixed! I could have broken my hip!"

"Psssst, Grams!" I whispered as she got closer. "I'll meet you at Maynard's."

She nodded once and kept on walking.

Is my grams cool, or what?

Anyway, when we met up at Maynard's, she asked, "Anything?" as I handed over her hat. So I told her about

135

the body parts in the Kojo cooler, then said, "But I don't think any of them's Dorito."

"Okay. So I think we were just overreacting, don't you?"

"But wait! The guy who chased me said, 'If I find cat again, I kill you!' And then he asked who was paying me. He wanted to know if it was the guy next door."

"Who?" Grams asked. "That Tiny character?"

"He could have meant someone on the other side." I thought for a minute. "But this isn't helping me get Dorito back!"

"Wouldn't it be something if Dorito was at the fire escape waiting for *us* to return?"

Suddenly I felt hopeful. "You think?"

"Could very well be."

So we hurried across Broadway, and then across Main, and while we were walking, Grams said, "I think I've pieced together most of what happened with the cats and all, but why didn't you tell me this yesterday?"

I just rolled my eyes and said, "'Cause you were all wrapped up in Lady *Lana,* and how grateful I should be that she popped in to tell me she's been lying to me for years."

Grams let out a heavy sigh and said, "Why does this all have to be so hard? And *please* don't go back to calling her Lady Lana. I thought we were past that. I thought you supported her wanting to make something of herself. She's doing her best to—"

"There you go again!" I said, spinning to face her.

"You're sticking up for her! Why can't you admit she was wrong to lie to me!"

"Of course she was wrong! But give her credit for agreeing it was time to make things right. She came a long way to talk to you, you know."

I started marching toward the Highrise. "Such a sacrifice."

"Samantha, come on."

I shook my head. "What were the two of you expecting? That I'd shrug and say, Oh hey, cool? Can't you understand that this makes everything *else* she's done come flooding back? She lies, she manipulates—"

"But she's trying to make things right, Samantha!"

I sighed. "Look, let's just drop it, okay? Thank you for being so nice about helping me find Dorito." I gave her a little smile. "And by the way, you look really great in high-tops and jeans . . ."

"As you do in pink."

We eyed each other a minute, then cracked up and headed home.

When we got to the fire escape, we discovered that Dorito was definitely not waiting for us. And after searching the area Grams finally said, "Let's take a break, okay? I think we could both use some dinner."

I shook my head. "I'm not hungry, Grams."

She sighed and said, "Well, you can stay out a while longer, but I'm going in."

So I moved into the shadows and watched as she went

up the fire escape, stopping at every level to scan the area for Dorito. Then I slid down the wall and kept a sharp eye out for him, hoping he wanted to come home as much as I wanted him to. But after a while my mind started wandering, and I couldn't help thinking how being thirteen all over again was already the worst luck ever.

I also remembered what Hudson and Meg and Vera had said, and really, I did try to think about the *good* things. But when you're stuck outside alone in the cold on your second thirteenth birthday, hoping that the cat you've told every single secret of your life to decides to maybe wander home, well, it's hard to focus on the positive.

And then, all of a sudden, out of the fog in my mind came Grams' voice. "Samantha?" It was floating above me . . . sort of a whisper. "Psssst. Samantha?"

I stood up and backed up so I could see the fifth-floor landing. "Over here!" I whispered.

She came pounding down the steps. "Great news!"

"What?"

It took forever for her to make it to the bottom. "Tony called!"

"Who?"

"Tornado Tony?"

"Oh."

"He found Dorito!"

"You're kidding!"

"No! Described him to a T. Says he'll be out in front of Slammin' Dave's in five minutes!"

I looked across the Highrise lawn and spotted Tony's

white van getting ready to turn onto Broadway from Wesler. "There he is now!"

But halfway across the lawn I had a terrible thought. I was already way ahead of Grams, but I stopped and waited for her. "He's not *dead*, is he?"

"Who?"

"Dorito!"

"Why would he be dead?"

Like little visual bites, finding Snowball, bagging Snowball, *delivering* Snowball played through my head. "Because . . . because . . ."

I couldn't stand it—I took off running. I tore across the grass, jaywalked Broadway, and practically ripped the passenger-door handle off Tony's van trying to get inside.

He came out the driver's side, Dorito in the crook of his arm. "This your boy?" he said with a grin.

"Dorito!" I tore around the front of the van and scooped him up. And after power-nuzzling him for a minute, I said to Tony, "Where did you find him?"

"I spotted him on Piños, just cruising." He nodded. "Buff cat. He'd have done fine on his own."

"Thank you! Oh, thank you thank you!"

I noticed that Grams was sort of stranded on the other side of the street, so I held up Dorito and signaled her to stay put. Then I shifted Dorito under one arm and dug in my jeans' pocket for the forty bucks.

He looked at it and said, "No way, Triple-T. Consider it my gift to you." He got in his van, saying, "But if the old lady ever needs some cleanin' done, you make sure she calls me, okay?"

"You got it! And thanks!"

He took off, and the minute there was a break in traffic, I ran back across the street, where Dorito and Grams had a nuzzle-nose reunion. "You naughty, naughty boy!" Grams cooed. "You gave us such a scare! Don't you ever do something like that again, you hear me?"

Dorito licked his paw like, Yeah, *right*.

When we got home, the phone was ringing. Grams hurried to the kitchen to answer it, and I could hear her say, "Oh, Holly! We have wonderful news. Dorito's back!...yes...yes...hold on, I'll let you talk to Samantha."

"Hey!" I said into the receiver.

"Where'd you find him?" she asked.

"Tornado Tony found him!"

"You're kidding."

"No! We ran into him when we were putting up posters. He said he'd keep an eye out, but I didn't really expect him to *find* him."

"Hey, that's great!"

Now, it's funny. Sometimes you can tell something's going on in someone's head, even when all you've got to work with is silence. Or a pause. And I could tell from the silence on the other end that the wheels inside Holly's head were definitely spinning. So I said, "But you weren't calling about Dorito, were you."

"Well, no. But that is great news!"

"So...?"

"So I saw El Gato out behind Slammin' Dave's."

"Yeah, and...?"

"And you won't believe who he was talking to."

"Who?"

"That crazy cat lady."

"What? Really? When?"

"About half an hour ago."

"Are you sure?"

She snorted. "There's no mistaking her. Or him."

"He was wearing the mask?"

"Of course."

"But Dave's isn't even open . . . is it?"

"Who knows. People come and go there at the weirdest times. It was just sort of freaky seeing the two of them together."

"Well, what were they doing?"

"I don't really know. I saw them out the kitchen window, but I couldn't really hear anything. It looked like they were just talking . . . then laughing."

"Laughing?"

I could practically see Holly shrug. "That's what it looked like."

"Hmm."

"But hey, who cares about wacky cat people, right? You've got your real cat back!"

I laughed. "That's right."

"Which means your birthday wasn't a complete disaster after all, right?"

I laughed again. "Right."

"Sorry we didn't get to do anything fun for it. Maybe tomorrow?"

"Maybe! Tony wouldn't take the reward money, so I've

still got forty bucks to buy something. I was thinking maybe a CD player."

"That'd be cool. Maybe I'll get you a CD."

"Hey, no way! You gave me the best birthday present possible—you helped me get Dorito back." Then a little uh-oh tickled through my brain, and I guess Holly could feel it across the line.

"What?" she asked.

"Oh. Well, I was just thinking I should go pull all those flyers down."

"Now?"

"Uh, I probably should. It's got our phone number on it, and Grams is worried about getting fined because posting flyers is against the law."

"Against the . . . what?"

"Yeah, I didn't know that, either, but you wouldn't believe how many people gave us grief about it."

Grams overheard my end of the conversation and said, "It's much too late to go back out tonight. Especially to that part of town. We'll take them down in the morning."

So I said into the phone. "Never mind. Grams says it's okay to wait until morning."

"You want to meet before school?"

"Seriously?"

"Sure."

"Okay! I'll come over. Is seven o'clock too early?"

"Nah, that's good."

So Grams and I ate birthday cake for dinner. It was so good! And I must've been beat to a pulp, because when

I snuggled up with Dorito on the couch, all I remember thinking was, I had my cat back and I still had forty bucks...maybe being thirteen didn't mean total bad luck after all.

FOURTEEN

What woke me in the morning wasn't the alarm clock. It was an itchy arm. A *really* itchy arm. Then my neck started itching. And my side. Then my *foot*. I was itchy all over, and when I finally got up and looked to see why, I discovered little red bumps, all over the place.

At first I thought I had the measles or chicken pox or smallpox or some other nasty rash disease. But weren't those, you know, obliterated? So maybe it was some other exotic rash disease.

But I didn't have a temperature. And I *felt* okay. Well, except for the itch. And the more I scratched, the worse it got. It was like a nursery of baby mosquitoes had smorgasborded on me.

But the minute Grams saw the bumps, she said, "Oh no!"

Her eyes were big. Her jaw was dropped. And for a second I just knew—I was gonna die. "What?"

"Fleas!"

"Fleas?"

She studied my arm. My foot. "Look at all these bites!" She wagged a finger at Dorito and said, "You naughty, *naughty* boy! Where did you go to pick up fleas?"

She scooped him up and tossed him in the bathroom. "You," she said to me, "take a shower." She tore my afghan off the couch. "I'll get this and your clothes washing."

So that's what we did. And later, when we met up in the kitchen, I heard her muttering about having to get flea powder and a flea collar and vacuuming twice a day for two weeks to make sure there weren't any flea eggs, and what a mess my mom had made of things, letting Dorito get away.

"What was that?" I asked, because I almost couldn't believe that she'd said anything negative about my mom.

"Never mind."

I got busy vacuuming and beating out the couch pillows and vacuuming some more. And by the time we'd tried a bunch of different salves on my bites to keep them from itching, it was already seven o'clock and I hadn't even had breakfast, let alone packed a lunch. "You want to write me an excuse for being tardy?" I asked. "'Cause I'm never gonna get all those flyers down before school."

"Don't worry about the flyers. I'll go take them down myself."

"By yourself?"

"Of course."

"You won't call Hudson?"

"No! I'll be fine."

Boy. People call *me* stubborn. And since there was obviously no talking her out of it, the only way to keep her from going to the West Side—through gang territory and who knows what else—was if I got the job done before school.

So I called Holly and told her I was running late, then powered through breakfast, threw some stuff together for lunch, and said, "Holly and I'll get it done, no sweat!" Then I tore out of the apartment before she could argue.

Holly and I did run around the neighborhoods as fast as we could, but we couldn't finish on time. Finally I looked at my watch and said, "You up for lunchroom?" because that's what Vice Principal Caan makes us do for tardy detention—eat lunch in a corner with other A.M. delinquents. Then he has us clean up the trash and slop left behind by everyone else. And believe me, if someone like Heather knows you've got tardy detention, she and all her friends make a righteous mess just for the fun of knowing you'll have to clean up after them.

Holly must have been thinking about scraping up mushy mashed potatoes, because her face crinkled and she said, "Can we finish after school?"

I nodded. "Let's go."

So we tore across town and managed to slide into homeroom just as the tardy bell was ringing. I was glad to see that Marissa was back from Las Vegas, but she was looking pretty tired in her seat across the room. I smiled and waved at her, then noticed Heather snarling at me from two rows up.

Now, Hudson's always telling me I should try killing Heather with kindness—that it's the only way of dealing with her. That's a tough thing to do, so I usually try to ignore her instead. And I don't know if it was because I

146

was all out of breath from running or what, but on impulse I smiled at her and gave a little wave.

And what I learned is that for such a smart guy, Hudson's clueless about people like Heather Acosta. I mean, talk about lighting a fuse! Heather sizzled and sputtered and had a mini spaz-out right there on the spot. And I could tell that any second she was going to explode in my direction, so I put my hands up and mouthed, "Chill!"

She mouthed something right back, and even though I couldn't exactly follow it, the meaning was loud and clear: She was gonna kill me. And no, she wasn't planning on doing it with kindness.

I rolled my eyes like, Oh right, then stood for the Pledge with the rest of the class. But inside, my stomach was churning. Heather may be mean, but she's also smart and sneaky, and that is one dangerous combination.

After homeroom I avoided her the best I could by taking different routes between classes and just ducking out of view when I spotted her in my vicinity. Then at lunch Holly and I pieced together for Marissa and Dot most of what had happened over the weekend. Marissa kept saying, "I can't believe I missed all this! I can't believe they made me miss your birthday! I can't believe you guys had so much fun without me!"

"Fun?" I asked. "You call digging up dead cats *fun*? You call losing your own cat *fun*? You call being thirteen twice *fun*?"

She scowled and said, "Better'n babysitting Mikey." And that's how it came out that pretty much all Marissa did in Las Vegas was look after her little brother while her parents went to shows and out for drinks and to the spa. "Even when we went swimming, *I* had to keep an eye on Mikey. The only thing I did that was any fun was go see Darren Cole and the Troublemakers with my mom."

"Darren Cole and the *Troublemakers*?" Holly asked.

Marissa laughed. "Yeah, I know. Apparently my mom had a crush on Darren Cole when she was young. The concert was pretty amazing, but that's basically the only fun I had."

So I actually wasn't thinking about Heather at all. But then Dot clears her throat, "Ahem," and that's when I notice that there's someone standing right behind me. "Oh hi, Casey," I say, turning beet red.

"Hi," he says back, then scoots his way onto the bench. "I was sorta waiting for a break in the conversation, but lunch is about over and you're still jabbering away."

"What's up?" I ask, because I can tell something is.

He grins around at the other three, saying, "I suppose she's told you that she and the Evil One have the same birthday?"

My friends nod, but I say, "I wasn't gossiping about Heather! I was talking about—"

"It's okay! I wouldn't blame you if you *were* talking about my sister. You should have seen her after brunch at the Inn—she spun into evil overdrive. If I were you, I'd definitely watch my back." He digs deep into his jeans pocket. "Which is why I brought you this."

"What is it?" I ask, and he shows me—a miniature horseshoe.

"Give me your shoe," he says.

"My shoe?"

"Uh-huh."

"Why my shoe?"

He rolls his eyes and looks at the others like, Is she always this cooperative?

They all laugh, so I say, "Hey! Stop that," which just makes them laugh some more.

Then Casey says to me, "Worried you got stinky feet?"

"No!"

"So give it here." He pulls my leg up so my foot's on the bench. And then—get this—he yanks the bow free and *fwip, fwip, fwip,* he starts unlacing my high-top.

I pull away. "Hey, what are you doing?"

He anchors my foot. "Trying to give you some good luck—would you quit fighting me?" Then he wags the horseshoe at me and says, "This is gonna stay right here on your shoe, neutralizing the bad luck that is thirteen."

"But—"

"So which way should it go? This way?" He holds it against my shoe so the U end points toward my toe. "Or this way?" He flips it around so the U end is facing up.

"Uh..."

"Some people think having the horseshoe point up keeps luck from running out. Other people think it's gotta face down so its luck can pour over you."

"Um..."

"Of course, people who bet on the horses think just touching a horseshoe makes you lucky." He held his chin a minute, looking down at my shoe, then suddenly got to work, threading the lace through nail holes in the horse-shoe so that the bottom of the U faced the toe of my shoe.

"So is that gonna keep the luck from running out?" I lifted my leg. "Or is it pouring over me?"

He laughed. "I guess it depends on your perspective. Or position." He grabbed my foot again and started threading the laces up the rest of my high-top. "Either way, it's got you covered. Plus, it's right where you can reach it, so basically this'll give you three-way luck." He finished lacing, tied a snug bow, then smiled at me and said, "Happy birthday."

I looked at him, then at my shoe. And honestly, I couldn't think of a thing to say. The horseshoe wasn't shiny. It wasn't fancy. It was kinda crude and almost rusty-looking. And if I'd seen it in a store window I would have thought, Who'd pay money for *that*? But looking at it on my shoe, I thought it was without a doubt the coolest thing anyone had ever given me.

But before I can figure out what to say, Holly says, "*Pssst,*" and nudges her nose across the lunch area.

And when I turn around, who do I see?

Sister Snot and the Snidettes.

"Oh no," Dot moans. "Not them again."

I look at Casey and say, "Lucky horseshoe, huh?"

He laughs and stands, saying, "Seriously. She won't be able to touch you."

I laugh, too. "Yeah, right."

"Believe!" he says all voodoo-like, then heads over to talk to his sister.

The minute he's gone, Dot and Marissa swarm around me like love-starved locusts. "Ohmygod," Marissa squeals. "That was romantic beyond . . . beyond comprehension!"

"Shut up, Marissa," I say through my teeth.

"That was so Romeo and Juliet!"

"Stop it! It's nothing like that! It was just a nice, you know, *gesture*."

Dot's shaking her head at me. "Oh no. He was dreamy."

"Dreamy? *Dreamy?*" I scrunch my face and look from Dot to Marissa and back again. "I can't believe you're being so juvenile!"

Marissa snickers. "You are so in denial."

"I am not!"

"Look, in the old days girls used to get pinned."

"Pinned? What's pinned?" I was trying to keep an eye on what was happening between Casey and Heather, but my friends were running serious interference.

"Guys would put a pin—you know, a brooch or some-thing—on a girl."

"Yeah," Dot says. "Or they'd give them a Saint Christopher necklace to wear . . ."

"A what?" I couldn't concentrate on pins or necklaces. Heather was shoving Casey . . . *hard* . . . but he was just laughing about it . . . walking away . . . and now . . . uh-oh, she was glaring at me again.

But that didn't stop Dot or Marissa from going on and on about signs of love.

"Some girls get a promise ring," Marissa whispered.

"Or a class ring!" Dot giggled.

Marissa grinned. "*You* got a horseshoe!"

"It's not *even* the same thing!" I said, trying to avoid Heather's glare. "He gave me a rusted piece of bent metal!"

"But it's something of *his*—"

"That you'll *wear*—"

"Oh please!" I cried. "You've lost it, you know that?" I wagged my high-top at them. "It's a bent piece of rusty metal! With holes!"

But then Holly said, "I don't know, Sammy. And I've got to say, the guy's pretty gutsy. He gave it to you in front of all of us."

"That's because we're just *friends*. He wasn't being all 'dreamy' or romantic or...or...*stupid*. He was just being nice."

Marissa giggled and said, "Maybe we should start calling you Lucky."

"Shut up!"

"Yeah," Dot chimed in, "Lucky Thirteen."

"I mean it!"

Holly grinned. "Sounds right to me."

I couldn't believe that Holly was joining in on this. *"What?"*

She shrugged. "Well, first you win forty bucks, then you get your cat back..."

Marissa nodded. "And now you've been horseshoed by a really hot guy."

That did it. I started whipping the laces out of my shoe, saying, "I give up. If you guys are bent on making this into something it's not—"

But Marissa and Dot *tackled* me, yanked my arms back, and retied my shoe. "We're sorry!" Marissa said. "We won't say another word about it. We won't mention it to an-y-bod-y!"

"Oh right."

"We promise!"

We stared at each other a minute, and finally I said, "Really?"

They all nodded. "Really."

"'Cause you know it was just a nice thing for him to do and . . . and I can use all the luck I can get."

"You can say that again," Holly muttered. She was looking across the lunch area, so we looked, too. Casey was long gone, but Heather was still there. And from the way she was still glaring at me as she huddled up with her friends, I could tell that surviving the day with her was going to take a whole lot more than luck.

FIFTEEN

Vice Principal Caan has slapped a little junior high restraining order on Heather that supposedly keeps her from getting within twenty-five feet of me during school. So it was probably more that than her brother's lucky horseshoe that kept her from actually touching me. Oh, her eyes sliced and diced me during science, and she walked past my lab table about twenty times trying to get a good look at my foot, but at the end of the day I was still in one piece.

So after we said bye to Dot, who was riding home with her dad, Holly, Marissa, and I headed across town to take down the rest of the Dorito flyers. And we were just moseying along collecting them when we came to a phone pole where I found *another* flyer posted above mine. "Hey," I said. "Check it out—someone else is missing their cat."

The new flyer was actually a lot better than mine because it had a picture. The cat was a tabby named Zippy, with white-tipped ears and a black star between the eyes.

"Oh, he's so cute," Holly said.

"Do you think it's that crazy cat lady's?" Marissa asked.

"You said you saw her on this side of town last night, right?"

I checked the phone number on the flyer. "It's not Psycho's number—I don't remember it exactly, but I know hers has three sevens in it." I pulled down my flyer and muttered, "But what's the deal with missing cats?"

As we continued walking, Marissa said, "Maybe you're just noticing it more?"

"What, you think there are always dead cats in trash bins, we just haven't noticed them?"

"No. But people lose their pets all the time."

"That's true," Holly said. "The Humane Society gets calls all the time. And the pound picks them up, too."

"But doesn't this seem like a lot?"

"You're always looking for the sinister," Marissa said.

"We found dead cats!"

"But you got Dorito back, alive and well! And this little Zippy kitty will probably turn up, too. Cats go missing all the time! There's no cat-hater conspiracy. And no one's skinning them alive and putting them out as buffet food—that's just an old folk tale."

"Oh, is that so," I said.

And Holly snapped, "So we're supposed to think it's *normal* to find dead cats in the trash?"

Marissa put both hands up. "Hey, sorry! I'm just saying maybe they got hit by a car. Or ate rat poison." She pushed her bike along, saying, "You know what rat poison does, don't you?"

"No, what?"

"It makes animals thirsty. They go crazy looking for

water. That's why people use it in their attics. Rats eat it, then they go outside looking for water and die."

"How does it kill them?" Holly asked.

Marissa shrugged. "I don't know. It explodes their insides or something. The point is, there is no cat-killing conspiracy."

"So you're saying you think finding dead, spazzed-out cats in trash cans *is* normal?"

Marissa stopped and looked right at me. "How should I know? I don't dig through trash!" The instant she said it she was sorry. "I . . . I didn't mean anything by that, okay? It's just not something I want to worry about. Dead cats. Dead mice. I don't like dead stuff."

"Neither do I," I said.

"Especially unnecessarily dead stuff," Holly muttered.

So the three of us walked along, taking down posters in silence for a while. And almost every place there was a Dorito poster, right next to it was a Zippy poster.

When we got to the brickyard, the place was bustling and loud. A big truck about ran us over turning into the yard, and a forklift beeped us out of the way as it moved a load of cinder blocks into the street and onto a flatbed truck.

"Good grief!" Marissa said as we hurried to the quiet safety of the Kustom Heat and Air property. "Were they trying to *kill* us?"

Holly laughed, "Seemed like!"

So we're just hurrying along when a voice behind us says, "Hey, chiquita, what brings you back to this wonderful part of town?"

We turn around and there's Tony, locking up the door to Kustom Heat and Air. "Oh hi," I tell him. "We're just taking down posters before someone calls the cops on us."

He nods and says, "Smart girl. I overheard the bank tellers at First Valley gossiping about it when I was cleaning there this morning."

"Really? *Why?*"

"You know those corporate types—they're big on rules."

"Well, I'll have all my flyers down soon, but somebody else's are up now."

He hesitates, then asks, "For another cat?"

"Yeah. Only their flyer's better because there's a picture." I point down the wall at the poster. "His name's Zippy—who knows? Maybe you'll spot him, too."

He shakes his head. "I'm not in the cat recovery business." Then he frowns and lowers his voice. "But I sure hope those rumors about the Kojo Buffet aren't true."

My eyes bug out. "You heard that, too?"

He nods. "In my line of work you hear a lot. And according to several of my customers, that's a place the cops ought to keep a better eye on." But then he smiles and says, "But hey. Cats run off every day. It's usually nothing. They get hungry, they come home."

"See?" Marissa says. "*That* makes sense."

Then Holly asks, "Hey, Tony? Have you happened to have heard anything about that El Gato dude?"

He shrugs. "Just rumors."

"Like?"

"You know. Obvious stuff—he's a criminal. He's a weirdo. He's in a cult...just stuff people say when they don't have much to work with." He waves. "Anyway, gotta get to my next job. Be cool!"

When he's gone, I say to Holly, "El Gato really creeps you out, huh?"

"Well, he seems to pop out of nowhere. And he *always* gives me the evil eye."

"He wears those cat-eye contacts, Holly. They're supposed to look, you know, dangerous."

Marissa says, "That guy sounds like a trip—when do I get to see him?"

Holly mutters, "He's probably there right now."

"Can we go look?"

Holly shrugs. "Sure, why not?"

Marissa giggles. "Cool!"

So we finish pulling down the rest of the flyers, then head east on Wesler Street and cut across the field behind the Pup Parlor. But as we're approaching the back door to Slammin' Dave's, I stop in my tracks. "Is that..."

Holly looks to where I'm pointing and gasps, "It is!"

"Who?" Marissa asks. "Where?"

"Crouched beside the trash can...see her?"

Marissa squints. "Who *is* that?"

"The crazy cat lady!" Holly says, then whispers, "What is she doing?"

I shrug. "Spying?" Then I tell Marissa, "Why don't you park your bike here so we can sneak up on her."

"But *why?*"

"Uh, because she's psycho?"

158

"Oh," she says. Like, yeah, that makes sense—even though it really didn't.

So she ditches her bike, and the three of us move in on the Psycho Kitty Queen, trying to get close enough to figure out what she's doing before she notices us.

And the funny thing is, she doesn't notice us. We circle way around her and are careful and everything, but still. Even when we're twenty feet from her...ten feet from her...even when the ground's crunching behind her and our shadows are falling over her, she doesn't turn around. She just keeps looking past the trash can into Slammin' Dave's.

So we sneak forward *another* few feet, and that's when I hear purring.

Purring.

And it's coming from the Psycho herself!

And then I see what she's watching.

Or, I should say, who.

It's the Tiger in Tights.

The Furball of Fight.

The one and only El Gato.

Holly puts it all together about the same time I do and looks at me, mouthing, "Oh my god!"

Then Marissa nudges me and mouths, "What?"

I shake my head at her, 'cause how can I explain that I haven't seen this kind of animal magnetism since a pig fell in love with a cop?

How can I explain something this bizarre?

But the more I listen to the purring, the more I know it's true.

Psycho Kitty's in love.

Now we manage to stifle our giggles for a solid minute, but finally I clear my throat and say, "Uh, Miss Kitty?"

She tries to jump up and spin around, but her circulation must have been pinched off from squatting for too long, because she winds up just falling over. And since Slammin' Dave's trash can is now empty, *it* falls over when she stumbles against it.

"Wh-what are you doing?" she stammers. "Why are you here?" She straightens her tiara and tries to stand, but her legs aren't quite ready.

"The real question is, what are *you* doing here?" Then, for once *I* lock eyes with *her*, and say with a grin, "But I think we've figured that out on our own."

She lost the stare-down almost instantly. "I don't know what you're talking about."

"You and El Gato?" I said with all sorts of *Espan-yolé* flair.

"Who?" she said, getting up.

From the skittery way she was looking at everything but me, it was easy to see she knew exactly who I meant. But she wouldn't fess up, so I said, "You know—the oversized cat in the ring?" Then I couldn't help it—I purred real loud and wiggled my eyebrows.

Marissa nudged me and whispered, "Sammy!"

The Psycho Kitty got all indignant. "I'm here because this is where you *claim* you found Snowball."

"So you and El Gato aren't, uh, *friends*?"

She crossed her arms. "No!"

"So why the little rendezvous with him last night?"

Her eyes shifted from side to side. Then she said, "It's true, isn't it? You killed Snowball and brought him to my house just to torture me!"

"What? Who told you that?"

"You think I don't know what a satanic cult is? How long do you think you can go on torturing cats before you get caught, huh? How long do you think you're going to get away with this? The police are on to you, I've made sure of *that*." She backed away from us, *hissed* at us, then she snarled, "Stay away from me and my cats, or *you'll . . . be . . . sorry!*"

There was a full minute of stunned silence as we watched her leave. And finally Marissa whispered, "You weren't kidding about her being psycho."

"I sure wasn't," I said, still all amazed.

Now, I guess our commotion caused some distraction inside Slammin' Dave's, because the next thing you know, El Gato is closing the back door. But before he does, he takes a few seconds to give each of us a hard stare. And maybe I should have pounced on him with, Hey! Did you tell her we belong to a satanic cult? but his eyes are so freaky, and he looks so spitting mad, that the door closes before I can get my act in gear.

"Wow," Marissa gasps. "Talk about a psycho kitty!"

Holly laughs. "Yeah. How would you like to live next door to *him*?" Then she says, "Hey, I've got to get to work. I'll see you guys tomorrow, okay?"

So Marissa and I retrieve her bike, then yak our way over to Main Street. And while we're waiting for the light to change, Marissa eyes Maynard's Market and says, "How about a Double Dynamo?"

I laugh, "Sounds good to me!" 'cause there's nothing like the world's biggest, chocolatiest, nuttiest ice cream cone to make you forget about wackos and psychos and school.

So we jet across Main Street, but when we pull on Maynard's door, it doesn't budge. "Huh?" Marissa says, and tries again.

Then we notice, clear as day, the sign in the window: CLOSED.

"Figures," I grumble, peering through the glass to see if I can spot T.J.

"We could get something at the mall . . . ," Marissa says.

"Nah. I should get home."

So she takes off, but as I'm crossing over Broadway, I notice that there's already a group of men smokin' and jokin' in front of the Red Coach down the street. And seeing them reminds me of seeing Candi Acosta go into the House of Astrology, which of course reminds me of Heather and how we have the same stupid birthday.

And all of a sudden I wonder what Gina's explanation to all this would be. I mean, if she's a star scientist like she says she is and not just some star *charlatan* like her made-up name suggests, then she has to be able to explain why Heather and I are so different, even though we were born under the same stars, or moon rising, or whatever.

And the more I think about it, the more I decide that yeah, this is a question I not only want to ask, but I want a real answer to.

So I truck down the street, right through the group of smokin', jokin' dudes, straight to Madame Nashira's House of Astrology.

Bells jingle as I push through the door, and as my eyes adjust to the darkness, I figure out that Gina is tied up with a customer, telling a fortune. I can't exactly *see* her, because she does her palm readings and fortune-tellings inside this gauzy curtained area, but I *can* see the shadows cast onto the curtain by the candles she's got burning, and with her hands moving over her crystal ball, it looks like an oversized Kabuki show.

Madame Nashira's voice—which is deeper and, well, *dreamier* than Gina's real voice—comes wafting through the gauze. "Haaave a seat. I'll be with you sooooon."

So I have a seat. First on her red velvet love seat, then, because I feel stupid sitting on a red velvet love seat, I move over to a cushy side chair that is nearer the gauze zone. And I'm trying to get comfortable in *that*, 'cause she's got three throw pillows on it and where's your body supposed to go with three throw pillows in the way? But as I'm wrestling around pillows, I notice that I can hear what Gina, uh, Madame Nashira, is saying.

"I see a struggle . . . and darkness . . . there are people around . . . angry people . . . and who's this? A man . . . holding cash . . . lots of cash!"

"What's he look like? Can you see?" It's a man's voice. Sort of tough.

And, it suddenly hits me, very familiar.

SIXTEEN

It's interesting enough, listening to a fortune-teller and all the bogus stuff they say, but when you realize that the person whose fortune is being told might be someone you know, well, your ears perk up, and forget about politeness—you listen.

Madame Nashira's voice massaged the air. "I can't see his face...there's too much...what's that? Aaah, it's money! Yes, he's handing it out...he's throwing it around..."

"When! When is this going to happen?"

"It feels very near..."

"Friday? Can you tell if it's Friday?" the man asks, and boy, does he sound spun up.

"Oh...," Madame Nashira says. "Oh dear, he's fading..."

"Wait! Can't you bring him back?"

"But someone else is appearing...Aaah, it's the same woman who appeared before...the one with the"—her hand swooshes around her head—*"hair."*

I snicker to myself as she drones on, saying, "And there you are beside her. She's reaching out...she's...oh, I see lips! Lots of lips!"

"Can you get back to the guy with the cash? I need to know more about—"

"Shhhhhh!" Madame Nashira whispers, swirling the air above the crystal ball. "I'm seeing lips, and...roses... and...white."

"White? You're seein' *white*?"

"Long...flowing...white." Her hands stop. "Are you considering marriage?"

"No!"

She swirls her hands over the crystal ball again. "So maybe it's a funeral."

"Same difference," the man grumbles.

"Oh...there she goes. She's floating...floating... floating away...!"

"And?"

"Oh, she's gone...," Gina says. Like she's so, *so* sorry. Then she sighs heavily and says, "I'm afraid the spirits have retreated. Perhaps next time."

After a minute the man stands and grumbles something as he hands over some cash of his own. She takes it and says, "I can only help summon the spirits. I cannot control them. But here's another discount card should you decide to come back again."

"Aw, come on. How long do you expect me to keep doin' this?"

"You can stop anytime," Gina says in her dreamy Madame Nashira voice. "It's entirely up to you. The spirits do seem to have a strong connection to you. They seem to be trying to tell you something." She laughs softly. "But life itself will tell you these things...in time."

The man grumbles something, but he takes the card anyway. Then the gauze curtain moves aside, and as they start coming through, I grab those three throw pillows, curl up in the chair, and cover myself the best I can. Then I hold my breath and wait. And when I see Gina's customer come through the gauze, I about bust up. I was right! And I'm dying to pop up and say, "Hey-hey, T.J.!" but I just stay curled up, holding my breath.

"Hello?" Gina's saying into the room. And lucky for me, it's a really dimly lit room with black walls, and she doesn't look my way. "Hello?" she says again, this time more firmly. And that's when I realize that she knows someone's still inside her House of Astrology because the bells on the door never jingled a second time, only that first time, when I'd come inside.

Now, if I was trying to hide from Gina I would have been sweating it out. But I only wanted to stay hidden long enough for T.J. to leave. So the second he's gone I pop up and say, "Psssst! Over here."

"Huh?" Gina whips around, and when she sees me, she clutches her heart and says in her normal voice, "Why do you *do* that?"

"Do what?"

"Sneak up on me!"

"I don't sneak up on you."

"The last time you were here you scared the livin' daylights out of me, too!"

I laughed. "You're just jumpy."

"I am not!"

I stood up. "So how often does T.J. come by?"

"More and more all the time." She grins. "That boy is hooked."

"You can say that again. And you were sure going for his weakness with all that guy-with-the-money mumbo jumbo—"

"Hey, hey. No insulting Madame Nashira!"

"No, I mean, you're good! You really had him going."

"Hmm," she says, and she's not looking too pleased with me.

So I say, "Sorry," because I do like Gina and don't want her to be insulted.

"Forget it," she says. "And thanks for staying hidden until he left. Spotting you would've made him quit for sure." She cocks her head. "So what brings you to the House of Astrology?"

I plop down in the chair again and grumble, "Heather Acosta."

"Heather Acosta," she murmurs, tapping her chin. "Why is that name so familiar?"

"Because you just did a birth chart on her. Remember? A rush job for a 'classy lady'?"

"Yeah, yeah, yeah!" she says, snapping her fingers. "So? You know the girl?"

"She happens to be my archenemy."

She studies me a minute, then sort of sways around. "So...?"

"So Heather's evil. Wicked. Spiteful. Malicious. Deceitful. Dishonest. *Mean*." I eye her. "Do I need to go on?"

"No, no. I get the picture."

"She also happens to have the same birthday as me."

A little light flickers to life inside Madame Nashira's eyes. "And you're wondering...?"

"Well, according to *you* the position of the moon and the stars and the planets and all that determines—"

"Ah-ah, they *influence*—"

"Okay, *influence* who we are."

"So...?"

"So how can two people who have the same birthday be so completely different?"

She shrugs. "I'd need your birth certificate to answer that."

"Why? I'm telling you—we were born on the same *day*."

"How many hours apart? Where was the moon? Where am I gonna put your horizon? How do you expect me to position the ascendant?" I just sit there blinking, so she swoops in a little closer. "Why are you so resistant to this? Just bring me the darn thing. I'll do your chart, okay?"

"Okay."

Just then the door jingles, and one of the guys who was hanging out in front of the Red Coach steps inside. He says, "Hiiii," and it hits me how amazing it is that you can tell from one little word that someone's ripped out of their mind.

"Yeah?" Gina says, ready to shoo him out.

He slurs, "You got time to read my palm?"

"You got ten bucks?" Gina shoots back.

He wrestles some crumpled bills out of his front jeans pocket, puts together ten bucks, and wags them in the air.

Gina looks at me and rolls her eyes a little, then gives me the time-to-scram nod. So I whisper, "How late you gonna be open?"

"Who knows?" she says through her teeth. "If I'm not here, just bring it to the Heavenly."

So I leave the House of Astrology and race over to the Highrise because by now I'm pretty late getting home. But when I get inside the apartment, Grams doesn't say, I've been so *worried*, or Where have you *been*? or What took you so long? She just asks, "So, where'd you go?"

Now, it's not that the question is so different, but the way she's asking it sure is. Instead of wringing her hands or buzzing around me, she's just seated at the table, flipping through a magazine, sipping from a glass of juice.

Then I notice the binoculars. "You were *spying* on me?"

"Hmm," she says, and takes an endless drink. "I wouldn't call it spying. I was just watching for you."

"Because?"

She puts down the glass. "Because I was worried that that horrible Heather might have caused you trouble."

"Clear out here? If you were really watching for that, you'd need binoculars that reached all the way to school!"

"As it turns out, I didn't need binoculars at all. I saw you and Marissa strolling along, right across the street."

"So? She wanted to check out Slammin' Dave's—so what?"

"My, my. No need to be so defensive. I'm just saying, I could see you. And I watched you try to go into

169

Maynard's, then cross the street. Marissa went one way, you went the other, and forty minutes later you're finally home." She looks right at me. "So? Where'd you go?"

I sat down across from her, laced my fingers together, and leaned in. "To Madame Nashira's House of Astrology."

Her face fell. Then she sighed and said, "I was really hoping you were going to say the mall. But I knew you would have gone with Marissa, so I was afraid it was somewhere . . . else."

"Aw c'mon, Grams. Gina's nice." And before she could argue, I added, "And I want her to do my birth chart."

"But why? You don't believe in—"

"Because I want her to explain how Heather and I can be so different if we were born on the exact same day."

"You don't need *her* to tell you that. It's simple—you have different genetics!"

I crossed my arms. "Well, okay. There's my mother—"

"Who called, by the way, and is really happy that Dorito's back."

I rolled my eyes. "I'll bet she is."

Grams frowned at me. "She said she'll try to reach you again later, and when she does, you've got to promise me you won't hang up on her."

"Whatever. The *point* is that if she's the X in my genetic equation, and neither of you will fill in the Y, I can't exactly solve the problem." I leaned in and slapped the table. "You're not giving me enough to work with!"

She put up a hand.

"So tell me who my father is."

"You know I can't do that."

"Then at least give me my birth certificate so Gina can do my birth chart—which, by the way, she's been offering to do for free since September."

Grams stared at me for a solid minute.

I stared right back.

Finally she pushed away from the table and said, "Fine."

"Fine?"

"Yes. I see no reason why you can't see your own birth certificate." She headed into her bedroom, saying, "If your mother has a problem with that, well, tough."

I couldn't believe my ears. I also couldn't believe she had my birth certificate in the apartment. Believe me, I know every square inch of the place, including the closet. So I was dying to spy on her and see where she had it hidden, because if she had my birth certificate stashed in her bedroom all this time, what else did she have hidden in there?

But I made myself just sit and wait, and about a minute later she was back with a little white piece of paper.

"That's it?" I asked when she handed it over. It seemed really...plain. I was expecting a scroll. With special seals and fancy writing and maybe even a little ribbon. But this was just a kinda rumpled piece of white paper—probably only one-third the size of a regular sheet of paper—with typed-in boxes and a couple of signatures.

"That's it," Grams said, then pointed to an embossed seal. "It's the original, too. Not the copy your mother changed."

I read it over and over again. I guess I was hoping to find out something about myself, but there wasn't much I didn't already know. The *Father of Child* box said "Unreported," which I guess about summed it up. And at least they hadn't been keeping me from a twin brother or sister or anything—Box 3A stated I was a "single" birth. And there in Box 4B was the time of birth: 0959. On a 24-hour clock, that meant I was born at 9:59 A.M.

I read every box three times, and finally I said, "Thanks, Grams."

Now, I guess it came out kind of choked up, because Grams asked, "Are you all right?"

I nodded. "Sure."

She reached over and held my hand, saying, "I will encourage her to talk to you about your father, okay?"

I nodded some more. "I just don't get what the big deal is."

She sighed. "I think it's your mother who isn't ready to discuss it, not you."

"So why don't *you* tell me?"

"Because it's not my place, and you know it."

"Neither is having to raise me, and you know *that*."

She sighed again. "Well, I hope the certificate is enough for now."

I nodded. "Thanks, Grams."

"So," she said, standing up. "How's the homework situation?"

"Moderate."

"Do you have time to help me with dinner?"

What I really wanted to do was zip over to the House

172

of Astrology with my birth certificate. But instead I said, "Sure."

So I helped fix dinner, and after we ate, I did the dishes and started on my homework. But really, my mind wasn't on factorials or lowest common denominators. I wanted to get over to Gina's to deliver my birth certificate. I wanted her to get going on my chart. Any explanation was better than the one I had—even if it came from a crazy star "scientist."

I kept peeking at my birth certificate, too. There wasn't anything else it could tell me, but it did make me feel somehow more connected. Maybe I didn't actually know any more about myself, but it felt like the answers were somehow closer.

It also made me feel like, okay—I wasn't found in a Dumpster. I wasn't adopted. I really was who I thought I was.

Which is something most kids never question, but with a mother like mine you learn to wonder.

So I was racking my brains for an excuse to get away from homework and over to the Heavenly—or the House of Astrology if Gina wasn't home—when the phone rang.

Grams answered it, but ten seconds later she was holding it out to me. "It's Holly. She needs help with her homework."

I took the phone and said "Hey" into it.

Holly whispered, "Sorry I kinda lied to her, but is there any way you can come over?"

"Uh . . ."

"He's here again. And he was nosing through our trash!"

"Who?" I whispered.

"El Gato!"

I looked over my shoulder. Grams was back in the living room, but still, I kept my voice down. "Your trash is empty, isn't it?"

"Pretty much, but he was pawing around in what *is* in it."

"I'll be right over."

I hung up, stuck my birth certificate in my pocket, and went into the living room. "Grams, I need to go over to Holly's for a minute. She's . . . she's got questions that I can't answer over the phone."

She looked up from her book. "Do you want me to check the hallway?"

"Nah. I'll be careful."

"Call if it gets late." She tapped her wristwatch. "No excuses."

I laughed and held up my wrist. "If the bat swings past the ball, I'll call."

She laughed, too. And with that I slipped out of the apartment and down the hall, wondering why El Gato was on the prowl.

SEVENTEEN

Holly was waiting for me at the Pup Parlor door. "Come on!" she said. "He's still there."

"Meg and Vera aren't home?" I asked as we charged upstairs.

"No! They're at some Groomers Club meeting in Santa Luisa."

Except for a light in the hallway, the apartment was totally dark. Holly led me into the kitchen, where we had a clear view of the alleyway. Slammin' Dave's back door was propped open, Tornado Tony's van was parked off to the side, and El Gato was back against the wall, lighting a cigarette.

Or at least trying. The cigarette didn't seem to want to light. And he kept checking the back door. "He's acting kinda amped, don't you think?" I whispered as he tossed down another match.

"He is so weird," Holly whispered back. "Why doesn't he just take off the mask?"

He threw down another match, and I said, "He's sure not acting like a smoker." Then I had an idea. "Maybe smoking's a diversion?"

"A diversion from what?"

"Got me. He's just not acting natural."

"What's natural about wearing a cat mask and spandex shorties?"

"Good point."

El Gato finally got the cigarette going, but he didn't puff on it. He just held it between his fingers and headed for Tony's van.

"Now what's he doing?" Holly whispered.

El Gato looked over both shoulders, then tried the driver's door. It was locked, so he shielded out the alley light with his hand and looked in the window.

"It looks like he's casing the van!" I whispered.

"What's he expecting to get out of a janitor's van?"

"Maybe the stereo?" Then I thought of something. "Hey. Do you know where Vera's camera is?" I knew she had an old manual one with a killer telephoto lens.

Holly glanced at me, then charged out of the kitchen. A few seconds later she was back. "There are two shots left."

"Do you know how to use it?"

"Yeah." She held the camera up, then zoomed in on him. There were no windows or doors on the side of Tony's van, so El Gato was now behind it, trying the back doors.

I whispered, "Is there enough light?" because he was sort of in the shadows.

"It's gonna have to be kind of a long exposure." She tweaked some knobs quick, then focused again, and *cl...ick,* the shutter opened and closed.

She'd barely taken the shot when El Gato went around

the van and out of view. Then a few seconds later *Tony* came out the back door of Slammin' Dave's. And I wanted to open the window and shout, "Hey! That El Gato creep is casing your van!" but Tony seemed to be looking for him, anyway. So I whispered to Holly, "Can we open the window a little?"

Very quietly she unlocked it and turned the crank. It made a little squeaking sound, but Tony didn't seem to notice. He was busy calling, "Hey! Hey, Cat Dude! Dave wants you inside. Where'd you go?"

El Gato's raspy voice came from down the alley. "Just havin' a smoke." He appeared from behind the van, then flicked the cigarette down and ground it out with his foot. "Thinkin' there's got to be a better way to make a buck."

"Amen to that." Tony laughed. "You wrestlers are nuts."

"Yeah, well, so are you. You work too much, you know that?"

Tony unlocked his van. "I'm not into power or glory. I just want the cash."

El Gato snorted. "Well, if you hear of any way *I* can make some quick cash, let me know about it, would ya?"

"Will do." Tony got inside his van and fired it up, then called out the window, "So you gonna quit wrestling?"

"Not until I figure out a better way of scoring some green."

"But you've gotta have a day job, right?"

"Yeah, and it stinks."

Tony nodded and started backing up. "Don't they all."

When they were both gone, I said, "What a jerk! First he tries to break into Tony's van, then he acts all chummy with him. How can people be like that?"

Holly closed the window and said, "Obviously, he's a criminal. And I think criminals just don't care." She held up the camera. "So? What do you think we should do with the picture? Give it to Tony? Give it to Dave? Give it to Officer Borsch?"

"Forget Officer Borsch. He'll just say, So the guy's hand was on the door—so what?"

"Okay, then Tony or Dave?"

"Maybe both?"

She nodded. "Maybe we should tell Dave, and he can warn Tony."

"Sounds good."

She let out a huge sigh. "I feel better already. I have a witness and at least *some* evidence as to why El Gato creeps me out." She smiled at me. "Thanks for coming over."

"Sure." Then I said, "Hey, I've got to go to the Heavenly for a minute. Want to come?"

"To the Heavenly?" She looked at me like I was asking her to eat slugs. "Why?"

I pulled my birth certificate out of my pocket. "I need to deliver this to Gina."

She saw what it was and laughed. "You're finally gonna let her do your birth chart?"

"Yup."

She hesitated a minute, then said, "You know, I've never actually been inside the Heavenly."

"It's no big deal, really. It's seedy, but André is cool and it's definitely worth the experience."

She laughed. "Well, okay then."

The worst thing about the Heavenly is the people who live there. They're like month-old produce at a farmers' market—they're shriveled and smelly, and believe me, nobody wants to take them home.

Which I guess is why they live at the Heavenly. I've heard that in the old days the hotel used to be *the* place to stay in Santa Martina, and the inside *is* pretty cool, especially the furniture. Carved feet. Pointy backs. It would actually be fancy furniture except the wood's all nicked and the upholstery's totally worn through, especially on the seats. You see those seats and you can't help wondering how many people have sat in them.

How many farts have been cut in them.

Which is maybe why the place stinks so bad.

"Pee-yew," Holly whispered when we walked through the door. "That's one serious smell!"

"Uh-huh." I headed for the reception counter, saying, "Don't worry. This shouldn't take long."

André grinned around the cigar that was clamped between his front teeth. "Hey, Sammy. How's life?"

"Better'n it was yesterday. How about you?"

"Can't complain. And what was yesterday?"

"Don't even ask." I pulled my birth certificate out of my pocket and said, "Gina home? I've got to give her this."

He started to reach for it, but I pulled back. "In person."

He rolled the cigar to the corner of his mouth. "She expecting you?"

"As a matter of fact, she is."

He dialed 4-2-3 on the desk phone, and when Gina picked up, he said, "Sammy and her friend are here with a personal delivery. You wanna come down, or you want me to send them up?"

A few seconds later we were heading for the elevator.

Now, the Heavenly's elevator is basically just a metal cage on pulleys. It's dank and musty, and you definitely want to keep your hands inside the cage. Holly looked around as we clanged and clattered up to the fourth floor. "I would hate to get trapped inside this thing! You think it's gonna make it?"

"Yeah," I laughed. "And it's probably less scary than taking the stairs."

"You've got to be kidding."

The elevator lurched, then thumped to a stop. "I'll show you on the way down."

Gina was waiting for us, leaning against her doorway, one hand on her hip, the other holding a cigarette. "Hey, girl," she said, blowing smoke in the air. "Deliverin' the goods?"

I tried to keep my distance as I handed over my birth certificate. "Right here."

"Whatsa matter? You're actin' like I bite."

"No, you smoke." Now, it came out sounding kinda mean, especially since she obviously thought she looked cool, standing there with a burning tube of toxic weeds between her fingers. So I added, "My, uh, my mom can smell it a mile away."

Gina held the cigarette back inside the room. "Oh, sorry," she said.

"So we'd better get going."

"Okay, then." She looked over my birth certificate. "Give me a week."

"A week? I was hoping—"

"Yeah, yeah, yeah," she said, waving me off. "First you think it's bogus, now you want it yesterday."

"But—"

She smiled at me. "I'll do what I can, girlfriend."

"Thanks." We started to leave, but I turned back and said, "Oh, and Gina?"

"Yeah?"

"Uh . . . that's my only copy."

"Got it."

Like I promised, I took Holly to the stairs. But when we turned into the stairwell, she pulled back and said, "Eeeegh."

I laughed and said, "Told you," because the Heavenly has the pukiest stairwell known to man. There are old, warped mirrors lining both sides from top to bottom, which makes weird reflections that go on for ever and ever in both directions.

Holly started down, saying, "It's making me seasick!" But once she got the hang of it, she said, "What a trip!" and moved a little faster.

So there we were, thumping along, joking about what drugs some interior decorator must've been on to actually *do* this, when all of a sudden me and my mutant reflections stopped dead in our tracks.

"What?" Holly asked. But then she saw him, too, coming *up* the stairs. "Who's that?" she mouthed.

"The Bulldog," I mouthed back.

"Who?"

He was close now, so I waited until we'd passed each other to whisper, "The guy I followed into Slammin' Dave's. When I hid under the ring, remember?"

"Oh right. But I thought you said that psycho cat lady said the guy who snatched her cat looked like a pit bull, not a bulldog."

"I know."

"So? Why'd you freeze up when you saw him?"

"I don't know. Something about him seems . . . off. Plus, I wasn't expecting him. It's like he disappeared inside Slammin' Dave's, and now *poof,* here he is walking up the steps of the Heavenly."

"Carrying a gym bag."

"And smelling like a shower . . ."

We both stopped and stared at each other.

"No . . . !" Holly whispered.

"Same build, same, you know, *demeanor.*"

"It's gotta be him!" she whispered.

I grinned. "El Gato is the Bulldog—kinda ironic, huh?"

"It fits, though."

"And it explains why he's at Dave's so much—he lives right next door!"

"Well!" she said. "Now we know who we're dealing with!"

I nodded. "And the cool thing is, he doesn't know *we* know."

Holly grinned. "He probably thinks we're just a couple of stupid kids."

I grinned back. "Ha!"

EIGHTEEN

By the time I got back to the apartment, the bat had swung past the ball, but not by much.

"I was just starting to worry," Grams said when I slipped through the door.

"Hey, I'm home on time," I said, and tapped my watch. "It's not a home-run watch—it's a run home watch. And when it was time to run home, I did."

She laughed and said, "Well, good!"

So I buckled down and did my homework while I ate a giant slab of leftover birthday cake. And by the time I'd taken a shower and put some more anti-itch stuff on my flea bites, it was way past time for bed.

The next morning started normally enough—I had to gobble down breakfast and ride like crazy to make it to homeroom before the tardy bell rang, Marissa waved at me, Holly waved at me, and Heather gave me the evil eye.

Definitely a typical morning.

But after that strange things began to happen.

First, I aced a math quiz. I got *none* wrong. And believe me, when it comes to pop quizzes, I never get 100 percent. Now, if everybody had done great on it, that would have been one thing. But half the class totally bombed it. Rick Lopez was the only other person to ace it, and as a reward Mr. Tiller gave Rick and me homework passes. That's like a get-out-of-jail-free card. Math homework is the worst.

So I left Mr. Tiller's classroom in a great mood, which only got better in history. Mr. Holgartner was absent. Absent! You have to understand—Mr. Holgartner is like the Noise Nazi. He sends you to the office for breathing too loud, which is a real hazard, seeing how his class is always a total snooze. But he was absent, and the substitute turned out to be a laid-back guy who let us work in groups. Marissa and I talked the whole class period.

Then after history I found a five-dollar bill on the ground. There was nobody around it or I might have said, Hey, is this yours? But it was all by its little lonesome, and since a five-dollar bill isn't exactly something you turn in to the Lost and Found, I stuck it in my pocket alongside the two twenties.

And as if that wasn't enough to keep me smiling for the rest of the day, Mr. Pence caught Heather copying homework during science and sent her to the office. I was so jazzed that he'd nailed her that I actually paid attention to his lecture on the anatomy of an amoeba.

So I had the most awesome day in junior high history. If every day could be like that, I would *love* school.

Then after school Holly went to work at the Humane Society, Dot went home with her dad, and Marissa and I went to the mall to buy me a CD player. And when I found a really great one on closeout, and the CD I wanted in the "Like New" section for half off, Marissa just shook her head and said, "You are having the luckiest day ever."

Up to that point we had used the words *awesome* and *amazing* and *unbelievable,* but no one had said *lucky.* But when Marissa used that word, we both stopped what we were doing, looked at each other, then looked at my shoe.

"Ohmygod!" Marissa whispered.

"It . . . it's just a coincidence."

"Oh right," she laughed. "Some coincidence."

I shook my head. "You watch. Any second now my life will go back to normal."

"Don't say that! Don't even think it. This is your new life. Embrace it! You now have unlimited luck."

I laughed. She was being so, you know, New Agey.

"Boy," she chuckled, "my dad could've used you in Las Vegas."

"What do you mean?"

Her voice dropped. "I'm not supposed to tell anyone, but I can tell you. He lost two thousand dollars at the roulette table."

I cringed. "Ouch."

"Double ouch after mom found out. She laid into him, and then he laid into her about acting like a stupid teenager over Darren Cole."

I shook my head. "Sounds like you did some real successful family bonding."

She snorted. "It was a disaster." Then she sighed and said, "I've gotta go kill some aliens—wanna come?"

So I went with her to the video arcade, and while she took out her frustrations on electro-badguys, I assembled my CD player, popped on the headphones, and let the sound of distorted guitars, driving bass, and bashing drums power-massage my brain. And by the time Marissa was out of quarters, I'd listened to the whole CD and had started over.

Marissa laughed. "You're going to be sick of that by tomorrow."

"It's so good!"

"Yeah, but I'll bring you some others tomorrow."

Then I noticed my watch. "Uh-oh! I'd better get home."

She held my wrist and said, "That is the coolest watch ever. Find out where she got it, okay?" She hesitated a second then said, "You wouldn't mind, would you? If I got one, too?"

"No! That'd be great. I was thinking we should get Ms. Rothhammer one next year if she coaches us again."

"Great idea!"

"Anyway, I've gotta go."

"Yeah, me too."

So off we went, me out the north end of the mall, Marissa out the south end. And I was having a great time cruising up to the intersection of Broadway and Main, listening to my very own CD on my very own player, when I noticed the Bulldog coming out of the Heavenly.

I peeled off my headphones and watched. Don't ask me why, but it seems you can *see* better if you can also *hear* what's going on around you.

The Bulldog had a black gym bag, but he wasn't heading north to Slammin' Dave's—he was walking south toward Main.

I couldn't help wondering where he was going. I mean, if he was working out, why wasn't he going to Slammin' Dave's? Did he have some other place he worked out, too?

Or maybe he was going someplace to switch into El Gato. If he didn't leave the Heavenly in his mask, where did he change? Some public bathroom? A gas station?

A phone booth?

I sort of hid behind the light post and waited out the light. And when the Bulldog got down to Main and turned west, I stuffed my CD player in my backpack, picked up my board, and crossed over Broadway.

The Bulldog was walking fast. And since I was on the opposite side of the street, I decided that I was being stupid, trying to keep up with him on foot. So I tossed down my skateboard and hopped on. It's amazing how you can just basically coast along on a skateboard and keep up with somebody trucking along on foot.

After I'd closed the gap a little, I noticed that his gym bag seemed heavy. Heavier than a cat suit and shoes, that's for sure. More like a cat suit and shoes and a dumbbell or something. Well, okay. Maybe not *that* dense, but, you know, heavy enough for him to switch hands a couple of times.

And then I swear I saw the gym bag twitch. Actually, it was more a *jolt*.

But . . . why would his gym bag be moving?

Well, just as I was formulating a horrible thought about what might be in his bag, *poof*, the Bulldog disappeared. One minute he was blocked from view by a tree, the next he was gone.

I figured out in a hurry that he had turned down the same driveway that I'd used to get away from Butcher Boy. So I cut across the street, wondering, Does he really have a *cat* in that bag?

I spotted him in time to see him turn left down the alley. So where was he going with his twitchy bag? To the Kojo Buffet? Did they *pay* him for cats?

But how stupid would that be? I mean, buying chickens had to be cheaper than paying someone to snag you cats. Unless . . . unless they were a delicacy. Or maybe the Bulldog hated cats so much that he just wanted to rid the world of them. But then why dress up like a cat? It didn't make sense.

Still. I was real careful going down the driveway toward the alley. I thought about ditching my backpack and my skateboard so I'd be more, you know, svelte, but decided against it. There wasn't a bush in sight, and the last thing I wanted was to lose my most prized possessions.

And I'm not talking homework books, believe me.

So I kept it all with me, but I knew it was going to make ducking out of view harder to do. So I was cautious. Careful.

And, it turns out, slow.

By the time I peeked around the corner and down the alley, he was gone. I moved out a few feet and checked left.

No Bulldog.

I checked right.

No Bulldog.

So I stepped forward a few feet, and when I didn't spot him further down the alley, I hurried to the back door of the Kojo Buffet.

The door was propped open, and I was careful going up to it because I didn't want Butcher Boy *or* the Bulldog to spot me, especially if a cat was changing hands. Who knows what they'd do to me? Maybe *I'd* wind up in the cooler, and get turned into sweet-and-sour Sammy. I could hear people now, going, "Mmmm... tastes like chicken."

But when I looked inside the Kojo kitchen, I didn't see the Bulldog. Just Butcher Boy and his helper chopping and stirring and making steam.

I watched for a minute or two, just in case, then gave up and moved up the alley, keeping my eyes peeled for the Bulldog. If he wasn't going to the Kojo Buffet, why did he cut to the alley? Had he spotted me tailing him?

At the end of the block I abandoned the alley and got on a regular street. And as I wound through the West Side, I tried to make sense of things. Why would a guy steal cats? It couldn't be like stealing babies, where someone would pay a lot of money for them—there were cats everywhere! So what would motivate a person to steal cats? Love? Money? Revenge? And why kill them? Why did the cats all look so... terrified? Was there a cult making animal sacrifices? Was there some *part* of a cat that people wanted?

The more I thought about it, the more nuts it made me. There had to be a reason. A *connection*.

But what?

When I came to the streets where I'd been with Holly and Marissa the day before, I noticed that the flyers for Zippy the Missing Cat were all taken down. But then I saw a lady across the street from the brickyard taping *up* a flyer. So I rode over and saw that they were flyers for...Zippy the Missing Cat. "Hey," I said, "I was hoping you'd found your cat. I noticed your flyers were all taken down."

"Some jerk *took* them down," she snapped.

"They did? Well, uh...did you know it was against the law?" She just stared at me, so I added, "To post flyers."

"What are you telling me?" She looked angry. Suspicious. Like she was thinking that *I* was the one who had taken them down.

So I said, "Stupid law, huh? I didn't know about it, either, but I found out when I put up flyers for *my* missing cat."

"*Your* missing cat?"

"Mine was the speckled orange one—you put your flyers right next to mine."

"Oh!" She smiled, and it changed her whole face. "Did you find him?"

"Yeah. I was so relieved." I laughed. "He was only missing for a few hours, but when we got him back he was, like, covered with fleas. But at least we got him back."

"So he was probably at the pound, then?"

"The pound? No, a guy who works around here found him over on Piños Street."

"Oh," she said. "When you said fleas I figured pound. They dump house cats in with mangy strays."

"I take it you've already checked there for Zippy?"

She nodded. "There wasn't one healthy-looking cat there. It was really sad."

"Well, I'll keep my eyes peeled for Zippy. He looks like a sweet cat." Then I added, "And if I were you, I'd keep breaking the law—it worked for me."

She looked down the street and shook her head. "Why would anyone care if you put up posters? Half these places are vacant anyway."

I snickered. "Welcome to Santa Martina." And I was about to take off, but stopped and said, "Hey, did a man with a blond buzz cut and a black gym bag happen to walk by here?"

She looked at me. "Yes!"

"Really? Did you see where he went?"

"Well, he . . ." She looked up the sidewalk. "He passed right by me, but no."

"Did he say anything to you?"

She shook her head.

"Did he read your poster?"

She shook her head again. "It was almost like I wasn't here. Who is he?"

Now, I didn't want to try and explain how he was El Gato the Cat-Stealing Cat because (a) I didn't know for sure that he stole cats, and (b) it sounded way too wacky.

So I just said, "I'm not sure, but you might want to be, you know, *wary* of him."

"Okaaaaay..."

I got on my board and pushed off, saying, "Anyway, I'll be on the lookout for Zippy."

"Thanks!" she called, and when I looked over my shoulder I saw that she'd gone back to taping up flyers.

That night I called Holly while Grams was in the tub and told her about running into Zippy's owner. She told me that she'd checked, but there weren't any cats like Zippy at the Humane Society. Then she asked, "But why were you back in that part of town?"

So I told her about following the Bulldog and about how it looked like his bag had jolted and all of that. And when I was done, she said, "So if it was a cat ... I mean, *why?*"

"Exactly."

We were both quiet a minute, and then she said, "I'm starting to think the guy's not just creepy—he's sick."

"It does seem weird."

"Well, I can't wait until tomorrow."

"What's happening tomorrow?"

"The pictures are going to be done. Vera took them in this morning."

"Great!"

"Yeah. I tried to get her to do one-hour, but she didn't think the picture sounded incriminating enough to waste the money."

"Oh well. Tomorrow's good. You want to go to Slammin' Dave's together?"

"Absolutely. You saw the whole thing, too."

"So after school?"

"Yeah."

"Cool."

So we hung up, but ten seconds after I put the phone down, it rang. And since I figured it was Holly calling me back to tell me something, and since Grams was still in the tub and couldn't exactly answer it herself, I broke a house rule—I picked up the phone.

But it wasn't Holly. It was a muffled voice that said, "Quit snoopin' around, kid, or I guarantee, you'll be sorry."

Now, right before the phone went dead, I heard a horn blare. And it took me a second to realize that what was weird about the horn was that I didn't just hear it through the phone.

I also heard it through the air.

I charged into Grams' bedroom, snagged the binoculars from underneath her bed, and scoured the area around the pay phone by Maynard's. I looked up and down Broadway, then Main. There were no cat dudes or bulldogs or psycho kitties out in front of Maynard's. Only T.J, standing in the doorway, having a smoke.

My brain did a double take. T.J.? But then I thought, Nah. T.J. was grumpy but harmless. Besides, how would he have my number?

Then I remembered—the flyers. He'd snagged one off the phone pole. Actually, now that I thought about it, *anyone* could have my number—we'd papered the whole West Side with flyers. Talk about a strategic mistake!

Grams was still in the bathroom, so I hurried back to the kitchen. Maybe I was also making a mistake about the Maynard's phone booth. Maybe the horn honk had been just a coincidence. After all, there were pay phones all over Santa Martina—lots of them near busy streets.

I picked up the phone and dialed *69, hoping I'd get lucky with automatic dial-back. Maybe I'd be able to figure out who had called, or from where.

The phone rang. And rang. And rang some more. But I just let it keep ringing. And then all of a sudden, somebody picks up. First there's the sound of exhaling. Then a voice says, "Hello?"

And my heart starts pounding, because even from that one little word, I know who's on the other end.

NINETEEN

I almost just hung up. But at the last second I gave my voice a Cockney accent and said, "'Ello, I'm tryin' to reach Maynard's Market."

There was a moment of silence, then T.J. said, "Well, ya just missed, lady. This is the pay phone *outside* the market."

"Ya don't say! Now, isn't that somethin'?" I forced a laugh, then said, "I'll look it up again, thank you," and hung up before he could say anything.

I jetted into Grams' bedroom, snagged the binoculars again, and looked down the street. Sure enough, T.J. was hanging up the phone. I watched him, thinking it was too bad he was such a pain in the glutes. I mean, if he and I were even halfway friendly, I'd race down and ask him if he'd seen anyone using the pay phone earlier.

But what if T.J. *had* called our number? What if he was . . . but that didn't make any sense, either. Why would he pick up the phone if he'd just placed a threatening call. He'd stay *away* from it. I mean, he had to know about *69.

Didn't he?

Besides, T.J. didn't have anything to do with bulldogs or cat dudes or missing kitties.

Did he?

Then all of a sudden I remembered how protective he'd been of his garbage. At the time I'd just thought it was T.J. being T.J., but now I started wondering.

I mean, had there been *cats* in his trash?

Grams' voice about shot me through the window. "I thought we agreed you wouldn't do that anymore."

I spun around. "I was...I was just looking down at Maynard's." I tried to relax. "T.J. was out front having a smoke."

"Oh, fascinating."

I put the binoculars back under her bed. I wanted to tell her what had happened, but all of a sudden I was just too tired. There's nothing more exhausting than having your grandmother cross-examine you about things you don't really understand yourself.

"So," she said, "I've been meaning to ask—what's that on your shoe?"

"Uh...it's a lucky horseshoe," I said, making my voice all perky. "And guess what? It works."

"Oh, pshaw."

"Seriously! I aced my math test and got a homework pass from Mr. Tiller, Heather got caught copying homework, and I found five bucks."

"All today?"

"Yup!" I scooted out of her bedroom, hoping she wouldn't ask me where I'd gotten it. "Marissa says I am now a lucky charm."

"Well! So much for thirteen being bad luck, huh?"

"I don't know about *that*." I eyed her over my shoulder. "I've got three hundred sixty-two days to go!"

The next day wasn't exactly lucky, but it still wasn't bad. Actually, I have to admit—it was really good. And believe it or not, it was good because of Heather.

She was totally and ridiculously tweaked over my horseshoe.

Now, if it had been a ring or a necklace or, you know, something *serious,* then yeah—I could see why she'd be a little spun up. Given how rational she is and all. But a bent piece of holey metal strapped to a worn-out sneaker? She was worried that what? This was a *romance*?

Please.

And I couldn't help thinking it was funny. I mean, Heather's not on the honor roll or anything, but she probably could be if she'd study even half as hard as she schemes.

What Heather *is,* though, is clever.

Wickedly clever.

And I don't know if she just happened to be clean out of cleverness or what, but when it came to the horseshoe, she couldn't seem to act anything but lame.

It started in homcroom, where she scowled at my foot and said, "What's up with that stupid horseshoe anyway, loser?"

I wiggled my high-top at her and smiled. "It protects me from evil."

She sneered at me. "Oh *right.*"

"Heath-errr," Mrs. Ambler warned, because by now teachers know—they're supposed to keep her *away* from me.

"See?" I whispered. "It's working."

Now, instead of just acting cool or like she didn't care, Heather had a mini spaz right there on the spot. Her nose wrinkled, her eyes sizzled, and from her neck up everything quivered. Her ears, her ear*rings,* her hair, her cheeks—everything sputtered and spattered. Like her head had been dipped into a deep fryer.

"Sammy?" Mrs. Ambler asked, and she was starting to look worried.

I put my hands up and said, "*I'm* in *my* seat, Mrs. Ambler."

"Heather!" she snapped. "Sit down."

So that was homeroom. Then later in the day Holly spotted Heather and her friends Tenille and Monet following us. Seriously, they were lurking in the shadows, hiding around the corner, spying on us between classes. Heather by herself might have been able to get away with it, but with Monet, and especially *Tenille?* What a joke. We ducked into the media center, zipped out a side door, and looped around. And while Heather and her friends were looking in the media-center door whispering frantically about where we'd gone, we were standing right behind them.

Finally I said, "Looking for someone?"

Heather spazzed out again.

I just laughed.

Then at lunch Marissa, Dot, Holly, and I found a nice shady spot on the front lawn and ate there. Everyone's supposed to be at the lunch tables or in the cafeteria, but it was so . . . *springy* out that we didn't want to eat in the cafeteria or be surrounded by cement. The grass was soft and cool, and smelled so good, plus there were other kids there, too. And since we were quiet and picked up our trash and all, nobody came and shooed us away. For thirty whole minutes the four of us caught each other up and totally forgot that we were in the middle of a school day.

It was nice.

Then on my way to science Casey ran up to me all out of breath, saying, "Hey, I thought maybe you were absent." He checked my foot, and when he saw the horseshoe was still there, he grinned and said, "So? Is it working?"

I stopped dead in my tracks. "Is this some voodoo magic horseshoe?"

He laughed. "Should I take that as a yes?"

We started walking again, and I said, "I don't believe in good luck charms or any superstitious stuff like that, but man, I had the best day yesterday." So I told him about the quiz and the homework pass and the money and the CD player, and I had to give him the super-speedy version because we were already in front of Mr. Pence's room, and Heather was lurking around.

"See?" he said, laughing. "What'd I tell you?"

"Yeah, yeah, right. If you ask me it's all a coincidence, but—"

He grabbed me by the shoulders and looked right into my eyes. "Sammy, you are lucky. L-U-C-K-Y. Believe!"

Now, in all the times I'd talked to Casey, I don't think—no, scratch that—I *know* I'd never been that, uh, face to face with him. And in all the times I'd talked to him, I'd never noticed that his eyes were brown. They could've been purple for all I knew.

But they're not purple. They're brown. A milk-chocolate brown, with maybe a little bittersweet mixed in. And they're clear. No specks at all. No yellow ring. Just a real smooth chocolaty brown.

And now I was definitely noticing them. There wasn't much room *not* to notice them—they were, like, six inches away from mine.

And you better believe, my brain was screaming, RUN, but as usual, the rest of me wasn't listening—I couldn't seem to blink, I couldn't seem to move, I couldn't seem to breathe. Then my mouth went dry, my lips pruned up, and my heart started duking it out with my chest.

I finally managed to say, "Lucky. Right. I'll remember that." Then I pulled away from him and beat it into the classroom.

So okay. I was a little spaced-out during science. My stomach was all, you know, fluttery. Not in a good way, either. More in an on-deck way, when the other team's pitcher is throwing a hundred miles an hour. You're afraid to swing 'cause you'll probably miss and totally embarrass yourself. And if you do actually connect, well, the force of the ball is going to send shock waves down the bat straight to your hands and arms.

Translation: it's going to hurt.

And then there's always the possibility that the ball will go wild and hit you in the head. Helmet or not, it'll probably kill you.

So no, I wasn't really focusing on the worksheet Mr.

Pence had passed out. And no, I wasn't paying attention to what was going on around me. I was too busy ducking wild pitches in my head. But then I crossed my legs, and *whack, clang* I kicked something that slammed into the metal table.

I looked underneath the table, and there, holding her head with a pained look on her face, was Heather.

"What are you *doing*?" I whispered, and Mr. Pence heard, because he came around from behind his desk, looked at the floor, and said, "Heather?"

She held her jaw and gave me a real lethal look as she backed out from under the table.

"Heather, what were you doing down there?" Mr. Pence asked.

"Uh..." She held her head with one hand as she slipped something into her back pocket with the other. "I...I dropped something—"

"Clear over *here*?" he asked.

She checked her hand for blood. "It was a...pearl..."

"A pearl?"

"It rolled and I..." She was feeling her head again, keeping her back turned away from me so I couldn't see her pocket. Then all of a sudden she turns on the doe eyes and says, "Oh, Mr. Pence, I feel like I'm going to...," and crumples into his arms.

He holds her for a second as she pretends to be all limp. "Heather?" He looks around, not knowing what to do, then eases her to the floor.

"Ooooh," she goes, all drama-queen-like. "What happened?"

"You fainted, Heather, now just stay put. Where did you hurt your head?"

"Right...here," she says, taking his hand and putting it on her head. "Ooooh, that hurts." Then she gives him the total damsel-in-distress routine, batting her lashes and looking at him like she's oh-so-grateful that he's saved her.

Now, I don't know if anyone in the class bought her act, but I can tell you this—Mr. Pence did. His scientific brain turned to mush. And yeah, I believe Heather hurt her head, but there's no chance her act was for real. The only reason Heather was being swoony was because she was trying to get out of having to explain what she was doing crawling around on the floor.

And what *was* she doing, crawling around under my table? And what had she hidden in her jeans?

When Mr. Pence finally helped her to her feet, she acted all wobbly and hung on him for support, but in the middle of all that she forgot to keep her backside turned away from me. And that's when I saw two little purple arcs peeking out the pocket of her designer jeans.

Scissors.

What was she doing with scissors?

Then it hit me. My horseshoe! She was planning to cut my laces and steal my horseshoe!

I looked down quick and let out a sigh of relief. It was still there. Good thing, too, 'cause I'd have tackled her sorry backside and shown her just how *un*lucky stealing someone's lucky charm can make you.

But I didn't have to tackle her. I just had to watch the

Swoon Show with the rest of the class until finally Mr. Pence decided to have Vanessa Pylor escort her to the office for medical attention.

Medical attention. Right.

But she was gone and that was fine with me. And the more I thought about Heather crawling around in her pricey jeans on the science room floor, the more I had to laugh. Do you know what gets spilled on the science room floor? Frog guts. Owl pellets. *Acid*. Talk about stooping low to get what you want!

But hey. All that got my mind off Casey's Easter-egg eyes. And gave me lots to laugh about with Holly and Marissa on the way home from school.

"She was seriously going to cut your laces to get it?" Marissa asked when we stopped at the intersection of Broadway and Cook.

"That's my theory."

Holly laughed. "Heather Scissorhands!" Then when the light changed, she looked at me and said, "You're coming with me to pick up the pictures, right?"

"Right."

"Are they at the mall?" Marissa asked.

"No. They're at Speedy Photo."

"That place up on Main? Clear past Miller?"

"Right."

Marissa sighed. "Well, I can't go. I've got to get home. I promised Mom that—oh!" She looked at me all wide-eyed, then started digging through her backpack.

"What?"

"I can't believe I forgot to give you these...." She

204

popped up with three CDs in her hand. "These two are from me...."

I checked them over—boy bands. "Uh, thanks," I said, as cheerfully as I could.

She scowled. "Give them a chance, would you?" Then she handed over the other CD and said, "And this one's from my mom."

"Your *mom*?" I asked. Then I looked at the CD and it made sense.

Darren Cole—Mr. Las Vegas.

Whoopee.

"She bought, like, *ten* of them." She tapped on the jewel case. "It's autographed, see?" Then she dropped her voice and grinned. "I think my dad wants them out of the house."

"Well, tell her I can't wait to hear what makes her go tick tock."

Marissa laughed and took off for home, and Holly and I headed up to Speedy Photo.

We were totally unaware that we were being followed.

TWENTY

The Santa Martina Town Center Mall has parking nearly clear around it. Some of it's regular parking-lot parking, and some of it's parking-structure parking. And to buffer the ugliness of all those cars and cement, there's a wide area around the whole mall that's landscaped with a windy walkway, little grassy hills, pine trees, and bushes. They've even put park benches along the walkway for people who get tired of circling the mall, trying to figure out how to get inside.

If you ask me, the best thing about the mall *is* the winding walkway. Give me a skateboard and a roller-coaster walkway over trendy clothes and household gadgets any day of the week.

Anyway, it was while Holly and I were carrying our skateboards across the little grassy hills to the winding walkway that I noticed we were being followed. "Psssst," I said to Holly. "Don't look now, but the Horseshoe Hustler and her posse are on our trail."

She started to look back but stopped. "Heather?"

"Yup. With Tenille and Monet."

"Where?"

"On the other side of Broadway."

"Are you sure they're following us? Maybe they're just going to the mall."

I bent down and retied my shoe, peeking under my armpit. The traffic light had changed, and Heather and her friends were moving fast across the street.

"Their eyes are glued on us," I said. "They're definitely up to something."

"So what do you want to do?"

The school buses roared by, blocking them from view, but I didn't want to make a break for it—I wanted to know what they were up to. So I stood up and said, "How about we ride slow for a little while and see if they follow us."

Holly shrugged. "I'm game."

So when we got to the windy walkway, we got on our skateboards and coasted along. And sure enough Heather and the others ran after us, Tenille carrying her shoes and Monet lagging behind, holding her side.

"We've gotta slow down," I said to Holly, "or we'll lose them."

"Don't we *want* to lose them?"

"Not yet."

So we rode along until we got to a place where the walkway takes a sharp right into a little amphitheater area and then goes up and around to Main Street. And the minute I knew we were out of view, I said, "Now!" and pushed hard through the amphitheater. Then right past a park bench on the other side I said, "In here!" and dove for some big bushes. Holly plowed in right beside me, then we both caught our breath and waited.

It seemed to take forever for Heather to come around

207

the corner, and when she did, she got all snappy with the others. "See? They're gone! Why do you have to be so slow?"

"How are we supposed to keep up with them?" Monet panted. "They have skateboards!"

"And my feet are *killing* me," Tenille cried.

"Besides," Monet said, gasping for air, "you'll never get it with *Holly* there."

"Yeah," Tenille said. "She's tough."

"Oh shut up, both of you." Heather took off running and said over her shoulder, "Stay here—I'm gonna see where those losers went."

She came back a couple of minutes later, looking really disgusted. "They're gone," she said, and plopped down on the bench right in front of us.

Tenille shook her head. "Why do you want it so bad, anyway? It's ugly!" Then she added, "If you ask me, your brother's weird."

Heather snorted. "Like this is news to me?"

"So?" Monet laughed. "Sammy and him make a perfect couple."

"He's not *that* weird! And they're not a couple! And they're not going to *be* a couple!"

"Is that why you want the horseshoe so bad?" Tenille asked. "So they're not a couple?"

"They're *not* a couple!"

"But," Monet said, "if you get it away from her, won't he just give her another one?"

Heather crossed her arms. "Look. If you don't get it, just shut up."

So Monet and Tenille sort of shuffled around the bench until Monet finally asked, "You don't really think it's *magic,* do you?"

"Or giving her luck?" Tenille asked.

"How many times do I have to tell you? She aced a test, she got out of homework, she found five bucks, and who knows what else? *I* got caught copying homework, flunked my English test, dropped my lunch tray, and banged my head!" Then she scowled and said, "Why'd he give it to *her* and not *me*? It's totally not fair."

"But . . ."

"So . . ."

Monet and Tenille looked at each other like they were out to sea on a very patchy life raft.

"Whatever," Heather said, standing up. "Let's get out of here."

When the coast was clear, Holly and I crawled out of the bushes. And as Holly was dusting off, she said, "That girl's got issues."

"No kidding."

We headed out toward Speedy Photo, slowly clicking along the walkway, side by side. "So what are you going to do?" Holly asked.

I shook my head. "I don't think it's the horseshoe *or* the luck. I think it's that Casey gave it to me."

"I agree."

"Why does everyone have to make such a big deal out of it?"

Holly shrugged. "I thought Marissa and Dot were really cool about it today. And I know *I* didn't say anything."

"Yeah, you're right. But still. Heather's sure blown the whole thing way out of proportion."

We rode along without saying anything for a while, and then she asked, "So you're going to keep wearing it?"

I glanced over at her. "Yeah, I'm going to keep wearing it!"

Taking it off had never even crossed my mind.

Speedy Photo uses a building that used to be a drive-through bank. And the way you get your pictures is, you go through the drive-through. And since there was no line, we just cruised around the building on our skateboards, went under the awning, up the corridor, and stopped at the window.

"Hello," Holly said to the lady inside. "I'm here to pick up pictures for Vera Talbrook." She pushed the claim slip under the window, and a minute later we were ripping the package open. "Yes!" Holly cried when she saw the picture of El Gato. "It's perfect!"

It was, too. The focus was sharp—she'd caught him with his hand on the door, and even wearing a mask, El Gato looked mighty shifty.

"Come on!" I said. "Let's show Dave!"

We made it back to Broadway in record time and went straight to Slammin' Dave's. We didn't bother to peek through the drapes or sneak around back, either. We just pulled open the door and went inside.

The Blitz and Ronnie Reaper and a handful of other students were listening to Slammin' Dave give them very intense instructions. It wasn't the kind of moment you should interrupt with your Kodak snapshots, so we stood off to the side for a few minutes and watched.

I loved the move he was showing them. He had a volunteer behind him who he drilled in the gut with his elbow, then when the guy doubled over, he whacked him in the face with the back of his fist. "You've got to move with it," he told the group, "or you're gonna be soakin' the mat with blood." He demonstrated again, saying, "Jab, whack! Jab, whack! See how he's moving with it?" The group nodded, so he said, "Okay! Partner up, give it a try, then switch. I want to see some motion! I want to see your pain!"

As soon as the wrestlers started practicing, Holly and I moved closer. "Ahem," I said. "Dave?"

He saw me and smiled. "Triple-T! How's the moves?"

I tried not to blush and got straight to the point. "Uh, we've got something we want to talk to you about."

Holly held the pack of pictures up. "And show you."

He spread his arms. "Talk and show away!"

"Uh..." I looked around. I didn't see El Gato anywhere, but I sure didn't want him pouncing on us from behind. "Can we go outside?"

He raised an eyebrow, then said, "How about we go into my office?"

"That would work."

So we followed him into the same room I'd snooped around after taking the bump, and when he closed the door, he said, "So? What's so hush-hush?"

"You know El Gato?" Holly asked.

He sat down in a roll-around chair. "Sure..."

Holly opened the package of pictures. "Well, he gives me the creeps."

Dave did a combination nod and shrug like, Yeah, so?

"And the other night we saw him trying to break into Tornado Tony's van."

That made Dave sit up a whole lot straighter. "What's that?"

"El Gato was outside pretending to have a smoke, but he was really casing Tony's van. He tried the doors, looked in the windows..."

"You both saw this?"

We nodded.

"Are you *sure* that's what he was doing?"

We nodded again, and Holly handed over the picture.

"Well," he said after studying it a minute. "No flies on you!" He looked up at Holly. "Can I have this?"

She nodded. "Can you get rid of the guy?"

He bit the inside of his cheek but didn't say anything.

So I asked, "Do you know who he is?"

He gave half a shrug. "I thought he was a determined, devoted student."

"But I mean when he signed up—he had to give you his real name, right? You made him sign waivers and agreements and all that kind of stuff, right?"

He gave me a sheepish grin. "I've been known not to argue with cash."

"So what you're saying is..."

He stood up. "What I'm saying is"—he wagged the picture at us—"I'll take care of things. And thanks for bringing it to my attention."

He was sort of hustling us out of the office, but I wasn't feeling too good about leaving just yet. "Well, don't you want to know who we think he is?"

"And what we think he's been up to?" Holly added.

"Uh, sure." He opened the door and ushered us out. "But make it quick—I've got to get back to my class."

So real fast I start to say, "We think he's this guy who comes here who looks like a—" Only just then I glance to my right and who do I see?

The Bulldog.

And my mouth totally drops open, because standing right beside him is the cat-eyed creep himself.

El Gato.

TWENTY-ONE

El Gato and the Bulldog were laughing.

Holly and I were staring.

"Girls?" Dave asked, but then he noticed El Gato, too. "Uh, maybe you should make yourselves scarce."

"Don't tell him we gave you the picture, okay?" Holly whispered.

"No problem."

So he created sort of a body block for us as we made a break for the front door. And once we were safely outside, Holly and I looked at each other all wide-eyed and said, "It's not him!"

"So who *is* he?" I whispered.

"Oh man, this is giving me the creeps."

My head was swimming, trying to sort through all the fragments that didn't seem to combine to any sort of whole. I'd felt better when I'd thought that El Gato *was* the Bulldog. It was like there were two shady characters spandexed into one. But now El Gato was just...El Gato. Some guy who'd given us the evil cat eye, had sort of threatened us, and had tried to get into Tony's van.

Maybe they weren't connected at all.

Maybe I was just imagining crimes where none existed.

But then why had someone called me?

Why had they "warned" me?

If they weren't trying to hide something, why did they care?

And what had I done that had made them so nervous?

"Sammy?" Holly asked. "What do you want to do?"

I snapped out of my thoughts and said, "I don't know. I was sure they were the same guy."

"Me too. And now I'm worried that El Gato's going to find out that I gave Dave the picture and do something, you know, to *us*."

"Like steal stuff from you?"

She shrugged. "I don't know. But whoever he is, I wouldn't recognize him without his mask. He could walk right into the Pup Parlor and . . . who knows what?"

"I don't know what to tell you." I thought a minute, then said, "Let's check back with Dave tomorrow—see what happens."

"I'm at the Humane Society after school tomorrow."

"Well, call me when you get home."

"Okay."

So she headed into the Pup Parlor while I got ready to jaywalk Broadway.

Now, normally it only takes a few seconds to get a safe break in traffic. But for some reason Broadway was really busy. And then I saw a cop car go by. It wasn't Officer Borsch, but still, between the cop and the traffic, it was enough to make me head down to the corner and use the crosswalk.

Now believe me, I was keeping my eyes peeled. I didn't

like the idea that someone might be watching or following me. And while I was at the intersection waiting for the
light to change, I noticed that a guy standing a few feet
away from me was dabbing at his upper arm with a
Kleenex. Like he'd been hurt or something.

I guess he saw me scoping him out, because he turned
and showed me the fierce-looking saber-toothed tiger
tattooed on his arm. "Cool, huh?" he said, grinning like
a little kid.

"Did you just get it?" I asked him.

"Yeah," he said, and went back to dabbing it. "Down
the street at Tiny's. He's awesome."

Now, seeing a big cat and talking about Tiny made a
little hiccup happen inside my brain—I'd never told Tiny
I'd found Dorito. So instead of crossing over Broadway I
headed up to the tattoo parlor.

I didn't see my flyer posted anywhere, but I did see
Tiny through the window. So I opened the door and
called, "Hey. I promised I'd tell you if I found my cat,
and I did."

He smiled and walked toward me. "I know. My janitor
saw the flyer and told me, which is why it's down. Don't
want you to think I was being heartless."

"No, I ... wait—your janitor?"

"Yeah."

"Is it Tornado Tony?"

"Exactly!"

"Well, he would know, he's the one who found my
cat."

"You're jiving me. Well, good deal." Then he leaned

out the doorway and said, "No grandma with you today?"

I shook my head.

"Interested in some body art? Maybe a butterfly? A little ankle rose? I could put it somewhere granny would never think to look."

I backed away, saying, "No thanks." But then I added, "You did a nice job on that saber-toothed tiger, though."

"You saw it? See? I'm good!"

"Still not interested, sorry. But thanks again for being nice about my flyer."

"Hey, no sweat. Glad you got your cat back. And come see me when you change your mind."

So I went back up to Broadway, but when I got to the light, I decided to take a little detour into Maynard's. I wasn't 100 percent convinced that T.J. *hadn't* called me from the pay phone, so I thought I'd sneak in, just to see what he was up to.

As usual T.J. was yakking on the phone as he was ringing up a customer. I tell you, we need some competition in the neighborhood. T.J.'s just rude—always on the phone trying to find a shortcut to some quick cash when he's supposed to be paying attention to his customers.

Anyway, by the time the customer was leaving, I'd crawled up to a carousel near the register so I could hear better, but T.J.'s conversation wasn't anything exciting or threatening or at all about cats. It was just, "Maybe next week. You need someone to vouch for you ... nuh-uh. Leo's getting me in ... yeah, sure. Sounds wild, I know, but I'm hopin' to make a bundle ... I'll tell you how it goes."

Typical T.J. stuff.

Then he saw me in the big shoplifter mirror and yelled, "Hey! Whaddya doin'?"

I stood up and said, "I dropped some change, Teej. Take it easy."

T.J. knew I was full of it, though. He leaned forward and said, "Scat, ya brat!"

Still. I took my ol' sweet time, stopping at the ice cream cooler on my way out. "Eat up all the Double Dynamos again, T.J.?"

"I said *scat!*"

So I scatted right over to the Highrise, making extra sure nobody was watching or following me.

Day five of being thirteen started out great, too. In homeroom the tardy bell rang, we said the Pledge, Mrs. Ambler read the announcements...Heather never showed up. And I figured that maybe she was just late, but I didn't see her strutting her stuff between classes, either. And believe me, if Heather's around, you'll know it. She's not what you'd call low profile.

When there was still no sign of her at lunch, it hit me that she was probably milking the whole "fainting" incident to get a day off from school.

Fine by me.

Anyway, we were having lunch on the grass again when Marissa asked me, "Hey, have you listened to the CDs I gave you?"

Before I had the chance to answer, Casey sat down beside me and said, "What CDs?"

That's the cool thing about Casey. Or at least one of the cool things. He's just...comfortable. It's like nothing weird had ever happened—we were just friends. So I hid the whole Easter-Egg Eyes incident in a distant, grassy corner of my mind, and laughed. "You don't want to know."

"Sure I do—let's see."

"Okaaaay," I said, then dug through my backpack and handed them over.

"Uh-huh," he said, looking at the first one. "They're okay," he said about the second one. But when he saw the Darren Cole CD, he said, "Now, *this* is cool."

"You've heard of him?" I asked.

Marissa seemed surprised, too. "How'd you know about him?"

He grinned at me. "I guess I'm a fan of Trouble-makers."

"Hey!"

He laughed and read through the song titles. "'Waitin' for Rain to Fall.'" He tapped the case. "One of my all-time favorite songs." Then all of a sudden he starts *singing*. "Maybe it's all been hard on you, Pushed against the wall, But there's no need to close your eyes, Waitin' for rain to fall..." Then he goes, *"Waah-waah-waaaaaaaaaah, waah-waah, whoa-whoa-waaaaaaaaaah-waah-waah,"* like some blues guitar. He looks at me and laughs. "See? Cool song."

Well, we were all just staring at him, so he laughs again and says, "I guess you've got to listen to the real thing." He starts handing over the CD but does a double take and pulls it back. "Is this a real autograph?"

Marissa bounces a little and says, "Yeah, it is! My mom and I saw him in concert in Las Vegas."

He cringes. "He's doing *Vegas*?"

"Yeah. But it wasn't schmarmy or anything. It was a real good concert."

"Wow," he says, shaking his head. "My mom would be green if she knew."

"Your *mom*?" I ask him.

"Uh, I should have kept that little piece of information to myself, huh? Forget I said it, okay? *I* think he's good." He hands back the CD. "Just listen to 'Waitin' for Rain to Fall,' you'll see."

So he's sort of getting up to go when Holly whispers, "Aren't you going to tell him about...," and then she makes a little scissors motion with her fingers.

I pull a face at her like, No! Because really, I don't need to go squealing on Heather to her brother. I can take care of her myself.

But Casey picks up on it and says, "About what?"

"Never mind."

But when Marissa whispers, "Sammy, tell him!" he sits back down and says, "Yeah, Sammy. Tell me!"

I roll my eyes. "It's no big deal. And believe me, you don't want to be in the middle of me and Heather."

"Like I'm not already?"

"Well, you don't want to be there any worse than you are."

Now *he* rolls *his* eyes. "Would you just tell me?"

So I explained what happened in science and how we

spotted Heather trailing us after school. And I did try to play it down, but Marissa and Dot and even Holly kept pumping it back up, saying stuff like, "Tell him what she did then" and "Tell him what she *said*" and "Wait, wait, you skipped the part where she said…" So in the end he got the Technicolor version instead of the black-and-white sketch I was planning to draw.

And you know, he didn't seem too happy. "She *said* that? And she was crawling on the floor with *scissors*?"

I nodded.

"This is so stupid I can't even believe it."

"Forget I told you, all right?"

He stood up. "No!"

"Look," I said, standing up, too. "She short-circuits around me, that's all. And I guess she thinks there's something, you know, *magic* about this horseshoe. Like it's really giving me good luck."

"Well, what if it is? The point is, she's got to stop messing with you."

He was walking away, so I grabbed his arm and said, "Casey, I can handle Heather."

"But why should you have to?"

I laughed. "Good question. But you talking to her will just make her madder." I let go of his arm. "Besides, she's absent today."

He looked right at me, which instantly mowed down the tall grass in the corner of my mind. "She is?"

My eyes broke away from his, and I tried to forget about all things chocolate. "Uh-huh."

"Are you sure?"

"Oh, I'm sure!" I wiggled my foot at him. "I figured it was just my lucky horseshoe, doing its thing."

He laughed and said, "Maybe so."

"So don't sweat Heather, okay? Just leave her alone and she'll eventually self-destruct."

He gave a little snort. "If you say so . . ."

"Trust me—it's the only way."

As it turns out, though, I was wrong.

TWENTY-TWO

If I'd been thinking at all, I'd have put two and two together. But there was so much else going on that I just chalked Heather's absence up to being lucky.

And, of course, I was dying to listen to "Waitin' for Rain to Fall." I wasn't expecting to love it or anything. I was just interested. I mean, usually kids hate the bands their parents liked, but Marissa said this guy was good, and Casey *really* seemed to think so.

So since Marissa had left school early for a dentist appointment and Holly was working at the Humane Society, after school I waved bye to Dot as she got into her dad's truck, then put on my headphones and hit the sidewalk.

I didn't search for "Waitin' for Rain," I just started at track one. And by the time I got to the fourth song, I had to admit—this Darren Cole guy was pretty good!

Then "Waitin' for Rain to Fall" started, and from the opening chords, I got goose bumps. I didn't even know it was "Waitin' for Rain" until the chorus. I just knew it had that magic combination of sweetness and pain. Then the chorus broke out of the verse, and I understood what Casey had been trying to explain. He was right about the guitar part, too—it was like a voice, squeezing all sorts of emotion out of one bending note.

So okay. I'm embarrassed to say—the song bowled me over. I cranked up the volume and listened to it again and again. And I was busy trekking across the mall lawn, listening to it *again*, when all of a sudden someone sneaks up from behind and *tackles* me. My skateboard goes flying, my headphones jolt off, and I smack the ground hard under the weight of my backpack.

I turn my head and there's Tenille jumping up and down next to Heather. And I can hear Monet yelling from down by my feet, "It's here! It's right here!"

"Well, get it!" Heather yells, then moves in to hold down the top half of me. But before either of them can do anything, I kick back with both feet like some kind of donkey-fish and smack Monet *hard*. And when she cries, "Ooooow!" and lets go, I wrestle out of my backpack and jump to my feet.

So now I'm face to face with Heather. I don't want to fight her, but I can't exactly run—they've got me surrounded. So I keep my eyes locked on Heather, turning as she circles me. "Heather, you're making a huge deal out of nothing."

"Shut up."

"Look. You can't really believe the horseshoe's lucky..."

"I said shut up!"

"And it doesn't mean Casey and I are going out—"

"I said *shut up*!"

"Why are you so bent out of shape over this?"

"Why am I so . . ." She snorts. Then her neck vultures forward and she spits out, "As if you weren't a big enough pain already, you had to go and steal my birthday—"

"Wait! I didn't—"

"*Then* you steal my brother—"

"I didn't steal your brother, either!"

"And then your *mother* steals my *father*—"

"My mother barely talked to your father!"

She looks vicious. Crazy. Like a caged animal starved for blood. Or freedom.

Or both.

Then, one syllable at a time, she spits out, "He said she was en*chan*ting!"

"But—"

"She ruined my birthday! *You* ruined my birthday! It was *my* day! *My* day! You stole it from me!"

"Hey, hold on! You think I like sharing *my* birthday with *you*?"

"Grab her!" she shouts at Monet and Tenille. "Grab her *now*." And before I can think of what to do, Monet and Tenille each grab an arm and Heather dives for my feet, pinning them down with her knees. And in the middle of all that, the school buses go by with kids hanging out of the windows, shouting, "Cat fight! Cat fight!"

I don't know how to explain the way that made me feel. Worse than suffocated. Suffocated and *angry*. It was a fierce, burning kind of angry, too. Like they were holding a branding iron to my soul.

In a flash my right elbow shoots backward into Tenille's stomach, which caves in like a giant marshmallow, gooey and soft. And as she groans and begins to double over, *whack*—my fist flies back and cracks into her face.

Tenille screams, then cries, "She broke my nose!" and when I glance over, sure enough, blood is gushing everywhere.

Now, I can tell Monet's freaked out, but she's not letting go. And Heather's got my feet pinned with her knees while she's frantically untying my high-top. And let me tell you—someone's knees drilling into your toes hurts! So I try to squirm free, but she shouts, "Hold her! Just hold her!" and drills down even harder.

I suppose I could've bent over and started flailing on Heather with one hand, but at this point, Monet's easy picking and I want her off of me so I can *really* deal with Heather.

So I twist around and *crack*—I catch Monet in the jaw with a solid right hook.

"Aaarrh!" she cries, and lets go.

"She broke my nose!" Tenille wails again.

My toes are screaming in pain, and Heather's actually whipping my laces out really fast, so I shove her off of me and say, "Forget your scissors?"

For a split second I'm free. But then Heather lunges for my ankle, crying, "Help me!" at Monet and Tenille.

I try to bash her in the head with my other foot. But before I can, Monet comes flying at me, gouging my neck with her fingernails as she pulls me over. And then, as I'm trying to wrestle away from *her*, Heather lets go of my foot and shouts, "I've got it! I've got it!"

She takes off running, just abandoning Monet and

Tenille. And I'm sorry, but I don't have time to pussy-foot around with Monet. I twist free and crunch her one good in the eye. And even though my toes are aching, I make myself run through the pain, charging after Heather.

Heather's not slow, but she's not as fast as me. Even with a half-tied shoe. So I close in on her, and then she starts zigzagging around the grassy knolls, trying to avoid me. "Help!" she screams, like I'm a mugger. "Somebody! Help me!"

I lunge and manage to grab ahold of her arm, and somewhere in the middle of *her* kicking and flailing and trying to get away from *me*, I remember another move I'd seen at Slammin' Dave's—the one Holly and I had actually practiced. So I apply the twisteroo–hammer-hold–make-'em-bite-the-grass move on Heather, and faster than you can say Screamin' Evil Ninny, Heather's on the ground.

I pry open her hand and take out my horseshoe, saying, "Fat lotta luck that brought you, huh, Heather?" Then I give her arm a final tweak and tell her, "You come near me again and I'll *break* something. You got it?"

"Let me go!" she screams into the grass.

"You got it?"

"I hate you!"

"Whatever," I said, and let go.

So I stuffed the horseshoe in my jeans pocket, then moved a few yards away from her before bending over to tie my shoe. I didn't thread the lace through the grommets or anything—I just wrapped it around my ankle and

227

tied it off quick. And I was getting up to go collect my stuff when—and you're not going to believe this—Heather charges me.

She was spitting mad, too, screaming, "If you think I'm going to let you get away with this...if you think you can just walk off without paying for what you've done..."

When she reaches me I sidestep away and warn her, "Heather..."

"You think you're so hot—" She lunges at me again.

I sidestep her again and start running toward my stuff.

But Heather's not giving up. She yells, "Get over here and help me!" to Monet and Tenille.

And I can't believe it—Monet and Tenille actually start hobbling over to help her. So since I don't want to have to deal with all three of them all over again, I turn around and hold my ground against Heather.

So there we are, face to face. And for a second she just stares. But then she charges, screeching, "I hate you, you stupid, ugly loser! I hate you for ruining my life!"

She starts flailing on me, but Heather doesn't punch with her knuckles. She uses the meaty part of her fist and *hammers*. So I manage to grab her wrist and get her in another twisteroo hold, only this time she starts twisting *with* it, running around me to avoid going down.

So I turn, too. And pretty soon I'm holding her wrist with both hands, going in a circle, faster and faster. It's like I'm the axle and she's the wheel. And the faster she runs to avoid the twist, the faster I move, until I realize that there's enough momentum going to actually yank her *off* the ground.

So that's what I do. I pull her up and fly her around and around in circles. And of course she's screaming her bratty banshee head off, but is that stopping me?

No way!

I speed up and keep her flying like a big ol' ball and chain while she's screaming, "Let me go! HEEELP! Let me go! POLIIICE! HEEELP! Let me goooo-oooo-oooo-o!"

So okay. I can't keep this up forever. She's heavy, I'm tired, and pretty soon I'm going to *have* to let go. So I finally do what she's been screaming for me to do.

I let go.

Now, I didn't *plan* this or anything, but I flew her right into Monet and Tenille. Even *I* said, "Whoa!" because Heather knocked them *flat*.

And I would have taken a minute to chuckle over the moaning, groaning mound of morons, only right then I heard something that let me know it was time to hightail it out of there.

Sirens.

TWENTY-THREE

Great. *Now* the police show up. Not that I could see them yet, but I recognize police sirens when I hear them.

Let's just say, I have experience.

So I'm trucking over to my stuff when I see someone charging toward me across the grass. His hair is wild, and believe me, he's not wearing a uniform.

"Sammy!" he calls.

"Hey, Casey," I say, picking up my backpack. "What's up?"

"What's *up?*" He looks over at the shrieking pileup of pinheads across the lawn. "Did you...?"

I shrug. "You obviously didn't beat up on her enough when you were kids. She's a terrible fighter. Dirty, but terrible." I keep on trucking. "So where'd you run from?"

He keeps looking over his shoulder as he tags along. "Uh, from the first bus stop. I saw what was going on when we drove by, but the stupid bus driver wouldn't pull over."

"I told you I could handle Heather." I smile at him. "But thanks, anyway."

Then he notices my shoe. "She got it?"

I nod, then grin and pull the horseshoe out of my pocket. "But I got it back."

He breaks into a smile, but then from across the lawn, Heather shouts, "Casey! Oh thank God. Casey! Grab her! She tried to kill us! I think my arm's broken!"

Casey shouts back, "You're an embarrassment, Heather."

"Caseeeey!"

Then I saw that the police car had parked illegally on Cook, and that the driver was getting out. "Uh-oh," I said, hurrying to collect my skateboard and CD player.

"What?"

"It's Officer Borsch."

"You know him?"

"Well enough to want to get out of here."

Now, call me dense, okay? But I figured Casey would check on his sister or talk to her or something. Instead, he kept walking with me. And the trouble with that was, where was I going? I couldn't go *home*. And I didn't have any reason to go to the mall. Besides, I didn't have any money, and there's nothing stupider than being a girl without money at a mall with a boy.

"Uh..." I looked over my shoulder. "If you want to stay and make sure—"

"No way. She's fine. And she got what she deserved."

So I decided to go where I always go when I need help—Hudson's.

I couldn't ride my skateboard because Casey was on foot, but I did want to put some distance between me and the Borschman, so I started walking really fast.

Casey kept up, asking, "How'd you learn to fight, anyway? Do you have brothers?"

"Nah."

"So?"

I shrugged. "I don't know." Then I laughed and said, "Holly and I have been spending a little too much time spying through the back door of Slammin' Dave's."

"That pro wrestling place?"

"Yeah. You should see some of the freaks who go there. It's very entertaining."

"Like, what do they do?"

So I told him about Ronnie Reaper and The Blitz and El Gato, and about how the wrestling ring is springier than it looks and all of that. And I was careful not to let out how I got caught under the ring, or took a bump, or any of the stuff that's too hard to explain in a way that makes sense. Unless you go back and tell the *whole* story, that is, and believe me, I wasn't up for that.

So instead I talked about how the wrestlers really do work out and really do have moves, but how they exaggerate everything to make it a better show. And he laughed and asked questions, trying to figure out if I was really *into* it or just entertained by it. And then, before I knew it, we were turning up Hudson's walkway.

"This is where you live?" he asks, taking the place in.

"Actually, it's my friend's house."

"Marissa's?"

"No. Hudson's."

"Hudson? Is that a guy?"

I laugh. "Yeah, he's a guy. A really smart one, too."

He stops walking. "So . . . maybe I should take off?"

I laugh again. "Actually, I'm thinking maybe he'll give you a ride home."

He follows me up the walkway. "Uh, that'd be cool . . ."

Lucky for me, Hudson was home. He opened the door and said, "Sammy!" then noticed Casey. Now, he tried to hold it back, but he was still a little too pleased for my comfort. "Well, hello, young man," he said, then they recognized each other. Casey said, "Hey, you were at the birthday bash," and Hudson nodded and said, "And you're Heather's brother, am I right?"

He laughed. "A fact I've been known to deny."

They shook hands, and Hudson asked, "Can I get you something to eat? Something to drink?"

"Sure!" Casey and I said together.

"Inside or out?"

"Out," I said, then looked at Casey. "This porch is my favorite place in the whole wide world."

Casey looked around. "Here?" Then he said to Hudson, "No offense, sir."

Hudson laughed. "Give it some time—it'll start to grow on you."

So while Hudson dug up snacks, I got comfy in my favorite chair and kicked my high-tops up on the railing.

Casey took a seat beside me. "Your favorite place, huh?"

I nodded. "This porch is magic."

He didn't get it, and that's okay. I've found that there's really no explaining a feeling you get from a *place*. You can put it into words, and people can actually understand it, but the feeling itself is still only felt by you. So I didn't even try to explain it. I just took in deep breaths and let them out, happy and slow. And somewhere in my deep breathing, Casey noticed my neck. "Wow. You got gouged."

I felt it and said, "Monet's stupid fingernails." Then I asked, "Is that why girl fights are called cat fights? 'Cause they hiss and scratch and pull hair and stuff?"

He nodded. "Yeah. And because a lot of girls are catty."

Hudson pushed through the screen door with a tray of drinks and brownies. "Wow," I told him, "that looks great!"

Trouble is, just as I'm reaching for a brownie, a car eases to an idle across the street. It's not just any car, either. And it's not just any driver.

It's the Man o' La Macho.

The Bruiser in a Cruiser.

"Oh rats," I mutter.

"What's wrong?" Hudson asks.

I tisk and sigh and pout, and finally just put down my brownie. "It's Officer Borsch."

"Ah," he says. Then as he watches Officer Borsch get out of his car and cross the street, he asks, "And this would have to do with . . . ?"

"Heather," I grumble.

Hudson's eyebrows go up as he looks from me to Casey, but he doesn't ask any questions.

Officer Borsch takes his ol' sweet time coming up the

walkway. He hikes up his gun belt. He fiddles with his baton. And yeah, he's looking at me the whole time.

When he finally gets to the porch, he stops and puts one foot on the bottom step, then leans against his knee with both arms. "So," he says, still looking right at me. "We've got a girl with a bloody nose, another with a black eye, and a third with a possibly fractured arm. They all have multiple contusions, and they all claim you caused the damage. Got anything to say about this?"

I shrug. "What are the odds of me wiping out three girls all by myself?"

He pushes his lips forward and nods. Then he eyes Casey and says, "I'm thinking maybe you had some help."

"No sir," Casey says, shaking his head. "I ran to help her, but I was too late." He looks at me. "She defended herself just fine."

"So," Officer Borsch says, sucking on a tooth, "is it your claim that they started it?"

Casey nods, and I jump in with, "Officer Borsch, don't tell me you didn't recognize Heather Acosta?" because the Borschman suffered some pretty embarrassing consequences from Heather's pranks back at Christmastime.

He lets a little grin slip through his grumpy façade. "Yeah, I recognized her." He stands straight and says, "But we can't have brawling in the streets, Sammy."

"But I didn't start it! And I swear, I tried *not* to fight them."

"Yeah, yeah, yeah," he says, and sort of waves it off.

"Are you saying you believe me?"

He nods. "You think I've forgotten the Christmas parade?"

"Thank you!" I could barely believe my ears—it all seemed too . . . easy.

Then he says, "Could I have a word with you? Alone?"

So I hop off the porch and have a little powwow with ol' Borschie right there in the middle of Hudson's walkway. And to my surprise he doesn't lecture me about leaving bruised and bloodied bodies on the lovely town-center lawn. What he says is, "I don't want you to worry about El Gato."

"Dave talked to you about him? Did he show you the picture?"

"Yes," he says, but it's a kind of hesitant yes. "And tomorrow will be El Gato's last day at Slammin' Dave's."

"Great! So who is he? Some parolee or something?"

He starts to say something but stops himself. "Sammy, it's police business and I can't really discuss it with you, but I want you to know that things are being taken care of and you have no reason to be worried."

"So he *is* a criminal! We knew it! The guy is so creepy. Have you talked to him? Well, you must have, right? If you're investigating him?"

"Sammy, Sammy, Sammy . . . just do me a favor— please, *please* stay out of it. And make sure Holly does the same. I haven't been able to talk to her in person, but give her the message, would you?"

"Sure. Oh, she'll be so happy to know El Gato's gonna

be out of there. He must've pooped his pants when he saw the picture. He did see the picture, right?"

Officer Borsch puts his finger in front of his mouth like, Shhh, then gives me a closed smile and says, "Police business, right?"

"Right."

He says, "Okay then," and starts to walk away, but then stops and turns. "What was the brawl with Heather about, anyway?"

I shrug. "She tried to steal my lucky horseshoe."

"Your lucky horseshoe," he says like, Uh-*huh*. Then he does the most surprising thing I've ever known Officer Borsch to do. He winks and says, "Well, unlucky her, huh?" then turns and walks away.

When I got back to the porch, Casey said, "He seemed pretty cool."

My jaw was still dangling. "You don't understand! Officer Borsch is . . . unreasonable! Grumpy! Bullheaded!"

Casey shrugged. "Didn't seem that way to me."

"Wow," I mumbled, taking the horseshoe out of my pocket. "First school, then Heather, now Officer Borsch?" I looked at Casey. "I'm beginning to think this thing *is* lucky."

"What is that?" Hudson asked, and when I showed it to him, he said, "Ah. A horseshoe amulet."

"Amulet?" I asked.

"A charm. Thought to be inscribed with a magic incantation to protect its owner from evil." He grinned. "A lucky horseshoe." He handed it back and said, "Where'd you get it?"

I hitched a thumb at Casey. "From him."

"Ah...," Hudson said again. And again he was looking a little too pleased for comfort.

So real fast I asked Casey, "Where'd *you* get it, anyway?"

He shifted in his seat. "Uh..."

He looked real uncomfortable, so I said, "It's not like I *care* where it came from. I'm just interested. Have you had it for a long time?"

He shook his head.

"Did you *find* it?"

He looked kind of sheepish, then nodded. "Last month. At the Renaissance Faire. I found it on the ground in the jousting arena."

I'd been to that Renaissance Faire. And even though I hadn't *wanted* to go, Marissa had dragged me along. And I'm glad she did, too. It was amazing! It was like being transported to a different place, a different time. Everyone talked in accents and acted like they were from Merry Olde England. It was a place where if you found a horseshoe, you could almost believe that it *was* magical.

Now Hudson could tell that Casey was sort of embarrassed, and great guy that he is, he tried to make him feel better by saying, "My understanding is that a horseshoe isn't lucky unless it *is* found."

"Yeah," I said, lacing it back on my shoe. "And I'm glad that's where it came from. That place was fun."

So Casey was okay about having given me something he'd found in the dirt. And after we finished our brownies, I helped Hudson carry things back inside. And when

I was sure Casey couldn't hear, I whispered, "Can you give him a ride out to Sisquane? Otherwise he's going to want to walk me home."

"Got it," Hudson said.

So we all piled into Hudson's car, and off we went to Sisquane. And when we got to Casey's house and he was getting out of the car, I said, "Oh! I almost forgot!"

"What?"

"That song is awesome!"

He grinned. "Told you."

So everything was, you know, cool. Only as Casey was thanking Hudson for the ride home, I saw the front door to his house open. "Uh-oh," I said, sort of slouching in my seat. Mr. Acosta had stepped outside and he was not looking too happy.

Casey glanced over his shoulder and said, "Don't worry about him. Dad's cool. When he hears what happened, he'll understand."

Only then we saw his *mother* step out beside him.

I slouched even farther, and Casey said, "Oh boy. This is gonna be fun...."

Hudson said, "Would you like me to speak with them?"

Casey shook his head. "No way. The best thing you can do is get out of here. But thanks again for the ride." Then he looked at me and said, "See you tomorrow."

He was already gone by the time I thought to lend him the horseshoe.

TWENTY-FOUR

Hudson gave me a ride home, too. He didn't say anything more than, "He seems like a fine young man" about Casey, which was a relief. Most grown-ups would quiz you from here to the moon, but Hudson's not like most grown-ups.

Which is probably why I like him so much.

Anyway, we were getting near the Highrise when he said, "By the way, Miss Kitty came over today."

"Oh yeah?"

"It seems she's missing another cat."

"Really?"

He nodded. "She was in tears. She's been to the pound, the Humane Society, the police...."

Then I had a thought. "You think someone has a big rat infestation?"

He shrugged. "Why *steal* cats? There are always plenty at the pound."

So he dropped me off, but the whole way up the fire escape his voice kind of echoed around in my head. *Why steal cats? There are always plenty at the pound....*

By the time I got home, there were a couple of phone calls I wanted to make. Questions I wanted to ask.

Trouble is, I didn't want to have to *answer* a bunch of questions about why I was *asking* the questions, and Grams would be sure to want to know.

But—lucky me—there was a note on the kitchen table: *Off to the market. Back soon. Love, Grams.*

I looked up the number for the Humane Society and dialed it quick. Holly was still there, so I asked her, "How many cats do you guys have there?"

"Uh, I think four," she told me. "And no, Zippy's not one of them."

"How many do you guys *usually* have there?"

"I don't know. It varies."

"More than four? Less than four?"

She hesitated, then asked, "Are you on to something?"

"I don't know. But can you find out?"

"Hang on."

So I waited, and a few minutes later she was back, saying, "Overall it's less than it used to be."

"Used to be, when?"

"She said three months ago they used to have at least ten, all the time. Sometimes up to twenty."

"Wow." My brain was racing, trying to figure out what to ask next. Finally I said, "What do the cats you have now have in common?"

"What do you mean?"

"Are they mangy? Are they ugly? Are they old? Is there a reason people *wouldn't* want them?

"Uh, let me go look at them again."

When she came back, she said, "One of them's pretty old, but the other three are cute."

"Cute as in small?"

"Yeah, one of them's still kind of a kitten."

"Are they females?"

"God, Sammy, what's it matter?"

"I don't know—I'm just trying to figure this out."

"Well, hold on, okay?"

"Fine."

Forever later she came back, saying, "They're all females except the kitten."

"Okay."

"Okay? That's it? What are you thinking?"

"I'm thinking that I'm going to call the pound."

"Sammy!"

"I've got to call before they close. I'll talk to you later, okay? And thanks!"

So I called the pound, and after a bunch of back-and-forthing with the lady on the other end, I found out that the pound had only three cats, that they were all kind of scrawny females.

"Is that all?" I asked. "I mean, is that usual?"

"We've got lots of *dogs* if you want a good selection."

"No. I want to know if you used to have more cats. Like, let's say six months ago?"

"Look, it's a *good* thing we don't have more of them. We used to have to destroy a lot more because nobody wanted them."

"So what's changed? Does someone come in to get cats? Like a repeat customer or something?"

"We do have people who rescue animals, sure. There's

one woman in particular. Actually, she came in for two today."

"Is she . . . does she go by Miss Kitty?"

"Why, yes!"

All of a sudden I felt terrible about hating the Psycho Kitty Queen. Here she had a whole plantation of cats, and why? Because she couldn't stand the thought of them getting gassed.

But I made myself focus on why I was calling. "I'm sorry for all the questions, but I'm trying to figure something out."

She laughed, but it wasn't a mean laugh. "Obviously."

"Are there other people who come in regularly?"

"Not really." Then she added, "Well, there was a fella who used to come in, but I haven't seen him in a while."

"A while as in . . . a month? Three months? Four?"

"Maybe four? He was another one who hated to see them destroyed. He didn't keep them himself, though. He found them homes."

"Can you tell me what he looked like?"

"I'm sorry, but you haven't told me why you're asking all this. And I don't know if I should give you that information."

"Okay, then just tell me this—was he about forty, with a husky build and a blond buzz cut?"

There was a moment of silence on the other end, and it was enough to make my heart start pounding.

And then, there it was, her voice in my ear, "Why . . . why, yes!"

*   *   *

That night when I went to bed, I lay there in the dark, trying to make sense of the pieces shuffling around in my head. Dead cats. Missing cats. Rescued cats. Returned cats. And I tried to fit them together with the people involved. The Psycho Kitty. El Gato. The Bulldog. Tornado Tony, Tiny, T.J.

Did they have *anything* to do with each other?

Things had made a lot more sense when I'd thought the Bulldog *was* El Gato. But now he was just a guy I'd followed across town. A guy with a twitching gym bag who had disappeared down an alley. Had he done that because he'd noticed me following him? Was he the one who'd called me? Was there any connection between him and the Kojo Buffet?

And who had taken down the Zippy flyers? Was it the same person who'd called me? I should have asked Officer Borsch about the flyers when I'd seen him at Hudson's, but I'd been too wrapped up in what had happened with Heather to think about it.

Maybe I was trying to take pieces of different puzzles and force them together. Maybe it was like El Gato *not* being the Bulldog. I'd tried to connect them when they didn't belong together.

Or maybe I was just obsessing about El Gato and the Bulldog and cats because I was trying to avoid thinking about Casey and Heather and the whole Acosta mess. I mean, what kind of trouble was Casey in right now? I could practically hear his parents: You went with *her* instead of helping your *sister*? Where are your priorities?

What were you *thinking*? Candi and Heather were sure to whip the whole thing into a frothy frenzy—especially if Mrs. Acosta was jealous of my mom.

Like I needed *that* thrown into an already unfactorable equation.

Anyway, I saw no solution to the Acosta problem, so I went back to puzzling about cats. In my gut it felt like there had to be a connection—that it all fit together somehow. But where were the border pieces? The edges. The anchor. I needed something to build on!

But wait! Maybe this was like one of those shaped puzzles, where there are no straight edges. Maybe the pieces formed some *thing*. Maybe they all fit together in the shape of a cat!

Okay, I was losing it. So I cuddled up with Dorito on the couch and just stroked him gently from head to tail, over and over. I was so glad to have him back. So glad he was safe and sound and not dead in some Dumpster somewhere . . .

The next thing I knew it was morning and Grams was shaking me gently, going, "Samantha? Samantha, wake up!"

"Huh? Huh? Oh!" My heart was pounding in my chest. I sat up quick and tried to catch my breath.

Grams held my arm. "It was just a dream."

I was still panting. My eyes were darting all around. It felt so . . . *real*.

"What was it?"

"Oh!"

"Tell me!"

"I was, um, I was stuck in an elevator..." I didn't want to tell her it was the Heavenly Hotel's elevator, but that's what it was, clear as day. "With Heather... and her friends."

"Oh," she laughed. "That *was* a nightmare."

I was having trouble catching my breath. I felt so claustrophobic. It was like I was still trapped in the elevator with them. I couldn't run, and they were all over me. Hissing. Clawing. Yanking my hair.

Grams sat down beside me. "Sweetheart, you look white as a ghost. It was just a dream..."

"I know." I got up and paced around. I couldn't seem to shake the feeling of... terror.

"Did something happen to make you dream about her? Is she causing you trouble at school again?"

I took a deep breath and tried to pull myself together. I hadn't told Grams what had happened after school because I knew she'd have a fit and maybe even call the school. But I was so out of sorts from my dream that I wasn't thinking fast enough to just say, Nah. Everything's cool. And then she noticed my neck. "Samantha? How'd you get those scratches?"

"Uh..." I was still wiped out from my dream and couldn't seem to think of a single Grams-worthy excuse. So after blinking at her a minute, I just gave in and said, "Heather happened to my neck. Actually, Monet did." Then I told her the whole story—how I was listening to a CD, how they ambushed me, how she pinned me down and tried to steal my horseshoe.

"Your horseshoe? Why your horseshoe?"

"Because she thinks it's bringing me good luck."

"But Samantha, that's ridiculous. To go through all that for a lucky charm? What am I missing?"

"Well . . . Casey gave it to me."

"Ohhhh," she said.

"But it's more than that. You should have heard her when she attacked me. She said I ruined her birthday— that I *stole* her birthday—and that Mom is now stealing her dad."

"*What?*"

"See? She's *losing* it. She said her dad is all 'enchanted' by Mom."

Grams shook her head. "That girl is poisoned by jealousy. And she *attacked* you." She stood up. "I'm going to call the police!"

"Grams, Grams, whoa, whoa! The police have already been called."

"And . . . ?"

"And they're not going to file any charges or anything against me."

"Against *you*? Why on earth would they file charges against *you*?"

I was starting to feel a whole lot better. Talking to Grams was like finding a way out of the elevator. So I shrugged and said, "Because I beat the three of them up."

"You *what*?"

So I gave her the blow-by-blow of the fight and told her about Casey showing up. And when I got to the part about Officer Borsch stopping by Hudson's, she said, "But how did he know to find you there?"

"He's seen me there before. I think he knows I hang out there."

When I'd finally gotten the whole story out and had answered all Grams' questions, she turned my head to the side and tisked over my neck. "Those catty girls."

Dorito hopped into my lap, and I stroked him, saying, "You're nothing like that, are you, boy?"

So, okay. I couldn't say Heather and her bratty friends hadn't put a scratch on me, but when I saw Tenille and Monet before school, I had to laugh. I mean, I wore a collared shirt, so you couldn't really see the marks on my neck, but even an inch of makeup couldn't conceal the black eye I'd given Monet, or the dark circles under *both* Tenille's eyes.

"Oh my *god,* Sammy!" Marissa said when she saw me on campus. "Everybody's saying you broke Tenille's nose! And you *did* break Heather's arm!"

"Oh, I did not...."

"You did! She's wearing a cast. I saw it with my own two eyes!"

I said, "Yeah, right. It's probably like the cast she wore on her nose, remember that?" because way back in September I got in a whole lot of trouble when she pretended I'd broken her nose.

"No! This is for real! And she's totally milking it! She's telling everyone you attacked her! Sammy, what happened? Why didn't you call me?"

Then Holly and Dot descended on us and started telling me exactly what Marissa had just told me. So I let out a big sigh and explained what had happened. And when I was all done, Marissa didn't focus on Casey coming to my rescue, or ask me anything I sort of expected her to ask. Instead, she said, "So wait a minute—the buses came by while they were ganging up on you?"

"Yeah."

"So there you go—you have nothing to worry about."

"What do you mean?"

"Kids saw! They know!"

"Yeah," Holly added. "Just stay cool and say Heather started it."

Dot nodded. "By the end of the day everyone'll know what really happened."

"Fat chance," I snorted.

But all day my friends hung close, and *they* told people the truth. And by lunch I noticed something very strange—kids were whispering about me, but it wasn't a backstabbing kind of whispering. It was more like they couldn't believe that someone as scrawny as me could take down cats as wild as Heather and her friends.

Then at lunch Vice Principal Caan came out to the grass where we were eating, and instead of shooing us back to the lunch tables, he took me aside and whispered, "Is it true?"

"Is what true?" I asked him, not really knowing what angle he was coming from.

"Did you really neutralize all three of them?"

I laughed. "I like the way you put that." Then I nodded and said, "I swear I didn't start it—they ganged up on me."

He nodded. "That's the word in the halls. And the bus drivers confirmed it."

My eyebrows went up. "Really?" And then my jaw dropped when Mr. Caan chuckled and whispered, "When is that girl going to learn?"

So things at school turned out a whole lot better than they might have. What I *was* sort of worried about, though, was Casey. I hadn't seen him all day. I even looked for him between classes and at the beginning of lunch, but I didn't spot him anywhere. I kept hoping he'd come by the lawn where he'd found us before, but finally I got fed up with hoping and said, "I'm gonna go find Casey."

Marissa bit down a smile. Dot did, too. And Holly looked away.

"Knock it off," I told them. "I just want to find out how much trouble he's in at home."

"Right."

"Sure."

"Uh-huh."

"Shut *up*!" I said, but they all just laughed.

I ran over to the cafeteria, but I didn't actually have to go inside. Casey was coming out just as I got to the door. "Oh hey!" he said. "I was just coming to see you." He looked over his shoulder, into the cafeteria. "Were you . . . ?" He looked back at me. "Are you getting something to eat?"

I felt myself turning red, but I said it anyway. "No, I was looking for you."

A little smile smoothed out his face. "Yeah?"

"Yeah. I want to know what happened with your parents. Are you in trouble?"

"Nah." Then he added, "Well, with my mom, yeah. And my sister"—he rolled his eyes—"majorly...but what else is new?" Then he grinned and said, "But I live with my dad, not them, so it's cool."

We started walking. And I don't even know where we were going. We just kind of walked around. Talking.

Laughing.

And I couldn't help feeling that I *was* lucky.

Really lucky.

How else could I explain a friend like Casey?

TWENTY-FIVE

It was Friday, so after school Marissa, Holly, and I all went to the mall. And while Marissa shot up aliens and other Creatures of Darkness in the video arcade, Holly and I sat nearby and traded off listening to CDs. And even though we were there a long time, I still didn't feel like going home when Marissa had to leave.

There's really not a whole lot happening in a seniors building.

So when Holly said, "You want to come over for a while? I'll probably have to do some chores, but...," I jumped on it. "Sure! I don't mind. Let's go sweep up some fur!"

She laughed and off we went. And I did call home to let Grams know where I was, but pretty soon I was calling her again, because Vera and Meg invited me to stay for pizza. Pizza! I love pizza. I hardly ever get it, though, because Grams is into steamed fish, broiled chicken, and broccoli. I don't care what you do to steamed fish, broiled chicken, or broccoli, it's never going to taste like pizza. And please, don't put those things *on* a pizza. That's like having to do homework at the movies.

Anyway, Meg and Vera ordered an extra large, extra

cheese, extra sausage pizza. And it turned out to be an extra fun dinner. We didn't bother with anything but pizza and soda, and we played rummy while we ate.

And then, when the pizza was about gone, Vera looked at Meg and said, "Remember how you used to have pajama parties when you were their age? Your girlfriends would come over and you'd giggle all night?"

"Sure," Meg said, breaking into a smile. "Some of the best times of my life."

Vera made little twitching faces at her. "So?"

Meg figured out what Vera was twitching about, because she said, "Say . . . I think that's a great idea." She turned to Holly and me. "What do you two think about having a slumber party tonight?"

Holly and I looked at each other and said, "Cool!"

So I called Grams *again*, and since she thought it was a fine idea, Holly and I set up sleeping bags on the floor in front of the TV while Meg and Vera cleaned up and then made themselves scarce.

Now, we didn't start off by watching TV. We played cards and talked, played backgammon and talked some more . . . and we covered everything from cats at the pound to "cats" at school. We even made a list of girls we thought were card-carrying members of the Cat Club.

Top of the list, of course, Heather.

But there were a lot more girls on the list than just Heather and her friends. And when we sat back and looked at it, Holly laughed and said, "Half these girls *hate* each other."

"Yeah," I said. "Could you see them calling the meeting

to order? It'd be like, *Rrrrrarrrrh! Rrrreeeerrrrh! Rrraaaahrrr!*"

"And *Hsssss! Hsssss! Hsssss!*" Holly said, putting up claws.

"A real claw-your-way-to-the-top club!"

"Yeah!"

So we laughed about that some, then Holly whispered, "I'm snacky, are you?"

I grinned. "Always."

"I wish we had some popcorn. We could stay up late and watch old movies or something." She flipped through the TV listings, and after a minute she said, "Hey! There's an *I Love Lucy* marathon on. You like her?"

"Sure."

She went into the kitchen and started rummaging though the cupboard. "We've got to have popcorn."

But they didn't. So I said, "Crackers are good."

"Nah. They fill you up too fast."

"How about those?" I said, pointing into the cupboard.

"Rice cakes?" She pulled a face. "Besides, I think they've been in there for, like, a year."

"Well, Maynard's is right down the street, but I've only got about thirty-two cents on me."

"That's not a problem." She opened a cookie tin and pulled out a five-dollar bill. "Let me ask Vera."

When she came back a few minutes later, she whispered, "They're both sacked out!"

"Really?" I looked at the clock—it was almost nine.

254

She nodded. "They get up at five, so they usually crash early—I guess I didn't know it was this late."

"So do you want to just forget it?"

"I'm not ready for bed...are you?"

I shook my head.

"So let's go."

She scrawled a note and we tiptoed down the stairs, through the Pup Parlor, and out the front door. And as we passed by Slammin' Dave's, I said, "Looks like they're closed for the night."

"Thank God," Holly muttered. "I sure hope Officer Borsch is right about today being El Gato's last day."

"He seemed real...determined about that."

"Well, good."

So we got to Maynard's without any detours, and zipped right in. And I was all prepared to get snapped and yapped at by T.J., only T.J. wasn't there.

An Elvis impersonator was.

No kidding. He had thick black sideburns, slicked-back hair, big fashion shades, and a sparkly white jumpsuit.

After I got over the shock of seeing Elvis behind the counter, I said, "Hey there."

He nodded, real cool-like. "Hey, little sister."

Holly gave me a secret roll of the eyes because the guy wasn't just trying to look like Elvis, he was trying to sound like him, too. "Where's he think he is?" she whispered. "Las Vegas?"

"Maybe he stowed away in the McKenzes' luggage," I whispered back.

So we chuckled about that a little, and when we

brought the popcorn up to the counter, I smiled at Elvis and said, "So what's T.J. up to tonight?"

"Why you askin' little sister? Are you lonesome tonight?"

I laughed. "I'm not big into Elvis, but that's a song title, right?"

He gave me a cockeyed grin. "Yes, it is. And your teddy bear's gone to the fights."

"The fights? Around *here*?"

He rang the popcorn through. "You ask a fool such as I?"

It was a weird conversation, but Holly whispered, "I think that's another song" as she handed him the money.

Then I remembered that T.J. had asked Gina—uh, Madame *Nashira*—whether he was going to win money on Friday. And there was this happy little hiccup in my brain when I realized I knew an Elvis song that fit perfectly. So I laughed and said, "Well, if he's got money riding on it, he'll be checking into the Heartbreak Hotel tonight—T.J. always loses!"

A smile spread wide across Elvis's face. But then he tried to look serious as he nodded and said, "Now, don't be cruel. That boy's no loser. Why, inside I'll bet he's a hunk-a hunk-a burnin' love."

"T.J?" I laughed. "He ain't nothin' but a hound dog!"

Well, Elvis just busted up. And as he gave Holly the change, he said, "There ain't nothin' I like more than a hard-headed woman—thanks for makin' my night."

It was the most fun I'd ever had at Maynard's Market, so I said, "Anytime, Elvis! Wish you worked here full-time."

We walked back up to the Pup Parlor, laughing about Elvis having landed in Santa Martina and how crazy it was that there were Elvis impersonators all over the globe, and what was the deal with Elvis anyway?

When we got back upstairs, we tried to quit laughing so we wouldn't wake Vera and Meg, and tiptoed through the darkness toward the kitchen. But just as Holly's getting ready to press on the stove light, there's this loud *thud* outside, followed by a crunching *slam*. So we zip over to the window and what do we see?

Tony and the Bulldog, getting into Tony's van.

The van fires up, does a quick three-point turn, and zooms up the alley toward Wesler Street.

I whisper, "You think they're stealing something from Slammin' Dave?"

"*Stealing* something?"

"Well, it sounded like they threw something heavy in the back of the van...didn't it? And he was with the Bulldog...."

Holly shrugs. "Maybe we've got the Bulldog all wrong. Maybe we thought he was a bad guy because we thought he was El Gato." She looks out the window again. "Besides, Dave's back door's not busted open or anything."

"But Tony has a key!"

"A key? Why would he have a key?"

"He's the janitor!"

"So? We sure wouldn't give him a key to the Pup Parlor if he was cleaning for us."

"But . . . but we saw him lock up that place across town, remember? That Kustom Heat and Air place?"

"Maybe *they* gave him a key, but we sure wouldn't. And I bet Dave wouldn't, either. I mean, why?"

"So what's he doing here then? With the *Bulldog*?"

"I have no idea. But I don't think he's stealing stuff. Maybe he's just giving the Bulldog a ride somewhere."

I look back out the window. "But why meet in a back alley? When Dave's is closed?"

We both stood there a minute, and finally Holly said, "Well, they're gone now. And what are we supposed to do? Call the police? What would we say? We heard a thump and saw a guy zoom off in his own van?"

She went over to the microwave, but I kept looking out the window. And when the popcorn was done and she'd shaken it into a big bowl, she said, "Look. Tomorrow we'll ask Dave if he's missing anything. If he is, we'll tell him what we saw, okay?"

"Yeah, you're right. . . ."

So we went into the living room, turned on the *I Love Lucy* marathon, got comfy, and munched on popcorn. Only I kept thinking about what I'd seen out the kitchen window. What were Tony and the Bulldog doing behind Slammin' Dave's? And what was the connection between *those* two? The Bulldog couldn't need Tony's professional services—he lived at the Heavenly Hotel! So what were they doing together in the alley on a Friday night? And what was that thud? Maybe a wrestling mat?

My mind kept wandering. Searching for an explanation. I played through the places I knew the Bulldog had been: Dave's. The Heavenly. The alley behind the Kojo Buffet. On the West Side near the brickyard . . .

And then I went through the places I'd seen Tony: At Dave's. On the West Side at Kustom Heat and Air. Delivering Dorito on Broadway . . . He was also the janitor for First Valley Bank and Tiny's Tattoo Parlor. And, according to him, for nearly everyone in the neighborhood.

So the things Tony and the Bulldog had in common were Dave's, the street with Kustom Heat and Air and the brickyard on it, and . . . that was about it. Well, there was cats, but that was sort of an iffy connection. I mean, Tony and I had *talked* about cats and the Kojo Buffet, and he had helped me find Dorito, but he didn't "rescue" them from the pound or haul them around in gym bags like the Bulldog.

Still, I sat there for the longest time, my mind going: Dave's, the brickyard, cats . . . Dave's, the brickyard, cats . . . Dave's, the brickyard, cats . . .

And then, very slowly, a chill worked its way up my spine. I let it tingle for a solid minute, and finally I whispered, "Holly . . . !"

She was laughing at Lucy, who was stuck out on a ledge.

"Holly!" I said louder.

"What?" Her eyes were still glued to the TV.

"They're doing something with cats."

She glanced at me. "Who is?"

"Tony and the Bulldog."

She muted the TV. "You look scary, Sammy. Are you okay?"

I didn't feel okay. "They're torturing them... they're ... they're ..."

She turned her whole body toward me. "Whoa! Sammy, calm down! You're letting your imagination go crazy. Tony *returned* your cat, remember?"

I nodded. And now I felt like my whole body had been lowered into ice water. "Because he *had* him. Probably with a bunch of other cats." I looked at her. "Which is why Dorito was covered with fleas."

"But...why would they be torturing cats? Do you think they're in a satanic cult? C'mon."

"No, I don't think *that*. But I do think they're doing *some*thing with them."

"Yeah? Like what? And where would you keep a bunch of flea-bitten cats? People would notice! They'd call the Humane Society."

I shook my head. "Not if they couldn't see them." My heart was racing now, tripping all over itself to beat faster. "Holly," I whispered. "Remember that Kustom Heat and Air place? The building we saw Tony come out of when we were taking down flyers?"

"Yeah..."

"Did you notice there was nobody there? The brick-yard next door was busy, but the only person who seemed to be around Kustom Heat and Air was Tony. And now that I think about it, there was nothing in the storage yard, either. And the big roll-up door was closed."

"Okaaaay...so...?"

I was warming up quick. "So why would a janitor be locking up a business in the middle of the day? Especially an industrial place like that?"

She shrugged and shook her head.

"Exactly! You wouldn't unless no one was coming and going. Unless the place was out of business!" I headed for the telephone. "Where's your phone book?"

"Right there," she said, pointing to a small bookcase.

I pawed through the pages until I found the listing.

"Who are you calling?" Holly asked as I dialed the number.

"Kustom Heat and Air." I waved her over and shared the phone as a mechanical voice came over the line. "The number you have dialed is no longer in service. If you feel you have reached this recording in error..."

"See?" I said, hanging up. "They're out of business! Why would a janitor be cleaning a place that's out of business?"

"Aw, Sammy, come on. Maybe the owners are getting ready for new tenants. Maybe it was a one-time job."

"I saw him there twice. And the day I talked to Zippy's owner, she said she saw the Bulldog on that street. Plus, it was after I followed the Bulldog that I got that phone call! Why would he threaten me if I wasn't getting too close for comfort?"

"Sammy, those are really weak connections. You don't know who called you. And so what if you saw Tony there twice? Maybe it takes him more than one day to do a one-time job."

"Or maybe he's the one who took down the Zippy flyers."

"But Sammy…"

"Maybe he didn't *want* those flyers up, Holly. Tony made a point of telling Tiny at the tattoo parlor that I'd found my cat. Maybe he *wanted* Tiny to take down my flyer so people wouldn't be on the lookout for cats. And hey! The only place we found cats in a sack was at Tiny's—and the garbage sack was just like the rest of the sacks in Tiny's trash!"

"But Sammy, doesn't that point to Tiny?"

"I think it points to his janitor. Plus, think about this— the places we found cats were all near places Tony cleans."

"He cleans everywhere!"

"Look. I know Tony acts like a nice guy and all of that, but there are too many things adding up to the fact that he's a cat killer!"

"A cat killer? But Sammy, *why?*"

I thought about it a minute, then stood up. "I don't know, but I think we should try to find out."

TWENTY-SIX

She finally agreed to come with me, *if* we took a baseball bat, and *if* we rode our skateboards. "It's the West Side, Sammy. It's night. I'm not going without a way to defend myself. And I'm not going to dawdle. I just want to cruise by the place and come home, okay?"

"Fine."

So we took off fast, and when we got to the street that Kustom Heat and Air was on, I slowed down and said, "This is it."

Now, in a residential area you expect there to be lots of cars parked along the street at night—everyone's home. But in an industrial area, the streets are usually deserted—everyone's *gone* home.

So the minute Holly and I turned the corner, we could tell that something was going on. There were cars parked on both sides of the street for as far as we could see. No people around, just cars. And all of a sudden our skateboards seemed really loud. So I hopped off mine and whispered, "Let's walk by, okay?"

So we were just walking along, keeping our eyes cranked and our ears perked, when I noticed a faded yellow El Camino. I pointed across the street and whispered, "Hey, look! That's T.J.'s car!"

Holly shook her head. "But Elvis said he went to a fight."

We walked along more slowly now. Carefully. But believe me, my mind was racing. "What if . . ."

"What if what?" Holly whispered, and I could tell she was nervous, too.

"Well, you remember what Meg said after I won forty bucks at Dave's?"

"No. What."

"She was upset because the wrestlers had bet on me, remember?"

"Yeah . . ."

"And she said how people bet on birds and bulls and . . . just about anything?"

"Oh yeah. She called them basement bookies."

"Exactly! Well, guess who took charge of the money the day I took a bump in the ring?"

"Dave?"

"You'd think, but no—Tony!"

"Really?"

"Uh-huh—and he seemed to know *exactly* what he was doing."

"So you're saying you think Tony is a basement bookie?"

"Or a warehouse bookie."

"And you think they're betting on . . . *cats*?"

For the first time since we'd found Snowball, things were making sense. "Uh-huh. Maybe he's doing something like cockfights, only with cats!"

"But—how do you *make* cats fight?"

A shadow appeared from around the corner of Kustom Heat and Air. So I yanked Holly into a niche by the north side of the building and said, "They've got someone staked out!" There wasn't much room because we were backed up against a short section of chain-link that marked off the property, but we held our skateboards close and sucked back.

A beefy man strolled out onto the sidewalk and looked both directions. He keyed a walkie-talkie and said something into it, then looked both directions again and strolled back.

When he was gone, Holly whispered, "What are we going to do?"

"Well, we can't go that way—not if someone's patrolling the place." I looked around. "Do you see Tony's van anywhere?"

She looked, too. "No." And when I didn't say anything, she said, "So you think maybe he's *not* involved in this? Whatever 'this' is?"

I started climbing the fence. "No, I think he is."

"Where are you *going*?"

"Around the back of the building."

"Why?"

"To see what I can see!" I looked down at her. "I'll be right back."

"Are you nuts? I'm not letting you go alone . . . !" She hesitated. "What about the skateboards?"

"Leave them." I reached out an arm. "But hand me the bat."

Holly was quick getting over the fence. And as we hurried along, she didn't complain once. We were real cautious when we got to the end of the building, too. But when we peeked around the corner, what did we see?

More of the same: Chain-link. A straight shot of block wall. No doors.

So we ran along, and as we neared the end of the wall, Holly asked, "So what exactly are we looking for?"

"Evidence that I'm not crazy."

Which is exactly what we got the minute we peeked around the next corner. Holly grabbed my arm and whispered, "Tony's van!"

The van was about thirty feet in front of us, parked close to the building alongside a door. It was the only vehicle inside the fenced yard.

"Now what?" Holly whispered.

"Let's check out the van. It's probably locked, but let's try. You take the passenger door, I'll try the other one."

So we waited for the guard to turn his back, then we snuck up, tried the doors, and met back behind the van.

"Locked," Holly whispered.

"Mine, too." I tried the handle to the back doors. It was locked, too.

I eyed the door to the building, and Holly could tell what I was thinking. She shook her head and whispered, "Not a good idea, Sammy. No one knows where we are. I say we leave."

I looked out at the guard. He had his walkie-talkie up to his mouth and was closing and locking the rolling gate. "Yeah," I whispered. "I've had enough."

But then a very scary thing happened. The guard started walking our way. And just as we're starting to panic, thinking that maybe he's spotted us, something bumps inside the van.

"What was that?" I whisper.

"I don't know!" Holly whispers back.

Then it happens again. *Thump. Thump-thump.*

So we've got a guard coming toward us and a van *thumping* at us, and I don't know what to do. I mean, the thumping doesn't sound random like a wagging tail or something. It sounds purposeful.

Human.

So I whisper, "Hello?" into the crack between the van's back doors. "Hello, can you hear me?"

Thump-thump-thump.

"Thump only once if you need help."

Thump.

My eyes bug out as I look at Holly. Then I whisper into the crack, "We'll try to help you, but don't make any noise! Someone's coming!"

The thumping stops, but the guard does not.

"What are we going to do?" Holly mouths.

"Stay behind the tire. If he comes this way, we'll go around the van that way."

She nods, and we can hear the guard's footsteps getting closer and closer.

And *closer*.

Finally we have to scoot around the van to avoid him. We can hear him jingling keys. Unlocking the van. Getting *inside* the van. Holly and I are stuck between the

267

building and the van, watching the front gate, then the van, worried that any second we'll be spotted. And since it's too far to run back the way we came, I do the only thing I can think to do—I try the doorknob behind me.

The door to the building is unlocked, so after Holly gives me the nod, we sneak through it. And when we get inside I'm shaking so bad the baseball bat's quivering in my hand. "Do you think he saw us?"

"I don't know."

Then we hear dogs barking in the distance.

"We've got to hide. At least for a few minutes, until we're sure he didn't see us."

We were in some kind of boiler room. There was a big tank and an exhaust fan, and then pipes and ductwork and metal tubing all over the place. There were also spools of electrical wires and, overhead, a bare bulb burning.

"They've got power," I whispered.

"So?"

"So maybe we can find the circuit breaker and shut the place down."

"You *want* them to find us? Let's just hide!"

So we moved through the boiler room to a short flight of stairs that went up to another door. Very carefully I peeked into the upstairs room. Nobody was there, so we went inside, and now we could hear the murmur of voices. Lots of voices. They sounded like they were coming from right next door.

We moved around the room and discovered a window. A window that overlooked the warehouse.

Holly and I both gasped when we looked down. There

were at least a hundred men below. They surrounded a wrestling ring that was like Slammin' Dave's, only old and tattered. Off to one side of the ring was a huge digital clock—like a scoreboard clock. And there was a microphone dangling from a roof joist.

But the really scary thing about the whole scene was the metal cage right in the middle of the ring. It was probably eight feet long, four feet high, and four feet wide, and had spikes sticking into it from all angles except the floor.

So Holly and I are just standing there, staring, trying to absorb what we're seeing below, when all of a sudden the Bulldog climbs into the ring. "There he is!" I whisper. "See if you can spot Tony."

But then the Bulldog opens the cage, and Holly gasps, "What are they going to do?"

We watch as another man leads a large dog into the ring. He and the Bulldog unmuzzle the dog and shove it inside the cage. Then the Bulldog grabs the microphone and says, "Bring on the contenders!"

Two cats get lifted into the ring by two men who have obviously spent a lot of time pumping iron. And while the men hold the cats by the nape of their necks and parade them around the ring, the Bulldog announces, "Gentlemen! Round-three contestants are: On my right—The Destroyer. He's won his bout three weeks running. On my left—The Claw. Crafty, streetwise, and the biggest tomcat we've seen to date."

The men with the cats circle the ring twice, then the Bulldog announces, "Gentlemen, place your bets."

Some men go over to a windowed booth. Others collect money on the spot. People start shouting numbers. Shouting names.

"Oh my *god*," Holly whimpers. "They put the cats in the cage with that *dog*?"

I felt like I was witnessing a nightmare come to life. "And let them fight to the death."

"So they bet on who dies first?" Holly choked out.

"Or who lives longer. Now I get why there were only scrawny cats left at the pound."

"This is *sick*."

"And this is what would have happened to Dorito," I whispered.

Holly was furious. "We've got to find the circuit breaker and stop them!"

"No," I said, heading for the door. "We've got to get the police."

TWENTY-SEVEN

The one time I decide to do the smart thing, some idiot tries to stop me. We didn't see the guard, but he sure saw us. "Hey!" he shouts when we're halfway down the stairs. "How'd you get in here?"

Holly and I freeze. "Uh...we're doing errands for Tony."

But the guard's not buying it—not for a second. "Get down here. Now!"

So we turn around and start back *up* the stairs, but he charges after us. And since I hadn't seen any other way out of the room we'd just been in, it hits me that we're running straight for a trap.

He's already right behind us, so I stop, turn, and ram him hard in the chest with the bat. He goes, *"Ooooof,"* and staggers backward, but he catches himself, then steadies himself.

"Uh-oh," Holly squeaks behind me when she sees the look on his face. And she's right—he looks like he's going to kill me.

Now, I can't jump. I can't hide. And I can't exactly *talk* my way out of the situation. This is a big-bucks operation, one they're not going to let a couple of junior high girls mess up. No, after what we'd seen, we'd probably wind up in a river somewhere.

Or maybe just a Dumpster.

Anyway, the guy's keeping an eye on the bat, but he's in a bad position and too mad for good judgment. So when he charges me again, I dig in the best I can, keep my eye on his head, and *swing*.

Ms. Rothhammer told us once that you can kill someone that way. And I wasn't trying to, but I couldn't _pussyfoot around worrying about it, either. And it's not like his head went flying or his skull caved in or anything. He didn't even go down right away. He staggered back and stumbled, hung on to the guardrail, tumbled a few steps, staggered to his feet, and then *finally* he collapsed.

"Wow," Holly gasped when he'd thudded to the ground. "He's tough."

I nodded. "That's definitely one thick skull."

We didn't waste any time. We ran down the stairs, and I started digging through his pockets. "You are one smart girl, Holly Janquell."

"Me?"

"Would *I* have taken a bat along?" I glanced at her. "No."

She smiled, but it was a very nervous smile. "What are you looking for?"

"Keys to the van."

"We're *driving* out of here?"

I pocketed the keys, grabbed his walkie-talkie, and grinned. "Not a bad idea."

"What if he wakes up?"

"Hmm." I looked around, then used a spool of electrical wire to bind the guard's hands behind his back. Holly got another spool and did the same thing to his feet. Then we twisted the two spools together tight and dragged him behind the boiler so no one would see him.

Outside, the coast seemed clear, so I whispered, "I want to unlock the van and help whoever's inside. Then let's go call the police."

"Why don't we just go call the police and tell them someone's in the van?"

"If it was you in there, what would you want?"

She thought for a second, then said, "You're right. Let's do it."

So we zip around the van, and while I'm fumbling through four or five different keys, Holly's whispering into the crack, "Hey, we're back. Can you hear me?"

For a second there's no answer. Then *thump-thump-thump*.

"Okay," Holly says. "Now, thump once for yes, twice for no. Are you tied up?"

Thump.

"Are you Slammin' Dave?"

I glanced at Holly, surprised. It made sense, of course, but I hadn't thought of it.

But then came the answer: *Thump-thump.*

"Do you promise not to hurt us if we let you go?"

Thump.

Finally I find a key that works. So quick as I can, I unlock the door and push down the handle. And when I open the van, who do we find bound and gagged, lying between cleaning supplies and pet carriers?

The Freaky Feline himself—El Gato.

Holly and I jump back. And Holly goes to slam the door closed, saying, "I'm not letting *him* out!"

But El Gato says, "Rrraaaammmy," and the funny thing is, I know what he's saying.

Sammy.

So I climb in the van and tell Holly, "Have the bat ready," because I'm not hot to set this creepy cat free, either. I mean, so what if he knows my name? What if it's a trick? Maybe this guy *deserves* to be tied up.

Then again, maybe he was on to Tony long before we were.

Still. I'm not taking any chances. I monkey-walk over to El Gato's head, because the idiot still has his mask on. And since the rag in his mouth is tied *over* the mask, I have to take the gag off first. So I bend down and untie it, and before he has the chance to say a word, I yank off his mask.

And there, looking up at me, panting for air, is Officer Borsch.

"It's Officer *Borsch*?" Holly cries.

"Quick! Help me untie him!"

"It's Officer *Borsch*?" Holly asks again, climbing into the van.

My brain was flying around, trying to make sense of things. "Were you working undercover?" I ask him, undoing the knots as fast as I can. "Where's your backup?"

He moans as the ropes loosen and his arms and legs are

freed. One of his wrists looks pretty badly chafed, and his whole body seems stiff as he sits up and mumbles, "I was working alone."

"*Alone?* Are you crazy? There's a hundred bloodthirsty guys inside that warehouse. They're killing cats as we speak!"

"Did you see?" he asks.

I nod. "They've got a whole boxing-ring setup—with a torture cage in the middle. They throw cats in with dogs and make them fight! It's sick!"

"Okay," he says, and starts untying his wrestling shoe.

"What are you *doing*? We've got to get out of here! The guard caught us inside and we knocked him out, but I don't know how long he's going to *stay* out."

Officer Borsch just keeps unlacing his shoe.

"Officer Borsch! Did you hear me? Follow us around the building—we know how to get out!"

"You girls have no idea how lucky you are to be alive." He yanks out the tongue of his shoe, and there, underneath it, is a small cell phone. He flips it open, saying, "Me, I know how lucky I am that you found me." He gives me a halfhearted grin. "And here I used to think you were nothing but bad luck."

Before he can finish punching in numbers, the guard's walkie-talkie crackles, and Tony's voice fills the van. "Mason, we still cool out there?"

"Pass it here!" Officer Borsch says.

So Holly scrambles for the walkie-talkie and tosses it to Officer Borsch.

He holds down a button and says, "Yeah, we're cool."

"No trouble from the narc?"

"Nah. He's a wimp."

Tony laughs, "We'll have fun gettin' rid of that one." Then he says, "What's the stats on the door."

Officer Borsch's eyes shift. "Uh . . . we're locked down tight."

"No! What's the numbers?"

Officer Borsch whispers, "How many people do you think were inside?"

"A hundred?" I look at Holly and she sort of shrugs and nods.

Officer Borsch keys the walkie-talkie and says, "Eighty-seven."

"That's it? Looks like more than that to me."

"Uh . . . I coulda lost count."

"Lost count? It's your *job* to count."

"And I counted eighty-seven."

"Look. I'll check in with you later. Keep an eye on the narc."

"No problem."

Beads of sweat are pouring down the Borschman's brow, but without wasting a second, he punches buttons on his cell phone and goes into total cop mode when someone picks up. "Gil Borsch here. I'm in a double-ought situation inside a white van at Kustom Air on the two-hundred block of North Depot. It's a ten-thirty-one involving animal gaming. We need all units to respond. Possible ten-thirty-four." He listens a second, then says, "At least a hundred. This is a high-stakes situation. . . ." He listens some more, then says, "Copy that," and hangs up.

"They're coming?"

"I'd give 'em two minutes." He takes the keys from me. "Meanwhile, let's see what we can do to trap *them* inside."

The van fires right up, but just as Officer Borsch is putting it in gear, the passenger door flies open. "Hey!" Tony yells, running alongside the van. "What are you doing in my van!" Then he must've noticed Officer Borsch's clothes, because he shouts, "You!"

Holly and I duck as Officer Borsch tries to peel away from him, but Tony jumps inside, slams the passenger door, and points a handgun at him. "Stop the van!"

Well, Officer Borsch guns it instead, swerving side to side, trying to keep Tony off balance. "I said stop!" Tony shouts, and I swear the second he can steady himself, he's going to pull the trigger. So I reach back quick and grab the bat, and before he even knows I'm there, I whack down on his hand.

The gun drops and Officer Borsch spins a U-ie, sending Tony flying against the passenger door while Officer Borsch stretches down and grabs the gun. Then he slams on the brakes, pins Tony's head to the windshield with the gun, and says, "Give me an excuse, creep. I'll tornado you straight to hell."

Sirens are wailing in the distance, and Tony knows it's all over—he just stays put, with his lips drawn tight and his hands up. So since I know Officer Borsch has him covered, and I know that help is on the way, I pull back and whisper, "Let's go" to Holly.

Officer Borsch is telling Tony, "You have the right to remain silent. Anything you say may be used against you in a court of law. You have the right to an attorney...," so I give him a quick wave and whisper, "We were never here," then hurry out the back of the van.

Holly follows me around the building the way we'd come, saying, "Why are we doing this *now*?"

"You want to be here all night? Answering police questions takes forever! Plus they'll want to call our *parents,* and besides, the last thing Officer Borsch needs is for it to get out that he was rescued by a couple of junior high girls. I want to make like we had nothing to do with this."

"Are you sure?"

"Trust me. I don't know what's going on at the police department, but do you think Officer Borsch would dress as a cat if he wasn't desperate to prove himself?"

"You've got a point."

So we jet around the building and climb the fence quick. Two policemen are already using bolt cutters on the locked gate, but we grab our skateboards and manage to sneak up the street without them seeing us. And by the time we're a safe block away, the Kustom Air place is swarming with cops.

Holly looks back and says, "So that's it? We're just going home? Don't you want to see them get caught? Can't we cruise around the block and check it out from the brickyard? Or from across the street?"

"You really want to?"

"Heck yeah!"

I grin at her. "Well, come on!"

It turned out to be a show worth watching.

TWENTY-EIGHT

I'd never seen so many cops in my life. I didn't even know Santa Martina *had* that much law enforcement. Every cop in the county must've been tuned into radio traffic and dropped what they were doing to help. There were fire trucks there, too.

And you should have seen it when the gamblers found out they were caught in a raid. They went wild trying to escape! They didn't get far, though. For one thing, they were surrounded. For another, the firemen hosed them down.

Holly and I loved every minute of it. And at one point it hit me that keeping all those bloodthirsty monsters inside the chain-linked yard looked like a huge version of what they'd done with the cats.

Too bad there wasn't a T. rex around to cut loose on them.

We didn't see Officer Borsch or Tony, or the Bulldog for that matter. But as they were piling people into a paddy wagon, Holly said, "They've got T.J.!" Then she laughed. "I guess he's gonna be doing the jailhouse rock tonight!"

So we watched a while longer, but when things settled

down a little, Holly and I headed home and snuck into bed. We had a real hard time falling asleep, but we agreed not to mention a word of what had happened to Vera and Meg. "They'd have a fit!" Holly said. "They'd never let you spend the night, ever again!"

Can't have that.

But in the morning Vera and Meg read all about it in the *Santa Martina Times*. Holly and I couldn't actually believe it had *made* the newspaper, considering how late the raid had happened and everything, but there it was on the front page, with a headline reading:

GAMBLING RING BUSTED

And underneath that:

Undercover Cop Cuffs Ringleader; Saves Cats

"Girls!" Vera called from the kitchen table. "You're not going to believe who El Gato is!"

"Who?" we asked, and tried to act surprised when she said, "Officer Borsch! He was working undercover!"

Grams called, too, wanting to know if we'd seen the paper. And when I told her we had, she said, "I can't believe it. That scoundrel was the ringleader! He probably had Dorito the whole time! Think what could have happened to him! What a cruel, vicious, despicable—"

"Stop, Grams, I know! Believe me, I've thought about it plenty."

"Well, I hope they lock him up for a good long time!"

"Yeah. In a nice, spiky cage."

But after I got off the phone, something was still bothering me. So when the Pup Parlor opened for business and Holly got tied up with chores, instead of going home I went next door to Slammin' Dave's.

. I was relieved to find the door open. I mean, if it was locked up, then maybe Dave was locked up, too. There had been so many people at the warehouse that he could have been among them, who knows?

Inside, the place was quiet. But when I called out, "Dave? Hey, Dave, are you here?" he came out of his office. "Triple-T, nice to see you."

Now, the way he said it was really subdued. Like he was totally depressed. So I said, "You okay?"

"Yeah," he grumbled. "Just disappointed in a few people."

"Like Tony?"

"You've seen the paper, I take it."

"Yeah."

He shook his head. "And I could have gotten that cop killed! I showed Tony the picture you girls took."

"So . . . you didn't know El Gato was a cop?"

"I had no idea." He shook his head and said, "I knew he was a little weird, but a cop? And he wouldn't explain the picture—he just said he wasn't a thief and asked me to trust him." Dave shrugged. "But I didn't."

"Well, I'm glad you didn't have anything to do with it."

"Me? Are you crazy? I like animals. And now I'm all embroiled in this mess because Tony hired some of my boys for muscle and had the nerve to steal my old equipment. Here I thought he was just an industrious guy, but instead he was piecing together his own sick operation. It's hard enough running a decent school without having to deal with this stuff."

"Well," I said, "*I* tell everyone you're cool."

He snickered. "Thanks, Triple-T."

"I'm serious. And by the way—I had occasion to use some of your moves the other day."

"What do you mean?"

"These girls attacked me down by the mall . . ."

"And?"

"And let's just say, they bit the mat and I didn't." I shrugged. "So thanks."

He laughed. "Hey, we don't call you Triple-T for nothing!"

I laughed and said, "Bye!" But when I got outside, I decided to take another detour before going home.

I found Hudson sitting on his porch, drinking tea, reading the newspaper. "Sammy!" he said when he saw me, but went right back to reading the paper. He didn't even offer me any tea.

"What's wrong?" I asked him.

He slapped the paper with the back of his hand. "Aside from this being unbelievable, it's unbelievable."

"What do you mean?"

"There are holes all over this story. There are parts that just don't make sense."

"It's the paper, Hudson. They get stuff wrong all the time. Besides, it happened late last night—I'm surprised they were able to report on it at all." Then I added, "But wasn't Officer Borsch great? I can't believe he was El Gato!"

Very slowly Hudson turned away from the paper and toward me. And the look on his face was the same look I get when things in *my* brain snap together.

But before he can start quizzing me, something bright orange catches the corner of my eye. "What was that?" I whisper.

"What was what?" Hudson whispers back.

And then the Psycho Kitty Queen comes around the corner. Her bottom half is still shrink-wrapped in denim. She's still wearing a halter top—this time bright orange. She's still got on twenty coats of makeup, and her tiara's still perched neatly on her Barbie-doll hair, but there's something different about her.

Something softer.

Something sad.

"Why, good morning, Miss Kitty," Hudson says as she walks up the side steps.

"Good morning, Hudson," she says quietly, then turns to me. "Good morning, Sammy."

Whoa now! This was weird. I didn't even know she knew my name.

Hudson asks, "Would you care for some tea?"

She shakes her head, and she keeps on looking at me, but not for a stare-down. She's just looking. And finally she simply says, "I'm sorry," then turns around and walks away.

I was stunned. But finally I stood up and called, "Wait!" I wanted to ask her if she'd gotten any of her cats back. I wanted to tell her that I was sorry, too—that I had no idea she had so many cats because she was rescuing them from the pound.

Unlike the Bulldog, who had rescued them just to kill them.

But she didn't wait, and Hudson held me back, saying, "Let her go, Sammy. She's a very complex person. And it seems to me she's in the middle of trying to figure things out for herself."

So she just walked away. And when she was gone, Hudson smiled at me and said, "So what does she know that I don't?"

"I . . . I really don't know."

"Well, then," he said, sitting down again. "Maybe you can start by telling me why you have your backpack with you on a Saturday."

"Uh, I spent the night at Holly's."

"And how about those scratches on your neck?"

My hand shot up to my neck. "Those didn't have anything to do with . . ." I almost said, last night, but caught myself in the nick of time. Trouble is, I couldn't think of how to finish the sentence.

"With . . . ?" he asked me, grinning.

So I broke down and told him. And when I was all done, he held his head in his hands and said, "No wonder you didn't want to tell me!"

"I haven't told Grams, either. And I think I probably shouldn't. You know how she gets."

"And with good reason! Do you realize how lucky you were?"

"Yeah," I said, then kicked my high-tops up on the rail. "Seems I've been lucky a lot lately."

On my way back to the Highrise, I stopped at Madame Nashira's House of Astrology. I wasn't really expecting Gina to be there, but there she was.

"Ooooh," she said when the sunlight streamed in. Then she saw it was me. "You're telling me it's morning already?"

I laughed. "Did you pull another all-nighter?"

"It's your fault," she said, hurrying over with a scroll in her hand. "This is fascinating! Absolutely fascinating!"

"What is?"

"You and Heather! You were born two minutes apart, in the same astral plane . . . you're like cosmic twins!"

"Cosmic . . . no, we're not!"

"Yes, you are!"

"You're *wrong*."

She put her hand on her hip and wobbled her head. "Don't you argue with Madame Nashira!"

"But Gina, she's evil!"

"Look at this! Just look at this." She spread the scroll and said, "This is a montage of the two of you."

"You put us *together*?"

"Don't worry, honey. I've got your individual birth chart done." She waved a hand behind her desk. "It's over there."

"So why'd you do this one?"

"Because it's *interesting*."

It was a birth chart, all right. With a wagon-wheel

design and signs of the zodiac and all the usual stuff. But this one looked like it should come with 3-D glasses. There were red markings and, sort of shadowing them, green markings.

She points and says, "You're the red one—"

"*I'm* the red one? Why'd you make *me* the red one?"

She rolls her eyes. "You are being so . . . annoyable."

"Heather should be red. She has red hair!"

"That's irrelevant." Then she eyes me and says, "And if it's anything like her mother's, it comes out of a bottle." She goes back to the chart. "But the point is, *look* at these!"

"What *about* them?"

"She is your shadow. She moves slightly behind you—"

"Through my whole life?" My whole face scrunched.

"Possibly."

"No! Don't *say* that!" I was shaking my head like crazy. "And this doesn't explain *any*thing!"

She rolled up the chart and frowned at me. "Fine. Be that way."

I followed her around her desk. "You don't understand! Heather's evil—I don't want her lurking around my whole life!"

Gina looked straight at me. "Well, she's your shadow sister."

"Sister? *Sister?*"

"That's what it's called."

"But you don't mean that *literally*, do you? I mean, she can't really be my sister, can she?" I was freaking out. Totally freaking out.

"Honey, honey, calm down. I can't tell you if she's your real sister or not. You're gonna have to have a heart-to-heart with your dad about that one." She sat down and said, "All I'm saying is, the two of you have a close *cosmic* connection. You were thrown into the cosmos in the same astral place and time." She leaned forward. "Avoiding her is as futile as avoiding your own shadow. Being *afraid* of her is as *ridiculous* as being afraid of your own shadow." She handed me my birth chart and birth certificate. *"Capisce?"*

I meant to say yes, but I shook my head. "No! I don't *capisce*!"

She laughed. "Well, honey, like it or not, that's what's in the stars."

When I finally made it back to the Highrise, I was more confused than ever about Heather. I was also beat. So I hid my birth chart under the couch, told Grams that yeah, I had had fun at Holly's but hadn't gotten enough sleep, then cuddled up with Dorito and took a nice long nap on the couch. And I probably would have slept clear to dinner, only at around three-thirty there was a soft *tap-tap-tap* at the door.

I did not feel like hiding in Grams' closet. I was way too wiped out for that. So when Grams gave me the signal to scoot along, I shook my head and whispered, "Can't I just be visiting you?"

She shrugged like, okay, then opened the door. Only the minute I heard "Hello, ma'am," I knew I should've dived for the closet.

Grams tried to sound calm. "Why, hello, officer. How can I help you?"

"I was hoping you'd let me have a word with Sammy."

"Oh," she said, fluttering a little, "you're in luck! She's here visiting me." She let him in, saying, "You're quite the community hero, aren't you?"

He didn't really say anything in reply. He just sort of gave a grunt.

I sat up straighter and tried to look awake. "Hi, Officer Borsch. How are you?"

He said, "Fine," but he looked really uncomfortable.

"Must've been a late night for you, huh?"

He nodded, then raised an eyebrow Grams' way. So I shook my head, letting him know that she didn't know I'd been involved in the raid.

That made him even more uncomfortable.

"Samantha's not in any trouble, is she?" Grams asks, and all of a sudden she's not looking too happy.

"No, ma'am," Officer Borsch says.

"Well, can I offer you something to drink? Coffee? Juice?"

"Maybe some water? My stomach's kinda . . ." He wobbles his hand.

So Grams scurries off, saying, "Have a seat."

He nods, then looks at his choices—the couch next to me, or an easy chair across the coffee table.

To my surprise he picks the couch.

And when he finally does speak, he sort of snorts first, then says, "You know, Sammy, I have a nephew and two nieces—they're all about your age, and they're brats."

He looks at me and says, "I also see a lot of the negative faction of society. A lot of kids gone bad. So, as I suppose you already know, I don't like kids."

I laughed. "I sort of picked up on that."

"What you may not know is that I've been passed up for sergeant five times in a row."

I didn't know what to say to *that*, so I just waited.

"And I've been pretty frustrated about it. So when I caught wind of a gambling ring, I foolishly decided to do a little legwork on my own—just to prove myself. I should have known they were on to me—I should have known Dave would show them the picture. But when Tony offered me a job, I wanted to believe I'd broken in. I wanted to believe I'd be able to get to the bottom of things, then spearhead a sting operation." He gave me a lopsided smile. "It didn't quite work out the way I'd planned. I almost wound up dead."

"But you didn't," I said, pulling a face to remind him to watch what he said. "And now, like Grams says, you're a community hero . . . and you *deserve* to be."

Grams handed him some water, saying, "Well, you're sure to get a promotion after this!"

He nodded and took a sip. "So it seems."

Then he just sat there for the longest time. Finally he put the glass down, took a deep breath, and held it a minute before saying, "So like I said, I don't like kids. Never *wanted* kids. *But*. . ." His chin quivered a little as his voice drifted off. But then he took another deep breath and said, "But if I had one like you, I wouldn't trade her for the world."

All of a sudden I had an enormous lump in my throat. I mean, I couldn't believe that Officer Borsch had actually *said* that. And I sure didn't know what to say in return, because if I had a dad like him, well, I *would* have traded him. In a hot second!

But right away he cleared his throat and stood up. "Well. That's what I came to say. Now I should be going."

I jumped up and said, "Wait! Uh...you can't just *go*...aren't you going to tell us what happened to those monsters you caught last night?" I looked at Grams and whispered, "Do we have any cookies or anything?"

"I'll check," she said, and hurried off to the kitchen.

So Officer Borsch sat back down and started talking. About how those cat-killing creeps'll be stuck in their own little cages for a while, about how good it felt to be able to return the cats they saved to their owners. And when I asked him, "Zippy? Do you know if one of them was named Zippy?" he said, "The one on the poster? Yeah, and he's fine."

And then, when I asked him if *he* was the one who had taken the posters down, he said, "Nah," and eyed Dorito. "I didn't take down the one for a speckled orange cat, either."

Normally that would have freaked me out, but now it didn't. Now I realized that Officer Borsch had known for quite some time where I lived, but I didn't have to worry about that anymore.

My secret was safe with him, just like his was safe with me.

And somewhere in the middle of us talking, Grams came in with cookies and two large glasses of milk, then disappeared into her bedroom. I guess she sensed we could talk better when she wasn't around. Later, though, there'd be no way to avoid telling her what had happened.

My grams is no dummy.

Then Officer Borsch explained that Tony had been spreading rumors about the Kojo Buffet as a way to get people to suspect them when it came to missing cats. He also told me that two of the cats they'd rescued were Miss Kitty's. "I had a little chat with her this morning, and without going into any real details, I told her that if it wasn't for you, her cats would be dead this morning." He shook his head. "I don't know if it sank in, but I tried."

"You know, I think it did. She apologized to me at Hudson's today."

"No kidding?"

"No kidding." Then I asked, "Was she embarrassed to see you?"

"Me? Why?"

I grinned. "Because she had the total hots for El Gato."

He made nervous little noises in his throat, then said, "Well, we all know the woman's nuts."

I laughed, then said, "Yeah, but I do feel kind of sorry for her."

"You feel sorry for a woman who hosed you down?"

"I know. I did used to think she was evil, but then I found out that the reason she's got so many cats is that she rescues them from the pound."

"Is that so?"

"Yeah. Plus Hudson says she's stuck in time, trying too hard to hang on to the past."

"Hmm," he said, then he stifled a grin and asked, "So who was that young man I saw you with on Hudson Graham's porch?"

I tried to stay cool as I answered, "Oh, just Heather Acosta's brother."

His eyes widened. "You don't say!" Then he chuckled and shook his head. "The plot thickens. . . ."

So there we were, Officer Borsch and me, having cookies and milk, actually *enjoying* each other. And I started wondering what this meant for the future, and also what it said about the past. I mean, how long had Officer Borsch known I lived with Grams? He couldn't *say* he knew, because I was breaking the law and he'd have to do something about it, but it was clear to me now—he knew.

But then I stopped myself from thinking about the past *or* the future. I stopped and just enjoyed the moment. After all, I was having cookies and milk with a cop in my secret hideaway.

How unreal is that?

So you know, I'm going to try to apply Hudson's advice to life in general. He told me that the best thing I can do for my happiness is live in the here and now, and I think he's right. Yeah, it'd be nice to go back in time to when I actually had a mother around. Yeah, I'm looking forward to being able to drive, and to having people not treat me like such a kid. But one's the past, and one's the future, and I can't be either place today.

Today, I'm here.

Today, I'm thirteen.

A week ago I thought that was the worst thing ever, but so far I can't complain. And who knows?

Thirteen may turn out to be the luckiest year of my life.

Have you read

sammy keyes
and the DEAD GIVEAWAY
yet?

Here's a sneak peek.

PROLOGUE

Grams says that most people have some sort of skeleton in their closet—something they really don't want other people to find out about. I always thought that was just grandma talk. Or, at least, her way of excusing the fact that *she's* got secrets from *me*.

"Skeletons are not just secrets, Samantha," she told me when I accused her of this. "They're life-*changing* secrets." Then she hurried to add, "And mind you, I'm not saying that *I* have skeletons in *my* closet, but if I did, that's exactly where I'd want them to stay."

I just laughed and said, "I bet you would!" 'cause I've learned that my grams can be pretty cagey—especially when it comes to things I'm dying to know about.

But shortly after our conversation I discovered what having a skeleton in your closet really means.

And how a closet isn't always a closet...

ONE

It's funny how you can think you know someone pretty well, and then something happens or they *do* something which makes you understand that you didn't really know them at all.

My homeroom teacher, Mrs. Ambler, is that way. I always figured she was just another long-suffering adult who was sick to death of dealing with junior high school kids. I also always thought that she was at least fifty. Probably well on her way to sixty. You know, *old*.

Then one day she came into homeroom with two lovebirds. I'm talking the feathered variety, not the gross pimply kind you see swapping spit behind the locker rooms.

Anyhow, these birds would've looked perfect on the shoulder of a midget pirate. They had orange faces, green bodies, a little splay of bright blue tail feathers, and I thought for sure they were baby parrots.

But when Mrs. Ambler parked the white domed cage on her desk and Tawnee Francisco asked, "Are they cockatiels?" Mrs. Ambler smiled at her and said, "No, they're lovebirds."

Now, this may seem like a perfectly normal exchange to you, but (a) I didn't even know there was actually such a thing as a lovebird, and (b) Mrs. Ambler's voice when she said "lovebirds" was all soft and sweet and . . . *feathery*.

Then I noticed her face. *It* was all soft. And sweet. And . . . well, not feathery, more *glowy*.

It was not the Mrs. Ambler I was used to seeing, that's for sure. I glanced at my best friend Marissa McKenze, who sits way up front in the corner, and she was sort of blinking at Mrs. Ambler, too.

Then Heather Acosta pipes up with, "*Love*birds, Mrs. Ambler? How *adorable*."

I rolled my eyes and Marissa did the same, because ever since end-of-the-year elections for Class Personalities started drawing near, Heather's been on the world's most revolting kiss-up campaign.

The whole idea of Class Personalities is stupid to begin with. It may be a "tradition" at William Rose Junior High School, but what it really is, is an overblown popularity contest. But since popularity is the pulse that drives Heather's blood, I guess that explains why she's dying to win something. Anything. You should see the way she's been circulating through campus lately, oozing a diabolically contagious form of congeniality. She's nice. She's sweet. She's helpful. She's concerned. And she's all that with such true-blue sincerity it's frightening.

Unfortunately for her, after nearly a full school year of her schemes and lies, I think that most people are smart enough to be suspicious, except for one thing—

Heather's also been acting contrite. You know—she's just so, *so* sorry for her part in any trouble this year. I've heard her tell teachers, "I know I made mistakes, but I've learned so much!" and "You know, I'm just so grateful for the experiences—I feel I've really grown as a human being!"

That's the kiss-up game she's been playing with other people, anyway. To *me* she's been whispering, "Count 'em and weep, loser."

Please. Like I care if she wins some stupid popularity contest?

She's not just after Friendliest Seventh Grader, either. Oh no. She's hedging her bets by going for Most Unique Style, too. One day she comes to school looking like a punk princess in black and chains and ratted red hair; the next she's all decked out like an old-time movie star, wearing satin shoes and a matching *hand*bag, her hair all smoothed back.

It's so transparent it's pathetic.

But anyway, the minute Heather finds out that Mrs. Ambler's birds are *love*birds, she kicks into total kiss-up mode. "Oh, how *adorable*," she gushes. Then she asks Mrs. Ambler, "Were they a gift from your husband?" like that would just have been the sweetest, dearest thing a man could do for his wife.

Well, Marissa and I may be able to see right through Heather, but not Mrs. Ambler. She goes from, like, forty watts of glow to about seventy-five and gives Heather the brightest smile. "How did you know?" Then she nuzzles her nose at the cage and says, "He gave them to me for our anniversary."

"How *romantic*," Heather sighs. "How long have you been married?"

Mrs. Ambler smiles at her again. "Fifteen years today."

"Fifteen years? Wow! And he buys you lovebirds? He must be terrific." Then she asks, "So how'd you meet?"

Mrs. Ambler keeps on letting herself be suckered. "In graduate school," she tells Heather. "We got married shortly after I got my master's degree."

Whoa now! A master's? A master's in *what*? Honestly, all I've ever seen Mrs. Ambler do is take roll and read the announcements and reprimand kids when they get out of line. I know she's in charge of the yearbook and has some class with special-ed kids. Oh, and she teaches eighth graders how to study or get focused on their goals or . . . I don't know what. But nothing that would seem to take a *master's* degree.

So while I'm busy trying to digest that, I'm also chewing on the math involved in this new Ambler Information. I mean, let's say you're twenty-two when you graduate from college. A master's is what? Two more years of college? So even if you tack an extra year on for good measure, Mrs. Ambler would have been at *most* twenty-five when she got married. And if she'd been married for fifteen years, that meant that this fifty-, well-on-her-way-to-sixty-year-old woman that I'd seen nearly every day for the whole school year was only . . . thirty-nine or forty?

I was stunned. I mean, forty is plenty old, but not

nearly as old as I'd *thought* she was. And she was probably also a lot *smarter* than I'd given her credit for. Plus,
at that moment she wasn't just my boring, worn-out
homeroom teacher, she was a woman who was embar-
rassingly in love with her husband.

"I hope I find a man like him someday," Heather was
saying. "Somebody that'll give me lovebirds after fifteen
years of marriage!"

She was laying it on thick, but Mrs. Ambler was obliv-
ious. "I hope you do, too, Heather."

Heather nodded at the birds. "So what did you name
them?"

"Tango and Hula."

Tango and Hula? Boy, this was getting weirder by the
minute! Did this mean she was into *dancing*? Did she and
her husband tango around the house?

Did she have a funny grass skirt in her closet?

Whatever. For the rest of the week Mrs. Ambler
brought the birds to school every day. She would park
them on her desk, where they'd flutter around the cage
during the day making chirping and chattering noises and
little *kissing* sounds, then she'd take them home at night.

They were actually pretty entertaining. Especially
Tango, who'd kind of spin around on the perch or just
hang upside down and make kissing noises up at Hula.

Mrs. Ambler became entertaining, too. Once when I
came into homeroom, I saw her nuzzling up to the wires
of the cage, cooing, "Who's so cute? Who's so sweet?
Who's got little angel feet?"

Angel feet?

She was also training them to perch on her shoulder, and you'd catch her cooing at them, saying stupid stuff like, "Hula-hoop, now don't you poop!" and "Does my little Tango want some mango?" She told us she didn't believe in clipping a bird's wings, so sometimes they'd flap around the room, but pretty much they stayed in their cage or on her shoulder.

Anyway, it was during lunch on our second Wednesday with birds that we found out that Heather's ridiculous Vote-for-Sweet-Little-Me campaign had worked.

I also discovered that I *did* care. I choked on my sandwich when they announced the seventh- and eighth-grade candidates in all Class Personality categories over the P.A.—Heather was on the seventh-grade ballot for Most Unique Style *and* Friendliest. I actually stood up and shouted, "You have got to be kidding!"

Holly and Dot pulled me back down and told me, "Just forget it. We know she's a phony, and so does everyone else."

"If everyone else knows she's a phony, then why is she on the ballot? *Twice?*"

"Why do you think she's been kissing up to Mrs. Ambler?" Marissa grumbled.

"Wait—Mrs. *Ambler* came up with the nominees?"

"I'm sure the other teachers helped," Marissa said, "but she *is* the one running the Class Personality elections."

"But...what does *she* know about us? Why didn't the seventh graders get to nominate?"

Marissa nodded. "It is totally lame, huh? I wonder if we should talk to the administration about it."

"Oh right." I snorted. "Like they're going to listen to *us*?"

So yeah, the whole thing made me spitting mad, especially since Heather came strutting into science whispering, "Count 'em and weep, loser" as she passed by. Couldn't the teachers see what Heather was doing? Did they sit around the faculty room going, "That Heather Acosta has certainly turned over a new leaf. I am so impressed with the manner in which she's been conducting herself lately...."

Did they *all* have master's?

In gullibility?

I brooded about it for the rest of school, wondering if the seventh graders were going to be as blind as Mrs. Ambler when it came time to vote.

After school I went over to Mrs. Willawago's house to walk her dog. It's a new, temporary job that doesn't pay squat, but thanks to Grams I'm on the hook to do it until Mrs. Willawago's recovered enough from her foot surgery to do it herself. Grams says I'm securing my place in heaven and that this is the kind of thing you're supposed to do for recently widowed senior citizens who've had foot surgery and go to the same church as you.

I say it's one more reason to avoid church.

Anyway, Marissa went with me the first couple of times but didn't like the way Mrs. Willawago is so over the top about God and the Bible. "I can't believe she's Catholic, Sammy. She seems like a total thumper to me."

Well she was right about that, but I sure wasn't going to risk asking about it. That'd be like walking straight into Sermon City. Besides, I don't really mind hearing "Praise the Lord" and "Amen" and all her other evangelistic expressions—I just kind of ignore them. You can get away with a lot of religious mumbo jumbo around me if you just don't preach.

And the truth is, going over to Mrs. Willawago's has kind of grown on me. For one thing, she's got the coolest house I've ever seen. I call it the Train House because even though it looks pretty normal from the street—well, except for the cowcatcher that ramps up to her porch—it's got an actual caboose attached to one side of the back of the house and an old parlor car attached to the other. The caboose she uses as a guest bedroom, and the parlor car is where she and her husband used to hold Bible meetings. It's the most luxurious room I've ever seen—rich wood panels, chandeliers, brass trim, green velvet seats.... It's hard to believe that it used to chug along a track, but Mrs. Willawago swears that it did.

And besides the total coolness of the train cars, the main part of the house is like a museum of railroad gadgets and furniture and signs and photographs and stuff. The more I go there, the more I learn about railroads and trains, and even though I didn't really care about any of that before, now I find it, you know, *interesting*.

But the *main* reason I don't mind going over to Mrs.

Willawago's came bounding across the house toward me as I stepped through the front door. "Captain Patch!" I cried as he yippy-yap-barked and dashed in a circle around me. "How are you, buddy?"

"Happy to see you, as usual," Mrs. Willawago said as she handed over the leash. "As am I, of course." Then she added, "Praise the Lord you're here. That dog needs a walk!"

Patch *is* kinda hyper and sniffs everything—not exactly the kind of dog you expect an old lady to have. He was a gift from Mrs. Willawago's kids, who live in different parts of the country and thought a dog would be good companionship for their mom after Mr. Willawago "went to be with the Lord." Supposedly he's a cross between an American foxhound and a golden retriever, but there's nothing furry or golden about him. He's got smooth brown fur and white paws and was named by one of the grandkids because of the big black patch of fur around his left eye.

Anyway, Patch always seems to get my mind off my problems at school and put me in a good mood, but not this time. This time when I walked him, I didn't forget about school, I obsessed about it. How could they have nominated Heather for Friendliest?

That's like nominating a vampire for Best Kisser!

Heather Acosta, Most Phony Seventh Grader—that was more like it! How come they didn't *see* that?

When I got back to the Train House, I guess Mrs. Willawago could tell I was upset, because after I let

Patch go in the backyard, she said, "I thank the Lord every day for your help, Samantha, but if you've had enough..."

"Huh? Oh no. That's okay. I don't mind."

Trouble is, it came out sounding really flat. Like I *did* mind. And the next thing I know, Mrs. Willawago's opening her purse, saying, "I told your grandmother that I was willing to pay you, but she insisted that I not."

"Wait! No. It doesn't have anything to do with that. It's just...it's just this girl at school that's got me all, you know, tweaked." And because I was embarrassed that she thought I was grumpy because she wasn't paying me, I wound up blurting out a whole lot more than I normally would have.

When I finally shut up about Heather Acosta, Mrs. Willawago let out a little cackle and said, "Heather sounds a lot like Coralee Lyon."

"Who?"

"Coralee Lyon. You don't read the paper?"

I scowled. "I live in this town—I sure don't want to read about it."

She nodded, then said, "Well, Coralee Lyon—or Coralee Abbot, as she'll always be to me—now rules the roost of our city council, but back in junior high school she was not pleased with her place in the pecking order. She did all manner of sinful things to remedy that." She gave me a knowing look. "Lucifer still dwells deep in Coralee's heart, but people don't see him because she's learned to disguise her tactics."

"Oh great," I grumbled. "So you're telling me Heather'll never change?"

She laughed. "Who but God can write history in advance? But until she walks through the door of repentance, it'd be easiest on you to simply avoid her. I haven't spoken to Coralee in years." She looked toward the ceiling. "Thanks be to God."

So you see how much help talking to Mrs. Willawago was. And talking to Grams wasn't much better. "Good heavens, Samantha," she said. "If her end goal is to win some popularity contest, let her. Besides, the popular people in *my* junior high and high school all fizzled."

"But what if she turns out like Coralee Lyon?"

"Who?"

"Some brat Mrs. Willawago went to school with who's now ruling the roost on the city council." I hesitated. "What *is* the city council, anyway?"

Grams laughed. "A group of people who make decisions about Santa Martina's growth and development." She eyed me. "In other words, she's not ruling much of a roost."

Still. I didn't sleep very well that night thinking about how people like Heather and Coralee Lyon shouldn't be allowed to rule roosts of *any* kind, even flea-infested ones like Santa Martina or William Rose Junior High.

The next morning I woke up ridiculously early and started brooding about the Class Personality nominations some more. And since there was no way I was going to get back to sleep, I finally just got up, took a shower, ate breakfast, packed a lunch, and went to school. And instead of tearing onto campus at the last second like I usually do, I arrived a whole fifteen minutes early.

There were other kids around and everything, but I didn't see my friends, so I decided to go drop off my backpack and skateboard in homeroom. That's one nice thing about Mrs. Ambler—unlike a lot of the other teachers, she unlocks the classroom early so you *can* drop off your backpack or just meet up with your friends and get in out of the cold. Usually she's at her desk grading papers or reading a book, but lots of times she's going between the classroom and the office, taking care of teacher business.

Now, since I was so early, it crossed my mind that I might have the chance to ask Mrs. Ambler how Heather got on the ballot. Or maybe I'd just ask her how kids on the ballot were nominated.

Of course on *second* thought, that might make it look like I was sore because *I* hadn't been nominated for anything, which I didn't care about, but I didn't want it to *seem* like I cared. I mean, *looking* like you care is way worse than actually caring.

It's truly... pathetic.

But thinking all that through turned out to be a big waste of mental energy, because when I arrived at the classroom, no one was there. Well, no *people,* anyway. The birds were there, but it wasn't until I was inside that I noticed that one of them was out of the cage. And flapping for the open door.

Fast.

The doors at my school are heavy-duty metal. Every one of them has a small wire-mesh window, a kick-down doorstop, and a hydraulic closer so it automatically shuts. Most of the classrooms have a whole wall of windows right next to the door, so I don't know *why* they're such heavy-duty doors, but they are.

And in all my junior high experience I can honestly say that I'd never been in a hurry to *close* a classroom door before. Open and dash in, yes. Close? Never.

So when I whipped around and pushed on the door to make sure the bird didn't escape, I learned something new about hydraulic closers—they can't be rushed. I mean, there I am, pushing like crazy on that door, but the stupid thing's fighting back, taking its old sweet time, closing at its own sweet pace.

So I drop my skateboard, plant both hands on the door, and really *lean* into it. And all of a sudden *shh-whack*, the closer gives way and the door slams shut.

Phew.

I look up for the flyaway bird but freeze with both hands still on the door. There, a foot above my head, is one beautiful, fluffy, blue-and-green bird butt sticking straight out of the doorjamb. And above it, pointing up to heaven, is one perfectly still, outstretched wing.

"Oh *no*," I cry, whipping the door back open. But with a little *thwump*, the bird drops to the floor.

I pick him up and whimper, "Oh no! Oh no, no, no!" but it's plain to see—little Tango has danced his last dance. I hold him in the palm of my hand and stare. There isn't even any blood. He's just kind of...broken. And inside *I* feel broken, too. How can this be?

And as I'm standing there, holding this poor broken bird in my hand, I glance up, and through the door's window I see someone coming up the walkway toward the classroom.

My heart stops midbeat.

It's not Mrs. Ambler.

No, it's someone much, *much* worse.